Under Saint Owain's Rock

Josh Langston & BJ Galler-Smith

Dedication

For lovers and dreamers everywhere, but
most especially for Annie and John.

Contents

Acknowledgments

We cannot say enough kind things about our many friends among the CompuServe IMPs who gave so freely of their time and talents to help us craft this tale. Rather than risk leaving anyone out, we offer blanket thanks in honor of

David "Duke" Bollinger

a talented writer, a dedicated teacher, a loving husband, an honorable and trusted friend. Duke will be missed by many, and the world is truly a poorer place without him.

Chapter One

Llancerriog, North Wales
August, 1307

Sainthood required more than a massive headstone and a dozen village idiots. Finally, Owain--*Saint* Owain--lay dead, and all Meleri could think was good riddance.

That didn't mean the truth had to be buried with him. She wrote a letter of confession meant for the Abbot of Sant Dewi's monastery, and for his eyes only.

Knowing her soul depended on its contents, she listed the name of every villager who had taken part in the affair and recorded, as faithfully as she could remember, the role each had played. When finished, she signed her name and affixed the family seal. All she needed was a safe place to hide the letter. If anyone asked about Saint Owain, she'd deliver it and let the world know the truth--though it ruin them all.

~*~

Llansantowain, North Wales
Spring, the present

Mali Rhys eyed the fourth rung from the top of the ladder, paying particular attention to the triple layer of duct tape. It should hold, for this job anyway. She scaled the ladder and worried a thin piece of slate into position. The first nail went in straight and true with two blows; the second seemed to duck sideways. The hammer skipped off the nail head and shattered the replacement tile.

"Hell," Mali muttered. She started down the ladder for another tile when she heard car tires crunching on the gravel drive behind her. She squeezed her eyes shut. "Please God, let it be anyone other than the Jamaican."

Leaving the hammer on the roof, she continued her descent but twisted around for a look at the vehicle. Instead of the Rastafarian's rusted Austin Healey, a dark green, Jaguar sedan rolled to a smooth stop in front of the cottage. The passenger door opened, and the vehicle disgorged a thin, balding, stork of a man she recognized instantly: Bertram Smythe-Webley, antiquities dealer.

"Bloody hell," she said, suddenly remembering his appointment.

"Good day, Miss Rhys," he called. "I've come for the letter."

Meleri's letter. "Bloody, bloody hell," she whispered. "Not today. Not yet." She continued to back down the ladder. The fourth rung sagged under her hand.

"Eighty thousand pounds is my final offer," he said. "It's more than generous." He peered at her expectantly as she brushed dust from her jeans.

Selling the letter was the last thing she wanted to do, at any price. She needed time. "More than generous? I might very well get a better offer." She led the way into the cottage, and the Londoner made straight for the display case.

"A better offer isn't likely without an open auction." Smythe-Webley looked into the case that housed the letter. "We aren't talking about used automobiles. Dealers in medieval manuscripts are nearly as rare as the manuscripts themselves. Besides--" he tapped the case lightly with his knuckle "--I'm the only person outside your family who's ever seen this one. We both know you could get a better price if you'd allow me to put it up at Sotheby's. Just say the word, and I'll make the arrangements."

"It's not just the money," Mali insisted. Someone like Smythe-Webley would never understand the effects her betrayal would have on the village. Not only would it put everyone in a terrible light, it would deprive them of their saint--their only claim to notoriety. And then there was Aunt Glynnis. Aunt Glynnis would rather burn the letter than sell it, no matter what its value.

"It's always about the money," he said. "There are universities, museums, and a dozen independent scholars who'd love to have a genuine 14th century document, especially one written in old Welsh by a woman." He flicked an invisible speck from one French cuff of his bone-colored shirt. "Nor should we overlook the private collectors. They're the most eager of all."

"You don't think they'd be put off by the content?"

Smythe-Webley twittered with amusement. "It would only add to its value. People love the prurient, and the seamier side of history holds special charm."

That was *exactly* what she was afraid of.

He arched one eyebrow, and for some moments Mali was without words.

"Would you like some tea?" she asked finally.

The antiquities dealer examined his had-to-be-genuine Gucci watch with a flamboyant flick of his wrist, and with long-suffering politeness, shook his head. "It's a long drive back to London, and my driver gets cranky if we get tied up in traffic."

"He won't mind getting back a bit late tonight," said a sing-song voice from the doorway. "I asked him." Glynnis Rhys stood with her hand on the driver's arm as if she was walking on ice and needed assistance. "I've made some lovely cucumber sandwiches." She dragged her eyes from the driver and batted them at Smythe-Webley, who stared back and blinked once. "We have company so rarely, you really must stay for a bite of lunch."

The Londoner glanced again at his watch. "We shouldn't, really."

Mali suddenly wished him miles away and wondered at her aunt's willingness to detain him. Surely Glynnis intended to sabotage the transaction. Perhaps she thought if the deal wasn't closed in private, it would never be closed in front of the chauffeur.

"If they must go, Aunt Glynnis...."

"Don't be silly. It's all prepared. If they don't join us, it'll just be wasted." Glynnis released the chauffeur, advanced on the dealer, and linked her arm in his. "Come now, the kitchen's this way. I've set a table with a charming view of the garden."

As if recognizing he faced an insurmountable foe, Smythe-Webley surrendered with only a brief hesitation and a resigned sigh. "Delighted."

Mali waved them on. "I'll join you in a moment," she said.

Glynnis gave her a bleak smile. "I'm sure you'll make the right decision. Take your time, dear." Then her smile ripened into something Mali had never seen from her aunt--the aspect of a woman on the prowl. "I'll do my utmost to entertain the gentlemen--the *Eisteddfod* is this coming August."

Mali felt a twinge of pity for her visitors. Glynnis had handily outflanked the pompous little Englishman and would soon be bending the ears of both men, probing their interest in the national cultural poetry competition for which she lived and breathed. If neither man evidenced any such interest, Glynnis would attempt to instill some. Not that she'd be boorish about it; Glynnis could be immensely genteel. Quick-witted and well-read, she hardly looked her sixty years and could positively exude charm.

Mali pulled a leather-topped stool to her desk and gazed down at the case that housed the precious document. It all seemed such a muddle. How much simpler life would have been if the letter had never been written. Though the content didn't matter to her, if it ever went public, neither Aunt Glynnis nor the townsfolk would ever live down the shame.

The popularity of history's seamier details wasn't limited to Smythe-Webley's collectors. Any scholar worth the title would instantly seize upon the scandalous story the letter told. The rest of the world might not care, but it'd set tongues wagging from Liverpool to Swansea.

It would be so much easier if she didn't have to face such horrid decisions all alone.

"Are you coming, Mali?" Glynnis stuck her head around the corner. "Those two are ravenous. If you don't hurry, there won't be anything left." She grimaced and lowered her voice conspiratorially. "It turns out Mr. Mayhew is something of a poet, but he's afraid to say a word around Mr. Smythe-Webley." She made another face. "You know how those old-money Englishmen can be!"

"Don't worry about me," Mali said. "I'm not hungry." Truth to tell, anxiety had killed her appetite. Her aunt called out for the benefit of their visitors, "Should I make another pot of tea, Mali? We've finished this one."

"I'll get something later," Mali said. *Bread and water, perhaps.* That was about all they'd be able to afford when she gave Smythe-Webley the news.

The antiquities dealer ambled back into the living room. "I can write you a check now, if you'd like," he said, "or you can just give me the letter on consignment. I'm quite certain it'll sell in a matter of days, and we'll both be the better off for it." He made a casual measurement of the case. I'll have Mayhew load it in the boot of my car."

Mali shook her head and straightened. "I've come to an unexpected decision. Your offer is indeed generous, and I'm sorely tempted to accept it, but I simply can't."

Smythe-Webley compressed his lips in a straight, flat seam and stared at her for a long moment before he spoke. "We had an understanding, Miss Rhys. I've come a very long way, and this is most distressing. You're making a mistake if you think I'll increase my offer."

"Your offer is entirely fair just as it is, but there are other circumstances involved, personal ones."

"People sell family heirlooms all the time," he said. "And when they do, the object is gone from them forever. But this is different, your family name will always be associated with this document, no matter where it ends up."

Mali laughed at the irony. "That's part of the problem, I'm afraid."

Smythe-Webley signaled for his driver. "You have my card," he said. "If you should change your mind, please let me know."

"I promise," Mali said. "And you will, of course, send me a bill for your expenses today?"

Smythe-Webley bowed--a crane stretching for a fish just out of reach. "Of course."

Mayhew, stuffing the remains of a cucumber sandwich into his mouth, fairly sprinted to reach the door before his employer and held it open for him. The dealer retreated into the afternoon, and Mali closed the door behind him, leaning heavily on it. The car doors slammed shut, and the Jaguar's engine roared. The diminishing crunch of tires on gravel told her when they'd gone. Mali made a mental note to let the dogs out of the tool shed. Though neither was vicious, they were enthusiastic in their exuberant efforts to protect the cottage.

"That Londoner's an odd duck," Glynnis said, wiping her hands on a tea towel covered with pictures of the Ffestiniog narrow gauge railway cars climbing Mt. Snowdon.

Mali felt a bit like her life was uphill all the way, too.

"But that driver now..." Glynnis' joy in meeting an agreeable fellow poet was evident.

"You're incorrigible," Mali said.

"I do my best." Glynnis flipped the cloth over her shoulder, her mood suddenly somber. "Now, I suppose you'll be running to the bank to deposit the check and put an end to the visits from that awful little man."

"Smythe-Webley's a bit peculiar, but I wouldn't say he's awful."

"Not him," Glynnis said. "The other little man. The black fellow with the odd hats. What'd you call him? The Rotarian?"

"Rastafarian," Mali said. "Sadly, we're quite likely to see him again. Him and his nasty companion." Her lips took on a slightly wry twist. "I'd better finish the roof before he can repossess the shingles."

"But, the letter. I thought..." Glynnis stared at the case still sitting on Mali's desk, a frown tugging at the corners of her mouth. "I don't understand."

"I didn't sell it."

Consternation briefly clouded Glynnis's face until replaced with a burgeoning smile as Mali's words sank in.

"When the time came, I just couldn't do it."

Tears welled in Glynnis's eyes, and she dabbed at them with the hem of her apron. "Oh, Mali, how proud I am of you! You've done the right thing." She gave her a hug. "Don't worry, dear, we'll manage. We always have.

"I've looked after you for so long," Glynnis continued, and hugged Mali tighter. "I sometimes forget you're all grown now. I do realize it's your decision to make. My job is to stand behind you, no matter what."

A burning welled in Mali's throat. Her aunt was worth it. She'd hold to the letter fast. "I only hope we haven't made a terrible mistake," she said morosely. "We still have a mountain of bills to pay."

Glynnis kissed her forehead. "I'm not in the least bit worried. Not a bit! The right will out--you'll see."

~*~

Atlanta, Georgia, USA
Spring, the present

Bill Thomas looked at his boss, David Jones, at ease in the client chair of Bill's cluttered office. Oversized ad samples, stacked publicity materials, and various products crowded the downtown Atlanta space where Bill spent roughly half his life. He spent the other half searching for business to bring back to it.

"You have a seriously Welsh name."

"I guess," Bill said. "I never thought about it."

David nodded like an old sage. "Where's your family from?"

"LA," Bill said.

"Los Angeles?"

"Lower Alabama."

The older man chuckled. "For how many generations?"

"I've no idea. Wetumpka is a great place to be from--way far away from."

"Didn't mean to push my obsession with ancestry on you. It's not why I'm here." He paused. "I've decided to retire."

Bill was flabbergasted. David had given no hint he might take such a step. "This is sudden! I thought you loved the business."

"I do, but I've had Wales on my mind for ages. Now I can go there and spend as much time as I want researching my roots."

"Congratulations!" Bill extended his hand, genuinely pleased for his boss and mentor, a man who'd become a friend. A sudden dread rose. "Are you planning to shut down the agency?"

"Decapitate my golden goose? Hardly. Jones and Associates will be around a long time. But I've made a decision about who's going to take the helm. I wanted to let you know before I made anything public."

Bill sat up straighter. "I'm flattered."

"I'm bringing my daughter into the business."

Bill covered his surprise with a cough. *"Rhia?"*

"Yes."

David couldn't be serious. Not the girl referred to by most of the male staff as TNT--Tits and Teeth.

"Are you okay?" David asked. "You look like you inhaled a bug."

Bill felt like it. He found his voice, and eased all the PR-neutral charm he could muster into it. "It's just... The last time I saw Rhia she was... in college."

During her two-month internship she'd destroyed one marriage and severely damaged another. She did acceptable work when she wasn't screwing around, but that seemed to be her specialty. He chose his words with care. "Are you sure she's, uhm, ready?"

"She's matured," David said. "She's practically run her mother's agency in New York for the past two years. She's really on top of things."

Bill knew exactly what kind of things Rhia liked to be on top of. Like mother, like daughter, and David's ex had worked more beds than a hotel maid. Not content to sleep with half his clients, she left David in the lurch and started her own business with many of her ex-lovers in tow.

"But is the agency ready for Rhia?" When David grimaced, Bill hastily went on. "Let's face it, you're conservative--strictly by-the-book. If she's not, the change will be a big shock to staff and clients alike." He forced a smile.

"She's been raised in the business, and she's no fool. She just needs a chance to prove herself," David concluded. "With a little cooperation from everyone here she'll do fine."

All things were possible, Bill thought, including those he considered damned unlikely. "She'll get our cooperation. Count on it."

"Excellent." David looked out the window for a moment before he continued. "I wanted to offer you the job, but frankly, you're too nice a guy. It's why our little accounts love you."

"Thanks, I guess," Bill said. So much for his chance to do something extraordinary.

"Another reason I'm bringing Rhia in is that lately

I haven't been doing my own job very well. Don't think it's a reflection of how I feel about the one you're doing."

Bill chewed on his lower lip. The last thing in the world he wanted to do was manage mom and pop accounts. If that was all he was destined for, he could've stayed in Wetumpka.

"Those little contracts keep us alive," David said. "If you want to play with the big boys, then be glad Rhia's coming. She's pulled off a coup or two in New York, and you know how competitive they are up there. You could learn a lot from her."

Bill knew the deck was stacked against him. Rhia had a face, figure, and friskiness against which he could not compete.

"She might just add the kind of pizzazz that'll take us to the New York level," David said. "Lord knows, I'm not getting it done." He stood up to leave. "She starts Monday."

So soon? "Great."

"And I'll be leaving soon after for Wales. I'm excited about studying my roots. Y'know, it wouldn't hurt you to get a feel for your own. Thousands of lives went into making you the person you are, whether you acknowledge them or not. A wise man knows where he's been as well as where he's going."

"Right," Bill said, not sure where he was heading and not wanting to think about where he was from.

~*~

Mali and Glynnis entered the crowded pub together, but once inside they went in opposite directions. Glynnis settled at a table with the usual crowd of critical observers who congregated beneath a huge, red-dragoned Welsh flag which covered the rear wall. Mali headed straight to the other side near the dartboard where she knew the head of the council, Dylan Davies, would be holding court in between turns. Dylan had just thrown and scowled at his score.

"Ah good, you're here then," he said when she reached him. He set a half-empty pint of brown ale on the varnished bar. "We can get started now." He gestured toward the dozen men and women sitting at nearby tables too small to accommodate them--legs stuck into the narrow spaces between the tables like fallen-log fencing. The tables, made of ancient and elbow-worn oak, shone in the dim light of the single bulb illuminating the dartboard. The villagers of Llansantowain had been holding meetings on those same tables for over four hundred years.

A smile tugged the corners of Mali's lips upwards. "I'm no celebrity, Dylan Davies, and y'know it. You can run your meetings when and as you like. You don't need me."

"You're wrong there, Mali Rhys," piped Brenna Parry, the pub's owner, from behind the bar. "Dylan was just sayin' how important you are to the whole scheme, weren't ye, Dylan?" She glanced back at Mali. "Can I get you anything, dear?"

"No, diolch. I'm not thirsty," Mali said as she settled into a seat opposite Dylan. "I'm afraid to ask what plan you've hatched this time."

"You'll like this one," he said. A number of other voices, male and female, rose in boisterous agreement.

Mali winced at the unguarded enthusiasm. "I quiver with anticipation."

Dylan rubbed his palms together as if to warm

them and when the onlookers cheered, pointed at the dartboard. Dai Thomas had just thrown a bull's eye. The craggy farmer stood with his huge callused hands on his hips, a grin splitting his weathered features.

"It's not that I begrudge you that throw, Dai, it's only that I hate losing so early in the evening." Dai laughed and without missing a breath, the council chairman turned his attention back to Mali. "It's a perfect plan," he said. "It'll solve all our problems."

"High goals, Dylan. You aren't going back to that *twp* notion of using tax money to buy lottery tickets, are you?" she asked.

The politician shook his head vigorously. "That was only pub talk, that was. I didn't mean it. I recall we all celebrated a bit more strenuously than usual that night."

"Good."

He leaned closer and lowered his voice conspiratorially. "It'd help if you quit bringing up that subject. People might get the wrong idea."

"Such as," she whispered back, "you had some idea of what you were doing?"

He straightened, but the smile on his face never faltered. Then he backed away and patted her on the head like a puppy. "You remind me more and more of your father. Irreverent as ever."

"I'll take that as a compliment."

"That's how 'twas meant, Mali. That's how 'twas meant."

She winked at Dai, and the older man winked back.

"Tell her your plan, Dylan," Brenna said. "She didn't come all the way here for her health."

He raised his glass. Those who saw him stopped talking, and soon the room fell quiet. "Most of you have already heard parts of the plan, but since there are a few who came in late, I'll start at the beginning." He took a long draught of the dark brew and wiped his mouth with the back of his hand.

Mali rolled her eyes at the theatrics. "Get on with it, then."

"I've exchanged a couple of letters with a fellow in the States. He--"

"How'd he get your name?" asked Caitlin Morgan, sitting in the back with Glynnis. As free with her style as Glynnis was reserved, Caitlin brought a bit of New Age cheer to the stuffy town meetings. Augmenting her hairdressing income with herbal remedies, she also had the distinction of being the local brewer. She pushed her unbound, silver-streaked, auburn hair away from her face and toyed with the quartz crystal dangling from a leather cord around her neck. "You haven't been to the States."

Dylan sniffed. "He didn't address it to me personally. He sent it to the mayor of Llansantowain. As chairman of the village council, I'm the closest thing we have to a mayor."

Caitlin appeared poised to ask something else when Mali glared at her. When that didn't work, Mali turned to Glynnis. Glynnis tapped Caitlin on the shoulder to get her attention, then threatened to drop a salt shaker into her beer. Caitlin rescued the glass with both hands and sat quietly.

"This fellow, David Jones his name is--a proper Welsh name if I've ever heard one--wants to come here to study a most distinguished person."

"Here? In Llansantowain?" Caitlin laughed, and titters of amusement drifted from every corner. "Since when did anyone like that live here?"

"It's been quite a while," Dylan said, glaring at her. "Something some foreigners wouldn't understand because they've only just arrived."

Several in the crowd chuckled.

"Aye," said Dai Thomas, "Cait's only lived here these twenty-odd years. She's still a newcomer." He tapped his temple and winked.

"Never mind all that," Mali said. "Who're you talking about?"

"Owain y'Craig," he said proudly.

"Our Owain?" Mali asked. "*Saint* Owain?"

"Aye," Dylan said.

Mali suddenly found breathing difficult.

Dylan continued. "I don't know why, but this fellow's got a burnin' interest in finding out all he can about Saint Owain--his story, his people, where he came from, everythin'."

"Fancy that. A Yank interested in our saint," Brenna said.

"Is he a scholar of some kind?" Mali asked, not eager for additional light on Owain's origins.

Dylan shook his head, a sly smile adding to the glint in his eye. "He's one of those advertising blokes. Owns an agency in Atlanta, wherever that is."

"That's crazy," Mali said. "What would he care about Owain? What is there around here for him to study?" It didn't seem likely someone had discovered the letter, but her suspicions fled to the only other person who knew about it, Smythe-Webley.

"I don't know what he hopes to find out," Dylan

said facing Mali. "He wants to learn everything he can, and he asked me to recommend someone local to help him."

Mali gasped. "You didn't!"

"Of course I did! You know more about local history than anyone else in the district."

"Well then, you'd best find another name, because I won't have anything to do with him. This is nonsense."

"I could use a tourist or two," Brenna piped in cheerily. "You could show him the murals upstairs."

"And take him out to see the Rock," added Dylan, at the mention of which, several villagers squirmed. "There's no harm in helping him and much to be gained."

She couldn't deny it, bringing in strangers and making them happy enough to tell their friends, was the best way to entice even more paying visitors. Lord knew they needed some. "And then?"

"You'll think of something, I'm sure. And if you don't, someone else will. I volunteered everyone in town to help."

"But, why? Why should we care what some silly Yank wants to study?"

"Because of what he offered in exchange," Dylan said.

He looked so smug, Mali knew the last detail would likely be as dreadful as the rest. "And that would be?"

"He's going to create an advertising campaign for us. All we have to do is assist him while he's here, and he'll give us our very own tourist industry!"

After a long moment of staring at him, Mali closed

her mouth. "You're mad."

"Don't be so narrow-minded! It's the answer to all our problems. We'll use tourist business to create jobs. Instead of watchin' our young people move away, we'll be watching new people move in!"

She turned to Brenna. "How much has he had to drink?"

Dylan spoke to her back. "I know we'll have to start small, maybe limit ourselves to T-shirts and souvenirs, but one day--"

"Souvenirs! Of *what?*" Mali asked, spinning back to face him. "Tourists want to see and do things. How many people are going to want to look at Owain's Rock?" She shook her head and gazed around the room. "How many of *us* want to see it? It looks like a giant--" She stopped in mid-sentence when she saw a look of horror twist Glynnis's face. "Body part," she added lamely.

"Caitlin Morgan and her crowd go there often," piped Michael Wills from a back corner. He spread his arms. "They put flowers in their hair, join hands, and dance around it naked."

"We do *not* dance naked!" Glynnis cried from a nearby table.

"There 'tis. The bit dog barks." Satisfied, Michael folded his arms.

Caitlin booed him. "If we did, Michael Wills, you'd be the one to spy on us. You'd not dare join us for fear of getting that cheeky face of yours slapped!"

"Aye, and it'd be as close as he's ever got to a woman," laughed Dai.

"Let me watch you dance naked, Cait, and you can slap me all you want." Michael gave her a distinctly evil grin. "There's nothin' in this world like a physical woman."

"Put a cork in it," Dylan said, then turned back to Mali. "It's perfect, my dear. We can build the whole thing around the legend of Owain. We'll start with the places where he performed his miracles. We'd have to spruce 'em up a bit, I know, but people would come for a look if they knew about it. That's where the adverts come in."

"They're just old stories," Mali said. "You can't even prove there ever was an Owain y'Craig."

"There must've been," Dai said, hanging eagerly at Dylan's elbow. "Else where would the stories come from?"

"The church probably has a record of him," Dylan said. "And there's that old statue in the cemetery. You could start by taking the Yank there."

"I'm not taking the Yank anywhere!" Mali said.

"Where's your sense of civic pride?" Dylan asked. "We need you, Mali. Now's the time to stand up and be counted."

"Oh, really? Then count me out."

The council chairman was undaunted. "I feared you might not welcome the idea, but what if there was money in it for you?"

"You're going to swindle the poor man?" Mali asked. She held her hands up, palms out. "I won't have any part of that!"

"The council voted this morning to establish a tourism board," he said. "The initial budget isn't great, but it should cover the cost of hiring an expert."

"The advertising man from America?"

"No. I mean you."

Mali's objections faltered. She needed the money, and if she controlled the stranger's visit, she could pick and choose what would be revealed to him.

Everyone waited in silence for her to respond. Even when a clock behind the bar chimed eight times, no one drifted away. Dinners would be late in Llansantowain that night.

"Oh, all right," Mali said with a resigned sigh. "But understand, I'm only doing it for the money." Not exactly a lie, she thought.

"I don't believe that for a second," Dylan replied, smiling. "Ye love us, Mali. Admit it!"

~*~

Bill didn't recognize the girl seated outside Rhia's office. She seemed out of place, her starched white shirt and neat black skirt too conservative for an ad agency, and the exact opposite of her new boss. She looked up slowly as he came to a halt in front of her desk. Adrift in a sea of file folders, notepads, and While-You-Were-Out slips, she seemed vaguely familiar.

"I'm Bill Thomas," he said, nodding his head slightly.

"Well, of course you are. How ya doin', Billy?"

Startled, Bill took a step back. He'd heard that sort of greeting all his life in Wetumpka, but only rarely in the city. And only one woman could put that special twang on it.

He squinted at her. *"Aunt Nell?"*

The girl grinned with unbridled enthusiasm. "Course not. I'm yer cousin, Stacey," she responded. "Nell's oldest. I saw you at Grampa Woodie's funeral."

It clicked. He remembered the down-to-earth girl

who glowered at her incorrigible twin brothers as much as their mother did. Stacey was easily ten years his junior, and had grown into an adult after he left home. He hadn't known her well. She'd seemed a sensible child, and had certainly grown into a sensible-looking young lady.

"You look...."

"Different?"

"Grown up. What're you doing here?"

She giggled. It was a hiccupy sound that must've driven Aunt Nell crazy. "I'm Miz Jones's new temp. I just got into town and found this job right away. It's amazing. Mama said city folk were mean, but so far, everyone's been nice as pie!" She paused and checked over her shoulder to see if anyone else was in earshot, then whispered, "'Cept for, you know, *her*."

Bill gave a sympathetic laugh. "Is Rhia in?"

"She's not back from lunch yet," Stacey said, putting her hands together in mock prayer. "Thank you, Jesus."

"Yeow. Bad day?"

"Bad week."

"Wanna compare horror stories? I lost two accounts in three days. I think that's a record."

"Maybe my week wasn't so bad after all," she said.

"Tell me about it."

She groaned. "It started on Tuesday. Rhia gave me hell for not calling her when I heard her father was in the hospital."

"David? My God! What--"

Stacey appeared stricken. "Was I supposed to call you, too?"

"No," he said quickly, trying to calm her fears.

"He's an old friend, and I've been on the road. What happened?"

"I don't know exactly, but he's okay now, stable. Something to do with his heart. I tried Rhia's cell phone when the hospital called, but she had it turned off. I left messages on her answering machine and a note on her desk. I wasn't here when she came in to tell her in person--nature calls, ya know--and she went volcanic."

Bill put his hand on her arm. "Don't let her get to you."

"Nobody gets to me like Mama. I can handle Miz Jones."

"Good," he said. "How 'bout a drink after work?" He paused suddenly. "You are old enough to drink, aren't you?"

"Yup. I've finished school and everything." She tilted her head. "Mama said if I saw you, to watch out--you had uppity ways and would introduce me to men of low character." Her grin turned sly. "Would you, please?"

"Definitely not. Nell would roast me alive. This is a Welcome to Hotlanta thing, a polite ritual."

"C'mon, cuz'! I want a date, not a Dad. Surely you know someone. I'm looking for Mr. Right, but I'd settle for Mr. Close."

"Sorry, kiddo. What kind of guy do you think I am?"

"He's a dangerous, unpredictable rogue, Stacey. I wouldn't go near him if I were you," said a rich baritone voice from the doorway.

Bill smiled at the dark brown face of his friend, Grady Banyon. "You're too late. We're having margaritas later."

The phone rang, and Stacey picked it up, listened briefly, then cut her eyes at them and silently mouthed Rhia's name.

Bill nodded and pulled Grady away. They walked down the hall, dodging the usual frantic mix of clerical and artistic staffers all of whom seemed dedicated to missions requiring that they exchange places.

"Why didn't you tell me about David's illness?"

Grady shrugged helplessly. "I'm sorry. I thought you knew."

They stopped outside the door to Grady's office as a diminutive assistant from the art department shoved an oversized envelope in Grady's hand. "Those are the proofs you wanted. Need 'em back in an hour." He disappeared without waiting for Grady's response.

"Gotta go, Bill. Rhia's on the warpath. I don't need to tell you to watch your back."

"Nope."

Grady frowned. "I'm really sorry for not telling you about David, but I've been up to my ass in alligators just dealing with Rhia's assault on the status quo. She says there's too much fat around here. Too much staff; not enough clients." Then he disappeared into his office.

Retreating to his own office with a growing sense of doom, Bill stared at the pile of email and miscellany crowding his in-box. In the short time she'd been back, Rhia had proven to be no different than she'd been as an intern, too intense and too--he looked up at the sound of the door--too in his office.

Closing the door behind her with practiced ease, Rhia leaned against it as if to absorb some of the deep-hued grain of the wood. He couldn't resist comparing them. One was a photo laminate glued to a slab of compressed sawdust and recycled milk cartons; the other was a complete fake.

"What can I do for you, Rhia?"

She batted long, dark eyelashes at him. Just as authentic as the door, he thought. She'd also had her teeth fixed. So much for the nickname.

"I'm concerned about your last few projects," she said.

"What about 'em?"

"They sucked."

Bill squinted at her. "The J&M series was good. It got an Addy nomination."

"Johnson and Malone," she mused, studying a manicured fingernail. "Wasn't that last year?"

He looked at her squarely and without apology. "Yeah. We had some delays."

"Right. I saw the file note. They wanted air time during the Super Bowl." She pressed her sinuous body away from the door. "You managed what--Saint Patrick's Day?"

"Super Bowl spots would've killed the budget," he said as she approached his desk. Her tight leather skirt ended well above her knees, way too short for office wear, but there was no denying she had the legs to make it work. He eased his eyes away from her to the poodle figurine a grateful pet groomer had given him in exchange for some free advice.

She tapped her perfectly white caps with a mauve fingernail that matched her outfit. "Did you expect that to balance out the two accounts you lost? 'Course, that's just since I've been here. Your record doesn't look terribly good." She pushed aside the piled paperwork on his desk, shifted one thigh upward and parked sidesaddle in front of him. "But let's not dwell on recent history."

He studied her intently, ignoring her deliberate positioning two feet over his head. Nothing about her made him feel anything but put upon, and a little sleazy being in the same business. He leaned back in his chair and met her gaze. Rhia arched her back, as if posing for *Playboy*. He wondered how many of her New York clients had gone after the bait in her blouse. "That's not entirely fair."

"Okay then, how would you describe your track record?"

He swept an arm toward his brag wall. Buried amid framed clippings, photos, and brass-on-pine attaboys were his Addy awards. He'd done good work and was proud of it. Rhia eased herself off his desk and slithered toward the wall, her finger lightly tracing the date on the latest trophy. "Got anything a little newer?" She lowered her brows and pressed her lips together in a parody of concentration. "God, I think I was still a virgin when you won this."

Bill coughed. It hadn't been *that* long.

She slid back onto his desk, this time with an air of conspiratorial camaraderie. "How'd you like a chance to redeem yourself?"

"If you're offering me a new client, sure," he said.

"Ever been to Wales?"

Bill chuckled. "I haven't taken a vacation since *I* was a virgin."

Rhia didn't laugh. "I didn't say anything about a vacation."

How was he supposed to work with her at all, much less give her the support David had asked of him? "I've never been to Wales," he said mildly. "Went to London once. Didn't much care for it--rained all week and no one knows how to cook barbeque."

"Wales is to London as Kansas is to New York."

"Only closer, I suspect."

She nodded. "Our client is a little town in northern Wales. They want to increase their tourist trade."

Great, thought Bill sourly, I'll never get out of the mom and pop accounts. "Sounds like a job for their Chamber of Commerce." He frowned. "Can they even afford us?"

"Think of it as *pro bono* work."

"Need I remind you we do advertising and PR? We aren't lawyers. We may share their lack of ethics, but--"

"Cute." She reached across the desk and punched his speakerphone to life, then entered her own extension.

"Hi, Billy," Stacey said. "You aren't calling to break our date, are you?"

Rhia arched an eyebrow at him. "A little office romance... 'Billy?' And with such a child. I'm shocked."

"What can I do for you, Miz Jones?"

Stacey's voice sounded tinny on the speakerphone. That she wasn't cowed by Rhia's unexpected presence spoke volumes of her upbringing. He was glad Stacey hadn't mentioned they were cousins. With her father out of the way, Rhia might suddenly dictate a policy forbidding relatives from working in the same office.

"That's *Miss* Jones, Stacey. You aren't working in the cotton fields anymore. There's a letter from Wales on my desk that's addressed to my father. I want it now."

"All righty," Stacey said as she hung up. Bill took small delight in seeing Rhia's eyes narrow. Few had the brass to hang up on her first. He liked Stacey all the more.

Rhia pretended not to notice. "I knew this job was right for you the minute I saw it."

Bill's bullshit detector clanged an alarm on multiple frequencies, but he kept a straight face by mentally cataloging the names of other firms that might be hiring.

After a perfunctory knock Stacey pushed the door open. She delivered the envelope, gave him a covert wink, and left.

Rhia rattled open a stiff page of paper and silently reviewed its contents. When finished, she tucked it back in the envelope and dropped it on his desk. He left it there.

"As you probably guessed, this is something Daddy put together. He was going to handle it himself before he got sick."

Bill frowned. "How's he doing? I need to drop by and see him."

"He'll pull through; no surgery required. You can see him when you've got this all wrapped up. I'm sure you'll want to tell him how successful you were."

"Right," he said, resigned to the inevitable. She seemed only too eager to begin the project, and he smelled a rodent. "So, what have they got that I can build a campaign on, and why is David so interested?"

"Oh, I'm interested, too. Very interested." She gave him her most dazzling smile--it chilled him to the marrow. "The town has an unofficial patron saint who Daddy was going to study. I want you to make him official--literally and figuratively."

"So much for question number one. They have a saint. How 'bout number two? What's in it for you?"

She kept the smile on at high voltage. "That saint and I are related."

Bill bit his lip in a conscious effort not to laugh.

She noticed. "I'm not making this up," she said petulantly. "It was Daddy's discovery." She pressed up against his desk, the hem of her skirt riding higher. "Pull this off, and I'll convince Daddy to make you a partner."

Now he knew she was lying, and annoyance reinforced his courage. "Aren't you afraid my presence might dim the glow from your halo?"

She reached across his desk and squeezed his cheek between her thumb and fingers, squishing his mouth into a goldfish kiss. He found himself staring at her perfectly painted, highly glossed lips. They moved. "Don't even think about screwing this up."

Chapter Two

One-Eyed Jack's Bar and Grill, a soothing little hole in the wall diner-turned-tavern that boasted ten stools along the dark wood bar and an ancient pool table, held far more patrons than the code allowed. Bill loved the place. He glanced up from his beer when the door opened. Grady quickly scanned the room until he spotted Bill, then escorted a worried-looking Stacey straight toward him.

"Just in time," Bill said, waving to the bartender. "Break open another keg!"

Grady shared Stacey's somber expression. "You may not feel like celebrating when you hear what she has to say."

"Party poopers. Where's my bon voyage?"

"I looked everywhere for you this afternoon," Stacey said. She eyed the tavern with concern. "You weren't here, were you?"

"I went to the library. Rhia knew. Did you ask her?"

Stacey shook her head. "I only talk to her when I have to."

"Of course," Bill said. "Anyway, I needed to do some research on Wales. I could be there a long while."

"Maybe that explains it," Stacey said.

"What?"

"What I tried to find you to tell you about."

"So tell me already!"

"Rhia had me reassign all your accounts. Grady got the big ones; all the--"

"I don't *have* any big ones."

"She gave me the biggest ones you had," Grady said, not meeting his gaze.

"What're friends for, right?"

Grady motioned to the bartender for a draft, then raised an eyebrow at Bill. "Even if I wasn't your friend, d'ya think I'd *want* your accounts?"

"Go ahead, twist the knife."

"C'mon you two, this is serious," Stacey said. "What're we gonna do?"

"There's only one thing we can do." Grady gathered them closer and lowered his voice. "We mutiny! Rally the troops at dawn and throw Captain Blitch overboard before she applies her second coat of make-up."

"Grady!"

"Relax, Stacey," Bill said. "Besides, my name's still on the office door, right?"

"The fasteners are Velcro."

"Accounts are reassigned all the time, especially

when someone's going out of town for a few weeks."

"So, it's no big deal?"

"Happens all the time."

She pursed her lips and looked at Grady. "Ya might've said something."

"Sorry. I'm a cad. It's what we do."

"Hmpf," Stacey said, rising. "I've gotta go. Can't keep Miz Hot Pants waitin'."

They waited until she was safely out of range, and Grady took delivery of his beer. "'Accounts are reassigned all the time'? Are you nuts?"

"I didn't want her to worry."

"Somebody should be."

"I'll deal with it."

Grady took a swallow of beer. "So, you found a library? Congrats!"

"I've got my very own library card," Bill said with a dramatic, wounded-pride sniff.

"Learn anything?"

"Yeah. Wales is really green. It has lots of sheep and castles. English-built castles, mostly. The king didn't trust the Welsh."

"It really sucks when you conquer somebody, and they just don't give up. What's with those people?"

"I think it's their language."

"What, no English? Hell, I thought they *were* English."

"Most do speak English, but many speak Welsh, too. Very strange language. There's a town over there whose only claim to fame is that it has the longest name anywhere in the world."

"And this is good to know because...."

"Because it's different. People like different." He

liked different. Maybe that's why he was so good with small accounts and not big ones. Maybe this trip would be good for him.

"You leave tomorrow?"

"Yeah," Bill said. The immediacy of the trip ate at him. Why the rush? The town had been without an ad campaign for a thousand years, what was one week more or less? "I'm flying into Manchester and renting a car."

"They drive on the left, ya know," Grady said.

"So I hear. I was hoping to catch a train or a bus, but nothing goes anywhere near Llansantowain."

"Land's End Town?"

"That's what it looks like to me. I have no idea how it's really pronounced. Anyway, the town's so small it's not even mentioned in the guide books. Back home, anybody with a 'possum ranch and a billboard can get into a guide book."

"You'll call me if you need help, right? This one's really important to Rhia."

Bill snorted. "I know it's important to David, but I don't believe for a skinny minute Rhia cares if I'm successful or not."

"She cares all right," Grady said. "Spin this saint thing right, and she'll nominate you for God."

"I'm doing it for David, not Rhia. And maybe one other."

Grady looked puzzled. "Who?"

"Me," Bill said.

~*~

The great stone building that had been in Mali's family for a score of generations stood forlorn and empty. The windows, shuttered with unfinished wood, worked in concert with warped and peeling trim to give the place a decayed look it didn't deserve. The foundation, walls, and floors were solid, a testament to years of her father's labor. Once he had died, Mali remained the only Rhys still interested in rescuing it. Aunt Glynnis humored her, and helped with the renovation fund where she could, but Mali was the driving force, albeit an underfinanced one. The last major advancement came when she had the roof restored, the cost of which she'd added to the lien and had paid against, more or less regularly, for five years.

Michael Wills, Llansantowain's sole electrician, strode toward her from inside the manor house. He wiped his grimy, long-fingered hands on his workpants and slicked his untidy black hair behind his ears.

"Well," Mali asked. "What do you think?"

He scratched his ribs under his shirt, a process which exposed more hirsute flesh than she cared to see.

"It won't be cheap."

"Aye, now there's a shocker!" She put her palm to her forehead. This was not the first time she wished she'd studied something useful instead of medieval Welsh history. Then she wouldn't be at the mercy of the likes of Michael.

"Can't wire an entire building for nothing," he said. "Especially one built long before anyone even thought about electricity. It'll take me some time to cost the job out."

He scratched again, and Mali closed her eyes. "Give me your best guess."

"It's going to run a thousand quid, at least."

"To run a few wires?"

"We aren't talkin' about stringin' Christmas lights."

"We might as well be," Mali said. Truly the manor was the bane of her financial existence. In the past, they'd always managed to find whatever money was needed, but now, without selling the letter, she'd never have enough to finish the work. Caught between Owain's Rock and the devil, she thought morosely.

"You wouldn't have to pay it all at once," Michael said. "We could work out some terms."

Mali shook her head, still engrossed in trying to resolve where she'd find a thousand pounds.

"There are other ways to pay off debts." Something in his voice brought her attention screeching back to the conversation.

She stepped away from him, put her hands on her hips, and raised an eyebrow. "What're you suggesting, Michael Wills?"

He straightened his shoulders and pulled in his stomach. "I'm a reasonable fellow, and I pay the taxman on time, but there are legal ways to leave the government out of our business." He adjusted the collar of his work shirt. "It's called barter."

"You want to trade electrical work for..." She looked at him skeptically. "I translate old documents. What possible--"

"I'm not talking about documents." His smile featured uneven teeth and a chin badly in need of a shave. "I'm interested in something much younger." His eyes dropped to the middle of her jumper.

"I'd appreciate it if you stopped talking to my

chest," she said.

He shrugged. "Your chest. My wiring...."

Her mouth dropped open in astonishment. "You slimy git!"

"Oh come on, Mali. It's not like you're married or anything. Who're you savin' it for? We could have a good time, you and me." He reached for her with both hands. "We could--"

Mali slapped his cheek as hard as she could.

Michael stood in shock, one hand still outstretched toward her, the other covering the bright red finger marks left on his cheek. "Mali, I--"

She pointed to the driveway. "Go!" she rasped. "Or I'll give you one to match the other, and set the dogs on you, too!"

Michael's eyes flashed in defiance. "And who d'ye think'll do your wiring, then?"

"I'll do it myself before I let you near me again, Michael Wills."

"You're not bein' reasonable, Mali. Listen..." His voice trailed away as she raised her hand for another swing. "All right. I'll just be goin' then." Still rubbing his jaw, he piled into his lorry, gunned the engine, and departed in a blue-gray cloud of exhaust. Mali didn't wait for the air to clear before she marched into the cottage and slammed the door behind her.

"What's the matter, dear?" Glynnis asked.

Mali huffed. "Nothing important."

"And the Queen's just another knobby old hen." She followed Mali into the kitchen. "You may as well tell me now and save us both the time and aggravation of waiting." Her face reflected amused disbelief.

"I asked Michael to give me an estimate for wiring

the big house."

Glynnis whistled long and low. "That must've been some price to make you so mad. I hope you told him no."

Mali laughed in spite of herself. "He quoted a thousand pounds. But even at half that, he knew I'd never be able to afford the work," Mali said. "So he suggested I pay him in bed."

Glynnis exhaled like a steam engine on the Snowdon run. "An utter pillock, that one. I'm not surprised. I shall have a few words with our Mr. Wills the next time I see him. You can be sure of that. I wonder what his mother would say if she knew what he's been up to?"

"You'd not tell his mother! He's a grown man--"

"All the more reason for him to know better!"

The way folk talked across the valley, Michael's mum--and everyone else in Llansantowain--would know of his offer to Mali before breakfast. She didn't envy him his mother's wrath. "Much as I look forward to hearing what she had to say to him, it doesn't solve our wiring problem. The job's just too expensive."

Glynnis briefly looked out the window, then began tidying loose newspapers. She was at her best when she could bustle around with her chores and still chat. "I'm sure we'll find someone to do it. There are plenty of able-bodied men about."

"Electricians by the dozen, I suppose?"

"Aye. And they'll likely know better how to treat a lady."

"Undoubtedly."

"You'll do better with the Yank when he arrives," Glynnis said as she fluffed the chair pillow.

Mali laughed at the notion. "That's hardly likely. He's your age, if not older. Maybe you'll hit it off with him."

"Stranger things have happened. I'm not too old for romance. You, on the other hand, oftentimes act like it."

"Me?" A slight warming at her cheeks made Mali turn away so her aunt would not see the blush. The kitchen offered a haven, and she put the kettle on for tea. Romance was fine for others, but she had no place for it in her own life.

"You're too picky," Glynnis called after her. "There are some good lads in the village. They aren't all like Mr. Wills. But, they won't last forever."

"I know them all," Mali said, "and I'm not interested." Most were nice enough, but none stirred her imagination, nor anything else. With that thought, the warmth in her cheeks blossomed full.

Mali retreated into her office. Glynnis trailed behind her, dusting knickknacks.

"Well, what does interest you, then?"

Mali stopped to think. "I don't know exactly, but I'd like to find someone who operates on a slightly larger stage than one crowded with only sheep or babies."

"You're almost thirty-two. You've turned down proposals far better than Michael's. What accounts for all of those?"

Mali shrugged. "I've been busy." She gave her aunt a sly look. "Not that you've done much better."

Glynnis nodded. "It's a couple of old spinsters we are."

"Do you think?"

"Could be," Glynnis said, resting her arm on Mali's shoulders. "When did you say that Yank would be here?"

~*~

Bill caught sight of a blue horizon that lasted all the way to Manchester. Instead of dingy warehouses he found a thriving city of modern architecture blended with the historical. In many ways, it was a lot like Atlanta--sprawling and busy, and he felt as if he understood it.

The Welsh countryside, however, bemused him. Dotted with villages, the region had nothing but endless miles of narrow winding roads through treeless green hills that led to heavily forested areas every bit as wild as the backwoods of the Appalachians. He no sooner realized he was in a town when it disappeared, and he was three miles from the next. He felt lightheaded from the notion he'd stepped across a threshold into the distant past. Modernism overlaid the ancient--roadways and power lines seemed to coexist with dirt tracks and ponies. The occasional road signs, mostly in Welsh, confused him no less. He stopped often, comparing the letters on the signs with those on his road map. According to the map, Llansantowain was next. Even so, if it hadn't been for the freshly painted sign near an old stone pub, Bill would have missed the town altogether.

He pulled to a stop in front of the pub and peered down the street. Not much there. No sign of a hotel-- only a few shops, and houses, some excessively old, and a smattering with the straight rectangular sides of new construction. If he'd blinked, or looked down at his map, he'd have driven right through the place. The pub, and the church opposite with a broad yard in front, formed the center of things. He wondered if that meant anything, or what order of importance the townspeople had--church then drink, or drink then church. He supposed there was little else to do. He'd never been in a place quite so small, including Wetumpka. And like the tiny Alabama town he was born in, this one would probably have a well-developed sense of us-versus-them, be it city folk and country folk or Yanks versus Brits.

He'd slept through most of the 6-hour flight from Atlanta, but the drive and the time change had caught up with him. A beer followed by a nap were the first things on his agenda, providing he could find a place to lie down. He contemplated doing just that in his rental car, but decided against it. Who knew what kinds of laws the Welsh had. Surely someone in the pub could point him toward a local inn.

The aging wooden sign over an equally ancient door bore a Welsh name he couldn't read and the crudely rendered figures of a rooster and a cow. At least, he thought it was a cow. *The Cow and Rooster? Or maybe The Cock and...* No, he decided, shaking his head. *They wouldn't.*

The tavern door opened silently on well-oiled hinges, and the competing aromas of heavy ale, roast lamb, and cigarette smoke washed over him.

A dozen people sat in clumps around a cozy room. Smooth wooden chairs or love-seat benches faced one another around tables no bigger than TV trays. He walked to the bar trying not to appear self-conscious despite the open-mouthed stares of everyone in the room.

"Americanoor," someone said. At least, that's what it sounded like, and someone else agreed with the assessment.

He nodded and grinned wearily. Of course the whole town would know he was coming.

The woman behind the bar seemed to recognize his discomfort and smiled warmly at him. *"Croeso!* I mean, welcome," she said. "You look like yer spittin' feathers."

"I... What?"

"You look thirsty. A touch dry."

"Tired mostly," he said, happy to return her smile. "I'm trying to find a hotel, but I'm not having much luck."

"I'm not surprised, since there is none in Llansantowain," she said. Her pronunciation wasn't as far from his own as he'd imagined it would be. She'd said something like clan-sant-oh-wan. "I've a few rooms for rent upstairs. They're not grand like you'd get in Llangollen or Betws-y-Coed, but the rooms are clean, and you can't hear much going on down here, especially if you're in the very back."

The lady spit the names of the towns out of the corners of her mouth, and he made a mental note not to stand too close to anyone speaking Welsh. "Then I'll take one in the very back."

Her smile faded. "Oh! On any other day, you could have your pick, but I'm holding that one for a special guest." She brightened. "Not that you aren't special, too!"

Spin, he thought, even way out here in the boondocks. A nice way to jack up the rent, even just a little. "It doesn't matter. I'm so tired, I'll be asleep before I close my eyes."

She reached under the bar and came up with a hefty and ornate key. A paper tag dangled from it, but Bill couldn't read the writing on it. "I'll need you to sign the register," she said, rummaging once again in the recesses beneath the counter. "Blast. I can't find it." She pulled a pen from her apron, added a napkin, and slid them across the bar. "Just jot your name down there for now. You can fill out the proper paperwork later." She handed him the key and pointed. "Up those stairs and to your right." She gave a sharp whistle. "Dai, you're doing nothing. Get the gentleman's bags, *os gwel wch yn dda.*"

A rough-hewn man in his thirties rose to his feet, slipped a gray woolen cap over his red hair, and sauntered out the door before Bill could tell him which car. Then it hit him. In a town this small, the man would instantly recognize an outsider's car.

He squinted once more at the tag on the key, then gave up. "I can't read the number."

Several in the room guffawed, including the woman behind the bar. "It's not a number, luv." She stared the others into silence. It says "*'y alltudiaeth'*-- the banishment. Each of the rooms is named after the paintings in them. In yours, Saint Owain is banishing devils from pagan women. Our village was named for him."

"That much I do know," Bill said. "It's why I'm here."

His announcement brought obvious surprise to the men and women listening intently to his conversation.

She looked confused. "*You're* David Jones, the

American? I expected someone older."

He laughed. "I work for David. Unfortunately, he has some health problems, so I'm here instead." He stretched out a hand. "I'm Bill Thomas."

"Pleased to meet you, William Thomas," she said, taking the fingers of his right hand and squeezing them once with a strong grip. "I'm Brenna Parry."

"We heard a Yank was comin'," said a man from the back of the room. He stood up, blocking the view of the enormous red dragon on the flag that covered the wall behind him. "Bren, I'd like to buy the chap an ale. Crack open an Owain for 'im."

She put her hands on her hips and faced him squarely. "I'd like to crack one over your head, Michael Wills."

"An Owain?" Bill asked. "Is that from a local brewery?"

"Aye," Michael said, ambling toward him, glass in hand. "Our very own Caitlin Morgan boils it up in a cauldron she keeps in that scary little cellar she has. She's a witch, you know." He winked as if to include Bill in some local joke.

"Sounds like fun." Bill turned back to the bar, picked up the pen, and prepared to sign the napkin.

"That's not necessary, William," Brenna said. "You're a guest of the town."

"Oh, but I insist."

She shook her head with finality. "I'll not have it."

"They're not bad beds," Michael said. "I've slept in 'em a time or two."

"You slept *near* one last time," Brenna said. "You knackered out halfway through the bedroom door."

"Saint Owain's ale," Bill said, thinking maybe he

wasn't so tired after all. "It's got a nice ring to it."

"You needn't drink it. I've got other brands to choose from," Brenna said, then turned to Dai who had one of Bill's bags in each of his callused hands. "Set 'em there, Dai, and have one on the town. This gentleman here is the Yank we've been expecting." She poured a glass of dark ale and pushed it across the bar to Dai. "Let me pour you a lager. I'm sure I've got something you'll like."

"And miss my chance to try the local brew? I couldn't. Let me take my bags upstairs, then I'll come back down and join you." He reached into his pocket for something to give Dai as a tip, but Brenna stayed his hand.

"He's drinkin' his reward," she said, then nodded toward the narrow stairwell. "Up we go then." She preceded him up the stairs with a set of towels and opened a door at the end of the hall. "The bath is in here. Your room is next to it. It's not the quietest, but it's close to the loo."

He nodded his thanks and opened the door to his room. Brenna reached past him to turn on the lights. A mural on the wall beside the bed dominated the room. It was obviously painted by the same person who'd done the sign outside the pub. In it, a man draped in a shapeless brown robe, his head encircled by a yellow blob that looked more like a happy face than the halo he presumed it to represent, waved his arms at a trio of--Bill squinted at the work--women. Wispy, ghostlike apparitions appeared to be leaking out of them like frosty breath on a cold morning.

"Interesting." It was all he could manage.

"My great-grandfather painted it," Brenna said.

"We say it's *hagr*."

"Hagger?"

"Yes. Hideous. But we leave it up because people still talk about how proud he was of it. That one and the others."

"I'd like to see them all," Bill said. "Tomorrow, perhaps?"

Brenna nodded. "Certainly, though you needn't hope the others have any more artistic merit than this one." She put the towels on a dresser and left. "See you downstairs."

Bill spent a few more moments examining the painting on the wall above the bed. It was painfully obvious the painter's motivation outdistanced his talent. He wondered what the art department at the agency could do with it. At the very least, they could make the women look more human. He dug his digital camera out of his bags and took a few snapshots. Hagr, he thought. *Yep. Hideous.*

Chuckling, he put on a golf shirt, then slipped into the tiny bathroom. Cold water flowed from both ancient taps, so he washed his face with a quick splash. He dried himself with a non-absorbent towel and vowed to buy a proper one at the earliest opportunity. Slightly refreshed, he went back downstairs.

When he returned, no one but Michael even looked at him. Unaccountably, it cheered him. *Maybe he was fitting in already.*

Michael waited with a glass of beer in one hand and an open bottle in the other. Bill accepted the bottle, and they both settled down at a table beside the bar. Bill put the bottle to his nose and sniffed deeply. He coughed, and his eyes watered. He heard amused snickers from the other patrons. He had no doubt every eye once more studied his every move.

"A bit fresh?" Michael asked.

Bill blinked. "That's not the word I had in mind." He smelled it again, though this time keeping his face several inches from the opening and fanning the fumes delicately toward his nose. No mistaking that aroma: *Quaker State. 30-weight, non-detergent.* He looked at the label--hand-drawn and duplicated on a copier--definitely a work in progress.

"Cheers," Michael said, raising his glass.

Bill clinked the glass with his bottle, put it to his lips, and drank. Then gagged. He desperately looked for a place to spit it out, but everyone in the room seemed to have rediscovered him. His taste buds screamed warnings, but he had little choice. He swallowed. It didn't go down easily. The beer was as hagr as the mural in his room.

He struggled to maintain an even expression, but nothing could hold back the tears.

"What d'ye think?" Michael asked, his face a serene mask.

Somehow, Bill managed to keep the stuff down and exhaled carefully. There was enough alcohol in it to pickle a lamb. "I've never had anything quite... like that."

Several patrons laughed outright.

"It's a man's drink, then?" Michael asked.

It's an idiot's drink. "It needs..." He struggled for the right word. "Toning down. I doubt it's going to become wildly popular as is." He set the bottle down and pushed it away.

"Caitlin says it's still in the experimental stage," Brenna said. "She didn't want to come up with just another ale. She said she wanted something that'd make a statement."

"More like a declaration," Bill said, hoping someday he'd be able to wash the taste out of his mouth. "You *like* this?"

"Lord, no," Michael said, shivering. "I wouldn't clean paint brushes with it."

"Nobody can stand the stuff," Brenna said, handing Bill a pint of ale before disappearing into a back room.

"I'm supposed to get in touch with a woman named Mali Rhys," Bill said to Michael. "Do you know her?"

Michael motioned for him to keep his voice low. "I can tell you anything you need to know about that one. But there's no need to bring up her name in a public place where people are trying to have a good time."

Bill frowned. He'd been hoping for someone congenial and helpful, but locals usually knew better, and he'd learned to listen to them. "I take it she's not well liked."

"Now don't get the wrong idea; she's a God-fearin' woman. She just takes it a little too far, if you know what I mean. *Miss* Rhys, we call her. She's quite particular about that. Won't let anyone get too close. Treats most of us like we've got some kind of disease."

Bill nodded. Just his luck to get saddled with a stick-up-her-butt school marm type.

"Maybe if she'd ever get down off her high horse and have a drink, she'd loosen up. But not our Miss

Right and Proper. You'd think she was a Royal the way she treats people. I don't envy you workin' with that one. No, sir. Not a bit. I'd sooner drink a case of Owain's and chase it w' dirt."

"I appreciate the warning," Bill said. "And this time, I mean it. Still, I'd better give her a call. I've come a long way and have a lot of work to do. I might as well see her early on and get it over with."

Michael put his hand on Bill's shoulder and looked him in the eye. "Best of luck to ya, then. Let me know if there's anything else I can do."

"You've been a big help already," Bill said.

Michael waved his beer at him and tottered off toward the back of the room. Bill stepped outside the bar and pulled a wireless phone from his pocket. Stacey had given him a number for the Rhys woman which he dialed. A female answered on the second ring.

"Good afternoon," he said. "I'm trying to reach Miss Rhys."

"I'm Miss Rhys," the woman said.

"I'm Bill Thomas, from Atlanta. I'm standing in for David Jones."

"Mr. Jones! Of course," she said. "You're the chap who's come to do our adverts."

"Correct, and may I say how pleased I am to talk with you? I've got so many questions I hardly know where to begin. Would it be possible for you to meet me tomorrow morning?"

"*Me?*"

"You're Miss Rhys, aren't you?"

"Well, yes, but--"

"Then you're the person I need to speak to." He

piled as much charm into his voice as he could. "Just tell me when and where."

"Very well then," she said. "Let's make it 11 o'clock in front of Caitlin Morgan's shop."

The name sounded awfully familiar. The beer! He shivered involuntarily. "I've already experienced some of her handiwork."

"That's odd," she said. "I didn't think she took male customers."

Bill wondered if he'd already made a tactical blunder in broaching the topic of Owain's Ale. It was bound to come up sooner or later, so he plunged ahead. "I meant, I'd had a taste of her uhm-- experimental beverage."

"I see." The woman didn't sound any less confused.

Oh, Lord. "I suspect it'll be my last."

"Indeed," she said. "So, 11 o'clock, it is, then?"

"Right. I'll be wearing a--"

"I'll know you," she said, warmth again suffusing her voice. "You'll be the person I don't recognize."

He chuckled. "Of course."

~*~

Afternoon sunlight streamed through a slit in the curtains and illuminated the letter case and Mali wondered, for at least the thousandth time that week, if she'd made a mistake by not turning it over to Smythe-Webley. But every time the urge to sell it became strong, she imagined how the media would jump on a story about a village named after the saint it had corrupted. They'd be a laughing stock. Such thoughts overcame any desire to allow the letter's contents to get out. Being the protector of the family secret threatened to crush her under a mountain of bills due and credit owing, yet she had little choice. There was no way she could allow the world to discover that Owain's miracles were lies--all of them-- stories fabricated from fragments of the truth and twisted into bizarre reversals of what really happened by ancestors more interested in self-preservation than piety. She picked up the case to put it away. Out of sight didn't mean out of mind, but at least that way it wasn't the focus of every glance.

"I'm off, dear," Glynnis said as she entered the room from the kitchen. "I'll be back sometime this afternoon." She raised an eyebrow at the case in Mali's hands. "You're not still worrying over that letter, are you?"

Mali nodded, unable to shake off the gloom the letter always seemed to give her. "Yes."

"Well, no one will ever know about it now. You've done the right thing, Mali." She patted at her curls.

"I still don't understand why Mr. Thomas asked to see you instead of me," Mali said. Americans could be perplexing; not that she had ever met any, but she imagined that's how they were.

"If you'd rather meet him yourself, I certainly don't mind. You'd be the better one to speak with him."

"No, no. He asked for you, and that's fine. Show him around; take him to the Rock; answer his questions. Tell him anything he wants to know about the legends." There was no point in cautioning her to avoid mentioning the letter. Glynnis would be the last person on Earth to reveal its secrets.

"Do you think Dylan will still pay if I go instead of

you?"

"He will if he knows what's good for him!" Mali bent to kiss her aunt's cheek, and the overwhelming aroma of cologne made her eyes water. "What in the world are you wearing?"

"It's called *Midnight in Marrakech*," Glynnis said. "Caitlin says it 'reflects the mysteries of the orient.'"

"Did she also suggest that you bathe in it?"

Glynnis clucked like a worried hen. "A bit strong, then?"

"That depends on the message you want to send."

"And that depends on how old he is," Glynnis said, with a playful wink. "Do you have any ideas?"

"Not a one."

"Well, I'll know soon enough. If he's the right age, I might just fancy him." She twirled around so Mali could give her a final inspection. "How do I look?"

"Magnificent," Mali said. "With charms like yours, the poor man doesn't stand a chance."

A look of quiet longing crossed Glynnis's face, replaced by an impish smile. "It's been a long, long time since I took a trip to the woods with--"

Mali held up her hands and turned her head away. She did not want to think of her aunt traipsing off into the woods for any reason.

"We all share the same urges, Mali," Glynnis said. "They don't go away just because we get older and lose our girlish figures." She patted Mali's shoulder. "But they're a might easier to do something about when you're young. Remember that next time you turn a man down."

"Aunt Glynnis!" Mali cried, her cheeks burning. She cruised out leaving Mali in a vapor trail of

Midnight in Marrakech.

"Wait!" Mali called just as her aunt left the cottage.

"What is it?"

"Leave a window rolled down during the drive."

~*~

From the outside, Morgana's House of Style looked like most of the buildings in the town--a stone front with glass windows so old Bill could see the flow marks. A closer inspection, however, suggested something more. Just what, he couldn't quite put his finger on. He peered inside, but a collection of new age posters obscured the view. He saw only an assortment of candles and a strikingly attractive flower arrangement. All in all, completely unlike any brewery he'd ever encountered but oddly fitting for the ale which shared the town's name. Lured by curiosity, he poked his head inside. Perhaps there were tastier beverages on the menu. He took a whiff, expecting at least the aroma of hops. Instead, he got a lung-full of perfume, hair spray, and the nose-wrinkling scent of something even more vile, all accompanied by Caitlin Morgan's laughter and an invitation for a wash and cut. He muttered a no-thanks, and quickly withdrew back into the fresh air. Taking a deep breath, he now understood how a brewery could manufacture a beer as nasty as Saint Owain's--a concoction better used to curl hair.

His watch read 10:59, and he wondered if Miss Mali Rhys was the sort to be on time, or if she would make him wait. According to Michael Wills, a hard-nosed prude like her would more likely do whatever was necessary to keep him off balance. He expected the worst--much as he would when he dealt with Rhia.

A tiny, ancient automobile careened down a road dusty from disuse. Clearly in need of some serious valve work, the car sputtered and coughed. He expected it to pass on through, but it slowed to a stop directly in front of him. A pleasant-looking woman of middle years waved, then rolled down her window and leaned out, as if he couldn't hear what she had to say unless her entire head protruded outside the vehicle.

"Bore da!" she said in a singsong.

Boedy da, to you, too, he started to say, then decided it might mean something like "Your fly is open." His fingers went to his belt to feel for the zipper pull, just in case. "Hello," he said simply.

"You must be Mr. Jones! I'm Miss Rhys," she said, with a blooming glow to her face. "You're remarkably well-looking for a man of your years, I must say!"

Nice way of putting it, he thought.

"I'm very happy to meet you, Miss Rhys, but sorry to disappoint you," he said. "I'm not David Jones. I'm Bill Thomas, David's associate. He was unable to come and sent me instead." She seemed more pleasant than Wills had suggested, nevertheless, he approached her warily.

She opened the car door to stand beside him. Short, incredibly cheery-faced, with rosy cheeks and a winning smile, she looked like a postcard for Welsh tourism. All she needed was a Mother Goose hat and a red cape to complete the picture. Not the woman described by Wills at all.

"William, is it?"

"Bill," he said. When she looked bewildered he

added, "My grandmother called me William."

"And so shall I," she said, patting at her hair. She took two deep breaths, brought back a natural expression of charm, and thrust her hand toward his in a no-nonsense way. He found himself liking her on the spot.

He took her hand, and she squeezed his fingers gently. "Happy to make your acquaintance, William," she said. "Well, we'd best get started." She unleashed another effervescent smile. "Let's start at the shrine, shall we?"

"Anywhere you suggest is fine."

"Then hop into the Mini, and we'll drive over. It's not so far, but I enjoy a drive as often as I can manage."

As he passed downwind and stepped close to her, her cologne mugged him. His eyes watered, and he held back a sneeze. He groped toward the car and suddenly realized the steering wheel was on his side. Miss Rhys said nothing, only gestured to the opposite door as the queen might gesture to a subject. It made her seem regal and grand, and while this may be the attitude Wills objected to, Bill didn't mind it at all. In her, it seemed to go with the territory. A younger woman would have had a harder time pulling it off.

He folded himself into the tiny confines of the car, squeezing his knees between his chest and the dash. Rolling the window down gave him a bit more breathing room, and he leaned toward the opening and the fresh air. Miss Rhys didn't move until he'd fastened his seat belt, then she freed the handbrake, raced the motor and slipped the car into gear. The drive lasted less than a minute, and most of that time

Miss Rhys spent turning around. They could have walked across the street faster. She parked in front of the church with a triumphant smile.

"It's not always easy to find a place to park here. We're a bit early yet for choir practice so we're lucky."

He hadn't seen another car, but he was quite happy to get out of hers.

She led him to a small statue in the corner of the Church garden. It faced the main square, and he imagined at one time it might have been the center of attraction for the town. For now, it only seemed to attract an assortment of little brown birds. The statue itself was unimposing, though the artistry was adequate. The sculptor had far more skill in rendering Saint Owain than did the painter at the hotel.

The stone Owain stood nearly five feet tall but, thanks to its pedestal, met Bill eye-to-eye. Owain's grimace of fierce determination gave his round face a look of wild-eyed fanaticism. Bill wondered if this was really the look the sculptor was aiming for. If memory served him, other saints were represented with far more serene expressions. St. Owain looked more constipated than holy.

"It's life-sized y'know," she said.

He frowned at the bird droppings that covered the head and shoulders of the saint. "At the very least, we'll need to clean him up a bit and possibly move him to a more accessible spot."

She looked dubious. "He's been standing right where he is for centuries, William."

"Maybe a change of scenery would do him good."

When she frowned, Bill smiled apologetically. "I admit my sense of tourism is probably much stronger than my sense of history." She returned his smile with her good-natured grin. Just as Llansantowain wasn't much of a town, the statue in the corner of the churchyard wasn't much of a monument. A stone alcove rose two feet overhead, and were it not for the single plastic flower gracing the feet of the statue, he'd never have known it for a shrine. It looked more like an elaborate tombstone.

"The flower was Caitlin's idea," she said brightly. "Adds a bit of color to the dour old fellow, I daresay."

"Are all saints dour? The painting in my room at the pub shows a man with a remarkably sour face casting out something from--" He turned to her with some trepidation. "May I be blunt?"

"By all means," she said calmly, but the sudden play of her fingers with one another suggested otherwise.

"It's just that the figures in the painting don't look like women, though that's what the lady at the pub said they were."

Rosy blushes flowered on her cheeks. "Oh, aye. We have to thank Bren Parry's great-grandfather, God rest him, for that. He was more blessed in his enthusiasm than he was in his ability. Brenna leaves them up not so much for our own sakes, as to honor the memory of two, uhm, remarkable men."

Her hesitation intrigued him. "Remarkable in what way?"

She glanced away for some time, and Bill could see the wheels turning. He hoped she'd tell him something juicy and worth using in the campaign.

"Saint Owain is known for several miracles, though it's quite likely he was responsible for much more than we credit him with today. The first was the casting out of demons from three sisters. They were village women who'd turned to a life of sin while their menfolk were off fighting in the Crusades. Owain cast out the demons which had turned them away from a godly life. Without him, they'd have gone to their graves as the handmaidens of greed, avarice, and vice."

"He cured them of greed?" Rhia wouldn't much care for that.

Miss Rhys cleared her throat and continued, but with some difficulty. "He cured them of using their feminine charms for financial gain."

"Ah," he said, failing to see how this was going to appeal to any but the most strait-laced of tourists. "What were the other miracles?"

She held up her hand. "You must get Brenna to show you the murals in the other guest rooms. The one in your room must be the casting out of demons. There's another showing Owain besting the devil in a drinking match."

Bill perked up. "A drinking match?"

"Aye. The winner would control the destiny of the town. It went on for hours, and Owain matched the devil drink for drink. The devil grew suspicious when he had trouble standing, and Owain remained cold sober. The devil demanded that Owain pour the next round, which he did. Well, the ale turned into milk in his mug as it had all along. The devil got sick when he took a drink and accused Owain of trying to poison him. In the mural, I believe the devil is throwing up."

"That's a charming image," Bill said. Owain's story was shaping up to offer more possibilities than he'd hoped. "There's more?"

"Oh yes, indeed. The devil ordered Owain to assemble all the women of the village and to separate the virtuous from those who... weren't."

Bill tried to picture the little man herding all the women from across the hills and valleys into one place at one time, especially for the reason given.

"While the women were summoned, Owain inquired where he might gather them all in private and conduct a great baptism. He reasoned that they'd then all be washed free of sin, and any who'd lost their virtue would have it restored."

"Sneaky guy," Bill said. "I'm liking him more and more."

"He found the perfect spot in an underground pool in a grotto not far from Owain's Rock. They called it the Devil's Finger back then, a towering stone which marked the way..." She paused, clearly uncomfortable. "To a place where he spent much time. Owain met the women of the village at the underground pool and baptized them one and all."

"An underground pool? Really? Does such a thing actually exist?"

Miss Rhys nodded sagely. "It most certainly does."

"I'd love to see it."

"I'm sure that can be arranged."

Now he had something to work with! "Excellent! Please continue."

Miss Rhys cleared her throat. "At the very end of the line came Old Nick himself, and once again he accused Owain of treachery. Vowing the pool would never again be used for baptisms, he jumped in and began splashing and carrying on as only a demon could. They say his skin was so fiery, and his anger so profound, that the water remains hot to this very day."

"Oh my God," Bill exclaimed, "it's a hot pool?"

"Quite."

"That's wonderful!" Tourists loved hot pools.

"It didn't prove so wonderful for Owain," she said, a hint of admonishment in her tone.

He frowned. "Why not?"

"The dip in the water didn't cool the devil off. He was still beside himself with anger and told Owain he'd have no more of his trickery. Owain could either meet him in a fair fight or watch him claim the souls of every living person in the village."

This kept getting better and better, and Bill grew more intrigued than he could have imagined. Why hadn't this extraordinary tale been contained in the tour guides?

"What kind of a fight? Swords and lances? A duel? How fair would that be, especially if Owain was neither knight nor soldier?"

"Nor was he either," Miss Rhys said, "and he told the devil so. But the evil one said they had no need of weapons. They'd wrestle to the death, and they'd do it in the shadow of the Devil's Finger."

"That's the second time you've mentioned the Devil's Finger. What is it, exactly? I don't suppose it still exists, does it?"

Her face clouded with distaste, but she nodded. "It's a standing stone, a big rock, though it's not standing anymore. Such things tend to last a long time."

He chuckled at the irony of the patient country woman explaining the obvious to a tourist. "I'm sorry to be such a rube."

A puzzled expression crossed her face then she went on. "I suppose you already know the rest."

"No," he admitted. "I'd love to hear it. You're quite the storyteller." Her smile broadened at that, and it pleased him to see it light her whole face.

"There's not much more," she said. "Owain spent a great deal of time in prayer. I suspect he was merely saving his strength while making the devil wait. They say he pranced around growing angrier and angrier, and whenever he demanded they begin, Owain found some new excuse to delay. Meanwhile, all the villagers and all the people living nearby gathered around the great stone to cheer Owain on.

"Finally, when the devil was all but overcome with his own impatience, Owain announced he was ready. They grappled and despite the terrible heat of the devil's skin, and the rending of his vile claws, Owain somehow hung on. In the painting at the pub, Owain is riding on the devil's back. Anyway, while he clung to Old Nick, he urged the townsfolk to push the great stone on top of them both. It was the only way he knew to defeat the devil, even though it'd cost him his own life in the bargain."

Bill shook his head in admiration. "Quite a guy, that Owain."

"That's why we call him a saint," she said.

"I've gotta see this stone," he said, looking in both directions. "Is it very far?"

The smile came back in full, and she pointed up the road on which she'd driven into town. "Not at all. It's just over the hill toward the big house. We can drive if you'd like." She gestured toward the Mini.

"Actually, a little walk in the fresh air would do me good."

"I don't suppose the air in America is quite like ours," she said.

He grinned at the pungent aroma of her cologne. "Not even close."

The walk from the church yard to the Rock of Saint Owain was less than a thousand yards, and nothing of the great stone could be seen even though the road ran right by it. A tall hedgerow and a copse of evergreen trees obscured the rock. The path turned and twisted through the little wood, and when they finally emerged into the sunlight, the stone lay only a few paces away.

Its sheer size awed him, for it was easily half as long as a city bus though not nearly as wide. As he walked around it and gained perspective he suddenly understood why someone had felt a need to plant the shielding vegetation. He struggled to control his laughter.

This was no classic standing stone as shown in the travel guides--certainly nothing similar to the storied monoliths of Stonehenge. Miss Rhys had been right about one thing; someone had knocked it down. What she hadn't mentioned was its shape. The Rock of Saint Owain resembled an enormous, erect, and anatomically correct penis. And in the crevice on the tip, a small bird had built a nest.

With ladylike gentility, Miss Rhys did not even smile, though the tips of her ears grew a couple of shades pinker.

"There it is," she said, gesturing broadly. "Just as it's been for over seven hundred years. The Devil's

Finger, indeed."

Bill nodded, still battling to maintain his composure lest he come off acting like a schoolboy. "And Saint Owain is buried under there?"

"Not so much buried as squashed, I imagine, but yes, he should still be there. He sacrificed himself for the village."

Weather-worn graffiti marred the stone in spots. Bill pointed to the carvings and gave Miss Rhys a questioning look.

"They're leftovers from the days when the village was a stop along the old trade route to the Irish Sea. The pub's been here at least that long, and there is the natural spring in the town center. As we were a good day's journey west of Llangollen, it drew travelers to stay here overnight. Now, the distance to the sea is more easily traveled. The main roadway bypassed us."

Bill pulled his camera out and took a dozen shots of the rock from different angles. Finally, his curiosity satisfied, he showed the photos to Miss Rhys.

"Digital. I just load them into my computer and voila'."

"Amazing. Truly amazing." She looked from the camera to the object of the photos. "Do you really think this rock, as a sacred place, might draw tourists? I just can't imagine a photo of it going in any guide book I'd want to look at."

"You never know. People will stop off to see the silliest things. I read of a popular roadside attraction in Canada where the only thing to do is have your picture taken beside a giant concrete moose. People are interested in the unique, especially if it's gargantuan." He coughed a little, suddenly embarrassed in front of this refined lady. He changed the topic. "You're sure he's still under there?"

At that she laughed heartily. "I doubt he crawled out, if that's what you mean."

"Has anyone ever dug under it to look for his remains?"

"Heaven's no! What a notion!"

"Well, if I'm going to prove Owain actually lived, and that there's reason to believe the legends about him are based on fact, it might be something we'll have to do."

"Oh dear. Mali won't like that!"

He started at her remark. *Mali?* He envisioned the harpy described by Michael Wills in the pub. So far Miss Rhys had been only helpful and congenial. No wonder--she wasn't the woman he was supposed to be talking to. "You aren't Mali Rhys?"

She laughed, a soprano tinkling sound full of amusement. "Gracious no, but I realize now where the error is. We're *both* Miss Rhys, you see. I'm Mali's aunt. If you want the finer details of Saint Owain's life, she's the one to ask."

Great, Bill thought. Just as Miss Rhys was beginning to charm him, he had to start all over again with a she-wolf.

Chapter Three

The six-hour time difference worked in Bill's favor as he dialed Atlanta from his room over the pub. He liked the idea of beating Rhia to work by nearly a whole day.

"She's not here yet," Stacey said. "Could be another hour. She doesn't have anything scheduled 'til 10."

"Guess I should consider myself lucky."

"Good idea. So, how's Wales? Pretty decadent?"

"Unbelievable. Full of sheep and very green. You should see what they do with stone carvings." He paused, trying to imagine how Stacey would react to Owain's Rock. Aunt Nell would have his head and mount it over the fireplace if he even suggested something like that to her daughter. "Can I bring you a souvenir?"

"Sure. If you see any cute, single Welsh guys, stuff

one in your bag for me."

"I'll see what I can do. But Customs may have a problem with contraband bodies in my luggage. How 'bout I bring you some photos."

She exaggerated a sigh into the phone. "I s'pose that'll have to do. Oh, you'll never guess who just walked in. Lemme put you on hold."

Elevator music. If he waited too long, it would put him to sleep. *C'mon, Rhia, get a move on!* Settling into her desk for the day was a production. She always hauled enough accessories to open a salon. He prepared for a long, dull wait. Some men might find that attractive, but he liked the kind of woman who... never mind. He was still trying to determine his type.

His gaze drifted to the garish mural on the wall over his bed. If this was the best, he wondered what the others held in store. He moved off the bed to view the painting straight on. No matter what angle he looked at it from, only upside down improved it. At least then it had some pleasing abstract shapes.

"Bill?"

Rhia caught him by surprise as he bent over and looked up at the painting. "Hey. How's your dad?"

"Wales must be pretty bad if you want to drag my father from his death bed to take your place."

"It's nice here. Pretty. And the natives haven't waved their spears at me, much. Seriously, how's David?"

"He says he's fine."

"And what do the doctors say?"

He recognized the note of impatience she attached to the simple act of exhaling. "You know how they are. It's all gobbledygook."

He figured that was Rhia's way of saying she hadn't bothered to understand them. "Well, say hi for me the next time you see him."

"Right. So, how's Lansdown? Found anything we can use in the campaign?"

"It's Clan-sant-owen," Bill said, "and it turns out there *is* some story material we can work with."

"No relics or a museum?"

"Not really." He thought about the morning he'd spent with Miss Rhys. "There's a statue, a handful of seriously bad paintings, and a rock."

"A rock?"

"Yeah. Big mother. Looks like a--" He paused, thinking of the words his companion had used that morning. "My guide described it as a 'gigantic winkie.'" He smiled thinking of how red-faced she'd grown. "Rhia? You still there?"

It took her a few more seconds to reply. "Do you mean what I think you mean?"

"Yup." Another stretch of trans-Atlantic silence followed his confirmation. *Rhia speechless? How often did that happen?*

"Tell me about this rock," she said finally.

"I took some photos," he said. "I'll E-mail them later."

"Fine, but for now just tell me about it."

Bill shrugged as if she could see him. "There's not a whole lot to tell. It appears to be granite, though the geology class I took in college was a long time ago."

"And it looks like a dick?"

"Pretty much, yeah."

"Aroused?"

He stared again at the phone. "Hardly. That sort of

thing doesn't do it for me."

"I meant the rock!"

"Yes," he said. The woman didn't have a humorous bone in her entire body. "It looks like a huge, gray, uncircumcised penis. Eighteen, twenty feet long."

Rhia was silent for a time, then asked, "Does it have, you know, testicles?"

"Yep, though they're partially buried in the turf." He closed his mouth and grinned.

"There's no way we can use that in the campaign."

"Gonna be hard not to. It's the only real artifact, and it's the site of Owain's finest moment. I don't see how it can be avoided. He's still under there y'know."

"He's *what?*"

"Legend has it that Owain was wrestling with Satan, and--"

"Are you shitting me?"

"Nope. Anyway, he was having a devil of a time, pardon the pun, and hanging on for dear life, so he told the villagers who were standing around watching to push the rock over on top of them to kill them both."

"And they did?"

"So I'm told. I asked if anyone had ever looked under the rock and got a quick no. I've gotta tell ya, though, it wouldn't be a bad way to go. That rock is huge!"

"Is there any angle we can use for filming?"

He'd wondered the same thing when Miss Rhys took him to see it. "It looks pretty much the same from all sides. You'll have the pictures soon. See for yourself."

She sighed. "Tell me about the paintings. Is there anything there we can use?"

"Like I said, the artwork is dreadful. Think grade school--early grade school--only more crude. But," he paused.

"But?"

"The stories that go with 'em are terrific. It seems Owain came here on a mission to save the people from themselves. Must've been a regular little Gomorrah. In addition to wrestling with the devil, he cast demons out of possessed women, drank the devil into a stupor and dunked him in an underground pool." Bill glanced up at the mural on his wall. "I haven't seen the pool yet, but I'm told it's been steaming hot ever since. If these hot springs pan out, they'd surely qualify as an artifact, too."

"Was it his self-sacrifice that made him a saint?"

"Technically, no. As I understand it, he was a saint before he got here. Owain was a church elder--a deacon or something--in a nearby town."

"I'm not sure that'll fit with the spots we're planning, but who knows."

Bill took a short, sharp breath. "You're already planning spots?"

"Yeah," Rhia said. "Get some shots of the paintings and send 'em with the pictures of the rock. Write up the legends. We'll do a series of short, punchy ads, each depicting one of these so-called miracles on location in Clantown."

"Clan-sant-owen."

"Whatever. I've got Alonzo Fernandez lined up to play the saint."

"A *Spanish* movie star?"

"He's hot. Women in our target audience love him. I've got the stats to prove it. I think it's his eyes, but ya never know. He's also got a great butt."

Bill stared at the phone. "A great butt is required for sainthood?"

"He's already agreed to do it," Rhia continued, her voice low and silky, "as a favor to me."

Bill could guess what favors she had done for him. "He was great in 'Zorro's Revenge,' but he's not Welsh. Casting him, or any foreigner, as their saint won't go over with the locals."

"Put locals in the bit parts," she said. "It'll help you stay in budget."

Just when he thought she couldn't surprise him more, she did. "We've got a budget already?"

"Of course," she said. "It's based on production of a handful of 30- and 60-second spots. By the way, you need to contact the owners of all the potential tourist attractions and get them to spruce up for the rush of new business. We'll do a media blitz, but not in the usual target areas; they're probably saturated with Welsh tourism stuff already. Instead, we go after Americans. The demographics are simple: we find rich churchy types of Welsh descent and pump our story right into their living rooms! Once the momentum's been established, we target the Vatican."

He stared at the phone as if it had come alive. "We can't 'target the Vatican.' That's not a market! What're you saying?"

She gave him a trademark sigh of impatience. "If we're gonna make this Orville guy--"

"Owain."

"--right. If we're gonna make him a real saint, the

Pope will have to buy in sooner or later."

"You're insane," Bill said, his voice trailing into a whisper.

Rhia plowed ahead, warming to her ideas. "Insanity is often confused with genius, and I'm counting on yours to pull this off. You're our point man. Hire locally as much as you can. Daddy's got deep pockets, but they aren't bottomless."

"You can't buy sainthood, Rhia."

There was a moment's hesitation before she responded. "But we can sway public opinion."

It was Bill's turn to sigh. "When it comes to little-known saints from the Welsh outback, the public doesn't have an opinion."

Rhia laughed. "Yet."

~*~

Bill flopped back on his bed, thoroughly frustrated by Rhia Jones. How could anyone manage to combine such a complete lack of taste with such an overblown self-image? Rhia was rapidly becoming a parody of herself. He stretched out, his hands behind his head.

His first full day in Wales and he'd already screwed up items one and two on his agenda--the meeting with Mali Rhys and the phone call to Rhia-- not that he had any control over his volatile new boss. The morning he'd spent with the charming Glynnis Rhys had been far from tiring, but he still hadn't recovered from the transatlantic flight or the late evening he'd spent in the pub downstairs. The pub had proved more useful than he'd imagined--he'd gained insights on Owain, the town, and many of its quirky inhabitants. What he wanted most now was the unfettered authority to do his job; what he *needed* most was a nap.

While lying on the bed he had little choice but to stare up at the mural. Owain, the saintly brown smudge, waved a cross at three darker smudges while yet another smudge hovered in the air above them like smog trapped under an inversion layer. Bill put his brain into neutral and let himself do a mental coast, a technique he'd often used to generate ideas. This time, however, he only succeeded in drifting off.

21st century north Wales faded and was replaced by a pale 14th century version which didn't look all that different....

Open countryside dotted with sheep flanked the dirt track on which he stood. Only his priest's clothing surprised him. An alb *covered his richly embroidered* chasuble; *his head was covered with a double pointed* mitre. *He was even more surprised that he knew the names of the religious vestments. Three peasant women, hands on hips and heads cocked at come-hither angles, stood in front of him.*

Two of them looked unaccountably familiar, but their wildly disheveled hair and ragged, yet revealing, garb suggested they intended to turn his thoughts to lustier pursuits than those suggested by his priestly robes. The first woman stepped forward with an exaggerated thrust of her hips which sent a seductive ripple through the abbreviated hem of her skirt. He knew he'd seen those *thighs before.*

"Can I show you a good time, honey?" Rhia's voice burst into his memory.

"I-- uh, no. Y'see, I-- Actually, you're not-- not

exactly my type." Denying himself the luxury of slapping his forehead, he nonetheless berated himself in silence. What was he thinking? *He felt for the crucifix hanging from a chain around his neck, then wondered how he knew it would be there.*

"Maybe I'm more your type," said the second woman. *The thin fabric of her shift was torn from neck to navel, and he marveled that it could hold together enough to pass the watchful eye of a network censor.*

Tearing his horrified gaze from her pierced bellybutton, he squinted at the cherubic face peeking out from behind a curtain of long, tangled, blonde hair. Stacey? Cousin Stacey?

She squinted back at him and spoke between firecracker-sharp pops of chewing gum. "I'll be anyone you want me to be, sweetie."

Bill deliberated whether to yank her home to Nell, or wave his cross at her. His resolve strengthened, and he gripped the cross. "You don't understand. I have a-- a mission!"

None of the women looked particularly impressed by this revelation, least of all the third one. Haughty, with a pinched nose and pursed lips, she stood unmoving in the center of the rude byway and stared straight into his eyes. Mali Rhys, he thought. Gotta be.

"What kind of mission?" she asked.

"I'm here to save the village from evil."

She cackled like any wicked witch ought to. "You?" *Something about her stood out, and he found himself tempted by her great doe eyes and a voluptuous roundness she kept barely covered.*

"Well, yeah," he said, hoping it didn't sound as laughable to them as it did to him. *This one could make him forget his saintly duties if he wasn't careful. Just the sort of woman he'd come to town to save.*

"He looks a bit bewildered here, eh, girls?" she said to her laughing companions.

Something dark in their eyes belied their apparent good humor, and their laughter held only bitterness. He staggered back as the awareness of their real problem sank in--they had no spark of life.

"You're possessed!"

They stared at him, silent and unmoving.

He stepped toward them and brandished the cross. "Can't you feel the weight of the demon bearing down on your souls?" Just as quickly, they stepped back.

"I can help you," he said, taking another step.

They retreated, again in silence.

"Really. Trust me."

Mali Rhys opened her mouth, but a new voice emerged, its baritone mocking and cruel. "Trust me!" it echoed. "Trust me!" A peal of cold, humorless laughter followed.

It made Bill shiver. He raised his eyes to the clouds and prayed for guidance. He'd never dealt with demonic possession before. Much to his surprise, the crucifix grew warm in his hand.

"Don't move!" he cried, flourishing the cross like a sword. As it began to glow, the women huddled together, their eyes wide. "Your immortal souls depend on it."

"They're mine!" said the demon, and it was plain Mali had no control over the words coming from her mouth.

Bill dropped to his knees, and thrust the crucifix toward them, praying as he'd never done before, praying in a sing-song chant that felt like Latin.

As he droned on, two of the women teetered and clung to each other for support. Then, one after another, they sank to their knees and slumped sideways to the ground, unconscious.

Despite Mali's inclination to sag along with her companions, the mocking voice of her possessor continued to ridicule Bill. He held the cross in both hands, knowing its heat must be raising blisters, yet he couldn't let go. The women needed him, and he wasn't about to let them down.

His strength failing, Bill fell forward onto the rough ground. He closed his eyes tight and continued his chant, the words right and magical and poetic and mysterious--and not a one of them made any sense to him. As the demon's disembodied voice grew louder and more threatening, Bill refused to give up.

"I will cast you into fires so hot your body will melt!" screamed the demon.

Bill chanted on. The women, including Mali, had grown exceedingly pale; a yellowish-brown cloud formed above them as if they exhaled a sulfurous smoke.

"Stop now, or I'll strike you down forever!" raged the demon.

Bill sensed the demon's growing weakness and poured on the chant. The demon's voice faltered, and the body it possessed swayed on her feet. It was weakening! Bill chanted the exorcism litany louder and brought the cross up into the demon's face. The cross burned, as if his palms were pressed against a red-hot skillet. He knew he'd never be able to use his hands again, yet he refused to let go. The souls of these women were at risk! Agonizing pain shot up his arms and drilled into his joints--wrists, elbows, shoulders--all trembled from the intensity of his effort.

"Be gone!" Bill commanded.

"No!" came a final, ear-piercing wail as the burgeoning sulfur cloud suddenly exploded, then drifted harmlessly away on the breeze.

Bill dropped the crucifix and let his head fall into the dirt. Too spent to move and too dazed to think, he lay waiting for whatever would come next.

The women stirred.

Bill felt suddenly refreshed and dared to look at his hands. No burns! Both were whole and healthy. He wiggled his fingers and made a fist, then laughed out loud in astonishment and joy. "I did it!"

The women gaped at him.

"We're free," said Rhia, clearly awestruck, her voice unnaturally soft.

Stacey put tentative fingers to her cheeks. Looking down, she quickly shifted her position to a demure pose which exposed less of herself, though her tattered frock lent scant assistance.

Mali appeared the most shaken of all. Her now-angelic face bore no trace of the demon. Lips once skewed into a sneer now seemed soft and ripe. She stood and bowed shyly to him before scampering away into the woods.

"Thank you," Rhia said as she helped Stacey to her feet. "I don't know who you are or why you're here, but thank you, brave priest."

"How can we ever repay you?" Stacey asked.

Nell would approve, he thought. "Your salvation is all the payment I require."

Rhia and Stacey turned to follow Mali, then stopped. Rhia looked back at him. "Who are you?" she asked.

"Owain," Bill said. "Owain y'Craig."

~*~

Bill napped most of the afternoon away and was shuffling between his room and the common bath when Brenna hailed him from the bottom of the stairs. "There was a call for you an hour or so ago. I knocked on your door, but when you didn't answer, I assumed you were out."

"Out cold," Bill said.

When a worried frown crossed her face, he smiled. "Exhaustion. I'm okay now. Who called--my office?"

"No," she said, wiping at a spot on the wooden handrail with a damp cloth. "It was Mali Rhys. She told me you'd spent the morning with her Aunt Glynnis--a grand woman, don't you think? Such a pity she never married. She'd be a fine catch." She paused for a breath. "Mali, of course, isn't married either."

Like the women of Wetumpka, the females here probably felt compelled to help each other find suitable mates. "Did she say what she wanted?"

"Glynnis?" The pub owner's face screwed up in bewilderment.

"Mali. She's the one who called, wasn't she?"

"Oh! Right!" She put a hand to her cheek, then brushed it as if to sweep away some imaginary cobweb. "Can't imagine where my mind went. She said she'd drop by this evenin' so the two of you could chat. She said Glynnis insisted that you get together as soon as possible. Of course, if you already have other plans I can call her back."

After the dream based on the painting in his room, he wanted to see if Mali lived up to the picture Michael Wells and his own imagination had painted. "There's no need. I don't have any plans other than cleaning up, then getting a bite to eat."

"I'll turn the hot water on in the bathroom for you, but you'll have to wait about twenty minutes. It'll take that long to heat up nicely."

He stifled his surprise at having to book hot water, but decided it made sense to conserve energy. "That'd be fine. And can you suggest a good restaurant?"

"Yes, depending on where you want to go."

"Preferably right around here. I'd rather not drive if I can avoid it."

Her eyes twinkled. "I can get you a table at the best one in town," she said.

"Excellent! Is it far? Can I walk?"

"I think you can manage. It's at the foot of these stairs." She waved the cloth at him as if it was a flag. "I've got meat and potato pie tonight, and you won't find any better without a good long drive."

It sounded perfect. "Sign me up!"

"D'ye want vegetables with that?"

"Sure. Y'know, I admire folks who're proud of their work. If you say yours is the best restaurant in town, I'll believe it."

"'Tis true, she said with a playful grin. 'Course it's also the *only* restaurant in town. I'll start loadin' up your plate when I hear the shower pipes stop rattling. It'll be cool enough to eat when you come downstairs."

"Ms. Parry?"

She turned and gave him a coquettish smile. "Brenna, please, or Bren."

He appreciated her helpfulness, and generous hospitality. He'd remember to make sure his expense account covered a big tip as well. "Bren. Did Miss Rhys say when she'd be here? Perhaps I could buy her dinner, too."

"She said she'd be along about eight. It may not be a good idea to wait. This is my biggest evenin' of the week. Darts night, y'know. The lads'll be goin' through that meat and potato pie pretty fast."

He nodded. "I like your original plan. I'll be down as quick as I can."

"Take your time."

He waited an extra five minutes before padding down the hall to the bath room. A cast iron, claw-footed tub dominated one end of the common bath. A massive rust stain beneath the green-tinged spigot stared up at him like a bulls-eye. He latched the door, slipped out of his robe and approached the tub. The white enameled handles squealed when turned, and though the water gushed forth in abundance, the temperature remained cool until he throttled the cold down to a trickle.

He climbed in, dragged a faded plastic shower curtain around the circular bar hovering above the tub like a great halo, then engaged the shower. Dodging the initial blast of frigid water, Bill danced on tip toes and shivered as he waited for the water to heat up. Suddenly, the antique showerhead belched forth clouds of steam, then vented scalding water directly on his feet. Yelping, he dropped his washcloth, dodged backwards, assumed a slew footed stance and twisted himself like a contortionist as he reached for the Hot and Cold knobs. With the washcloth clogging the drain, the hot water level rose rapidly forcing him further backwards. With a grunt and a curse he twisted both knobs. As quickly as the hot water appeared it went back into hiding, and a steady stream of cold briefly soothed his tortured feet. Rather than tempt fate twice, he shut the water off completely and listened as the pipes rattled out the message Bren predicted. He made a mental note to discuss the advantages of modern plumbing with her. He put a rubber plug into the bulls-eye, extracted his washcloth and wiped himself down using the water that had accumulated in the bottom of the tub. It would have to do until he could master the secrets of the shower.

He dressed in a light sweater and slacks. He didn't want to appear too formal when he met Mali Rhys. His dream, and the image of her in it, had clung to him even through his shower escapade. He knew she'd likely be as proper as her aunt, and he couldn't shake the notion his evening was about to be spent with a haughty, pinch-nosed spinster. He hoped she was at least half as friendly and outgoing as her aunt.

When he went downstairs, Bren handed him a tray bearing a steaming bowl of meat with gravy covered by an inch-thick layer of mashed potatoes, a pint of dark beer, and several slabs of warm, fresh bread slathered with butter. He eyed the huge baked potato which filled a side plate. He'd expected something greener. "Didn't you say something about vegetables?" he asked.

Her eyebrows formed a sharp V. "Aye. Don't ye like potatoes?"

"Absolutely," he said. "They're my favorite."

At that her eyebrows resumed a straight line while the corners of her mouth turned up.

Grinning, he carried the provender to a corner table which, though out of the way, still afforded a good view of the door and anyone who entered.

Despite his encounter with the shower and the overdose of tuberous vegetables, Bill felt relaxed and at ease. He only wished he had someone he could share the feeling with, but the pub remained empty. He considered asking Brenna to join him, but opted not to slow her down as she prepared for the anticipated crowd. Instead, he took his time and worked his way through the simple meal.

Eventually the locals began drifting in, and Bill recognized several from his first night in town. Michael Wells and Dai Thomas breezed in amidst a cloud of cigarette smoke along with a handful of weather-beaten men he assumed were farmers. They congregated around the dartboards at the far end of the pub. Michael waved in recognition, then stepped up to the throwing line and concentrated on his game.

Bill glanced at his watch: eight o'clock and still no sign of Miss Rhys, though the pub had grown quite crowded. He watched the locals engage in what must be a centuries-old ritual involving darts, laughter, and considerable quantities of ale. It was a rite they all knew by heart, but one which--being conducted entirely in Welsh--left him bewildered and feeling distinctly left out.

Intent on Michael's throwing technique, Bill

nearly missed seeing the attractive dark-haired woman who stepped up to the bar and took a seat beside Dai.

She chatted with Bren, Dai, and others, often turning towards him as if to say something. In her late twenties or early thirties, she looked like she'd spent a lot of time hiking through the countryside. Considerably shorter than Bren, and with her long brown hair tucked behind her ears, she had a country look that appealed to him. Neither her faded jeans nor a thick woolen sweater could disguise her trim figure.

He tried not to be too obvious in his examination, though when she turned and looked directly into his eyes an unexpected flush of excitement coursed through him. He drained his beer for cover, and she gestured towards him with her half-pint glass. He smiled and ruefully looked at his empty glass on the table. Better not have another if Mali Rhys was arriving any moment.

He glanced at the woman's left hand. Good news-- no wedding band. Of course, Llansantowain was a far cry from Wetumpka, and certainly far from Buckhead or any of the other upscale neighborhoods in Atlanta; customs here could differ. Still, it wasn't a bad sign. She intrigued him. He moved beside her, and Bren handed him another glass of foaming lager. He exchanged smiles with the brunette then walked back to the corner table he'd been sitting in all evening. Much to his surprise, she followed him and made herself comfortable in the table's only other chair.

"Welcome to Wales," she said, coolly looking him up and down with rich, hazel eyes.

"Do I stand out that much?"

She shook her head gently, and he resisted the urge to reach out and touch the resulting dark wave which framed her face. "The only way to truly blend in is to be born here," she said.

"Were you?"

She nodded. "Lived here all my life. I know everyone in town. I'm related to most of 'em."

He looked from her to Dai refusing to believe they shared any genes. "What do you do around here?"

"For a living or for entertainment?"

"Either. Both."

When she smiled, one side of her mouth curled higher than the other. It was a warm smile. Genuine. Inviting. Definitely a smile he wanted to see more of.

"I work at home," she said, "but I get out often enough. This isn't a bad place to spend an evening. Especially when Dai is throwing well. It annoys Michael, and that amuses me."

"I wish I could stay longer, but I've got an appointment, and I'd best wait outside."

"Why?"

There was a sparkle in her eye he found difficult to resist. "Well, for one thing, I heard the person I'm waiting for doesn't drink. Very straight-laced. Bookish, I'm told."

She raised a skeptical eyebrow. "Indeed?"

He nodded, stood and started away then turned back, somewhat surprised he didn't want to leave her sitting alone. "What would be my chances of finding you here after my meeting?"

"Pretty good," she replied with a wink. "It's the only pub in town."

"Great!" he said, extending his hand. "I'm Bill. Bill

Thomas."

"My apologies, Mr. Thomas, for not coming straight to you earlier, but you seemed so intent on the darts I didn't want to interrupt. I'm Mali."

It took Bill a few seconds to register the name. Then he stiffened and stared at her. "*You're* Mali Rhys?"

Her nod didn't disguise her impishness. "Aye. Perhaps you'd allow a bookish, tea-totaling historian to buy you a beer?"

"I--uhm--obviously got some bad information." He turned to glare at Michael, but found the man studying something fascinating on the toes of his boots.

"It pays to know your source," Mali said, her eyes twinkling.

"No kidding," Bill groaned. "And yes, I'd love a beer."

~*~

"Hey, Billy! How's Wales?"

In his wireless phone, Stacey sounded every bit as far away as Georgia, but it was still good to hear her voice. "It's still very green. And the people are great. Odd, but great."

"Caught up on your sleep yet?"

"No, but this Owain legend gave me the strangest dream yesterday," Bill said.

"Unless it's about me or that you're the reincarnation of Martin Luther King, Jr., I'm not terribly interested," Rhia interrupted. "By the way, I looked over the photos you sent. There's no way in hell we can use that stupid rock in any of our ads--the Bible Belt will eat us alive even if California loves it. We'll have to fabricate something that doesn't look quite so... phallic. Have you got anything else we can use?"

Bill paused, his sinuses signaling an imminent threat. "Yeah, I've--" He covered the phone and sneezed. The steady drizzle which had begun the night before must be getting to him. "Sorry. Anyway, that's what I'm trying to tell you. I do have something else." He longed for a box of Kleenex.

"I don't know if it's you or a bad connection. You sound lousy."

"I feel lousy, but I reckon I'll live." Failing to find his travel-sized tissues he settled for a paper napkin.

"I love it when you use that folksy lingo. I'll bet it plays well with the sheep herders."

He wiped his nose, crumpled the napkin, and tossed it toward the trash can, but missed. "My idea was inspired by the mural in my room."

"I looked at the pictures of that, too. I thought at first it might be graffiti, except there weren't any words. The art department printed an enlargement of it. Bleah. Chuck said-- You know Chuck, right?"

"Sort of. I got your father to hire him."

"I figured you knew him; he's been here forever. Anyway, Chuck said he'd seen inkblots with more artistic expression."

That sounded like something Chuck would say, but purged of the expletives he usually threw in. Bill plunged ahead. "I dreamed I was Saint Owain and saved those women from the devil."

"What women?"

"The three from the mural in my room. One of 'em looked like you."

"Which one?"

He felt like saying "The one with the price list tattooed on her tail," but managed to resist the urge. "Not any one in particular, just a woman in uhm... period costume." He thought back to the dream, parts of which remained quite vivid. Mali's parts especially. "It wouldn't be difficult to portray Owain in such a saintly role."

"I hadn't thought about putting myself in the spots," Rhia said, missing his point. "You don't think that'd be a little over the top?"

"Hitchcock set the precedent."

"But he was a director. I told you about Alonzo Fernandez, didn't I?"

Bill grimaced. "I wish you'd let me talk you out of that. I still can't see him as a Welsh saint."

"Trust me," Rhia said. "The women in our target audience would line up to be saved by him. He really is divine." She chuckled. "Saved. Divine. Get it?"

"Yeah. You're killin' me." Bill sneezed again, this time not bothering to do more than turn his head away from the phone. He opened the door and padded toward the lavatory to grab a handful of the tough material masquerading as toilet tissue. "Anyway," he said between sniffs, "it was an incredibly vivid dream, and I think it has great dramatic potential, though I don't see how we could do it justice in a 60-second spot."

"I'm thinking 30-second spots."

"30s! We aren't selling aspirin. We'll need time to tell this story. The details alone--"

"Aren't terribly important. We can always make up what we need."

Bill glowered at the phone in his hand. "Then why

bother having me look around here at all?"

"So you'll get to know the place. The story should *feel* authentic even if we have to fudge a detail or two."

Bill felt another sneeze coming on and wondered idly if he should launch it straight into the receiver as a kind of protest. "You just said we could make everything up. Which is it?"

Rhia exhaled loudly, her growing pique evident in her condescending tone. "Don't be argumentative. You're the one who isn't making much progress. Do I need to send someone else?"

"No," he said, not doubting for an instant she'd fire him if she thought she could get the idea past her father. He refused to give her any justification. "I've got it under control. Today I have an appointment with the woman who knows the most about the saint stories." He and Mali had barely begun talking when Dylan Davies, the head of the town council, had joined them. They agreed to discuss the whole thing in the council chambers--Bren's pub--later that day. "I've also arranged a meeting with the top elected official to see about using locals as extras. I'm sure we can get a film crew from as close as Cardiff."

"Don't bother," she said. "Alonzo says he knows exactly who to use. He says they can even do post-production on site. Can you imagine?"

Bill sighed. Rhia would have her own way, despite rational planning. "Good old Alonzo."

"Send more details on the saint stories as soon as you have 'em. We'll use what we can. I'm really eager to get something scripted. Alonzo's got a break in his shooting schedule, and he wants to squeeze us in."

"Maybe if we took a little more time--"

Rhia cut the connection.

"And to think I saved you from the devil," he mused out loud. He didn't fight the sneeze.

~*~

Bill checked his watch before going downstairs to meet the head of the town council. Eleven o'clock. He'd slept later than intended, and the call to Rhia had left him in a foul mood. He tried to shake it off, reminding himself he needed to stop letting her get under his skin. If this ad campaign fell apart it wouldn't be because he didn't give it his best. Still, David would be disappointed--something Bill would work hard to avoid. Nor would David be the only one disappointed. He thought of the people from Llansantowain who'd hired him to put them on the map, not make them look foolish. How would they react to ads that featured some hotshot American executive's wise ass idea of how their patron saint lived and died? He didn't even want to think how they'd react when they found out a foreigner would play the part of Owain.

When he reached the bottom of the stairs he sneezed again, hard.

"God bless you," called out a round-bellied, narrow-shouldered man who stood at the bar nursing a tall, dark brew.

Bill recognized Dylan Davies, the town councilor, from their brief encounter the previous evening. The man wore a work shirt and a knitted wool cap that blended into his heavy, gray-tinged sideburns. Heavy jowls matched dark circles under his eyes. The center of attention, the man was flanked by a number of villagers, including Michael Wells and, of course, Mali

Rhys. In the morning light, Bill glimpsed golden highlights in her hair. "Hello again."

"Come join us, William," Davies said. "I was just about to ask Mali here what you two accomplished yesterday."

Mali gestured toward Brenna who uncapped one of Caitlin's vile brews and set it gently in front of Michael.

He eased away from the odor. "I guess I earned this."

"Indeed," Brenna said. "Let me know when you're done with it, and we'll find you a proper one."

"You don't really have to drink that," Mali said.

Brenna shushed her. "He certainly does. One of life's most valuable lessons is that there are consequences. Isn't that right, Mister Wells?" She glanced at Michael who looked up sheepishly. A reddish hand print colored one side of his face.

"What happened to him?" Bill asked.

"He got a little fresh when I asked him for a quote on some plumbing work," Brenna said. She looked at Mali. "By the way, that scruffy chap from Bedgelert was by here asking about you."

Mali swallowed. "The Rastafarian?"

"That's him. He was drivin' that rusted out little sportster with the top down, and he had that great mass of hair tucked into a baggy cap. Might've been brightly colored once, but it's so faded now it's almost white. He looked like a ruddy Q-Tip."

"What'd he want?" Mali asked.

Brenna gave her an understanding smile. "You know what he wants, we all do. It's why we're givin' Dylan and his daft scheme more than the time o' day."

"Thanks for the warnin', Bren."

"It's good to see everyone getting along so well," Davies said. "Especially if we're going to be working together." He clapped Bill on the shoulder. "That's what you wanted to discuss, isn't it?"

"Yes," Bill said. "We're going to be filming a few commercials for distribution in the States pretty soon, and I wanted to get the word out that we'd like to use some local actors."

Everyone in the room, except Mali, sat a little straighter, and most of the men pulled in their stomachs.

"Is there any money in it?" Davies asked.

"Probably not much--whatever is the local scale for extras," Bill said. "We need to keep the budget within reason."

Everyone else started talking and quickly drowned Bill out.

"Here now," Davies said with authority, "settle down. You don't want to scare our Yank away, do you?"

"There's not much chance of that," Bill said. He tilted his head for a closer look at Mali. Her lips pursed, and her gaze rested on something outside the open window. She seemed entirely disinterested in their conversation. "Don't you want to be in the films, Mali?"

She shrugged. "I'm not convinced it's a good idea to even make the bloody things." She swept her hand around the room. "Have any of you lot given any consideration at all to what could happen to this town if these adverts are successful?"

"We'll get our share of the tourists!" bellowed

Michael from the back of the room. "And not a moment too soon."

"Is that what you really want?" she asked, her voice rising with the question. "And just where will these tourists stay? What will they eat? What will they see? Are you going to build a Saint Owain amusement park complete with a Ferris wheel and a carousel?" She stood, made a circle with her arms, and turned in place. "Here's the Saint Owain ride, step right up! Have some candy floss and a three-by-five color postcard featuring the great stone penis Owain's buried under. Oh, I can see it now: stores will line the street selling stone penis key chains and stone penis pens and--who knows--maybe even some little penises made out of Welsh slate. Fancy that, a whole new cottage industry."

"Mali," Davies said, drawing out her name. "We get the idea."

"Do you? Because I'm just getting warmed up. Think of the opportunities! Penis T-shirts. Penis baby bibs. Penis hats. How long do you think it'll be before we'll have to change the town name? How does Llanpenis sound?"

"It doesn't have to be that way," Bill said, trying not to laugh at the image she'd painted.

She was on a roll. "There could be other consequences. What if this campaign actually works the way you intend it to? Who hasn't been to Betws-y-Coed, or Beddgelert, or any of the other towns that hardly have any Welshmen living in them anymore? Property values go up, people sell their homes to Englanders who want to convert them to Bed and Breakfasts, and before you know it, none of us lives here anymore 'cause none of us can afford it!"

Davies raised his hands and waved down the cacophony of voices that followed Mali's tirade. "Now, now, aren't you gettin' a little carried away?" he asked. "Some of what you say might even come true, but I don't believe much harm can come from creatin' a few new jobs."

"Exactly," Michael said. "Why have you spent so much time tryin' to finish the work your father started on the manor house if you didn't hope to open your own hotel one day?"

Mali fell silent, but glared open-mouthed.

"'Cause she wants all the business for herself," he added.

Mali turned on him. "I'll give you the business, Michael Wells!"

"You'll have to wait your turn," Brenna said, rolling up her sleeves.

"Ladies, please." Davies forced laughter into his voice. "We needn't assume the worst--from any of us. Besides, we're not talking about making any major changes around here. We'll only need to spruce up around the rock, open a pasture for caravans to park overnight, and maybe add a coat of paint here and there."

"You'll also need to do something about the road into town," Bill said.

"Like what?" asked Davies, though everyone turned towards Bill as if to share the question.

"Like widen it. It's only one lane."

Gasps in unison rose from those gathered. "Impossible!" Dai said.

"Radical," said a man in the back.

"And possibly subversive," muttered Michael.

"Welsh roads tend to be narrow," Mali said. "It's part of their charm." Heads nodded in agreement.

"Well then, make them one-way, or you're going to have some absolutely charming traffic jams. God help you if anyone ever calls an ambulance."

Davies nodded. "I admit there may be some things I hadn't considered, but that doesn't mean we should give up on the idea. What choice do we have? This town has slowly withered away since the slate mine closed. Do ye want to see it die completely?"

His view seemed to garner a consensus.

"The idea has merit," Bill said, "and we're making progress. In fact, we've already arranged for a film crew." The comment got everyone's attention; Davies was clearly relieved.

Most everyone in the room clamored to shake Bill's hand, and he promised them all he'd give them plenty of warning before they held auditions. "We'll start filming as soon as the scripts are approved and the pre-production stuff has been taken care of."

"The scripts are already being written?" Mali asked with obvious surprise. "I didn't think my aunt could've given you enough details."

"No, she didn't, and yes, the scripts are being written, but I could use more information. Lots more. Hold on a minute, will you?" He gestured for Davies to lean closer. "If I tell you a little secret, will you draw the crowd away so I can have a word or two with Miss Rhys alone?"

A smile crept across the politician's face. "Is this the sort of secret that has to stay a secret for very long?"

"Only long enough for you to get these folks out of here," Bill said.

"I'm yer man then," he said, gently pushing bodies away even as he leaned in closer.

"Are you familiar with Alonzo Fernandez, the famous actor?"

The mayor's eyebrows dropped into a deep crease. "Don't believe I am."

Bill frowned. "He's been in loads of movies. 'The Return of Zorro's Brother', 'Escape from Zanzibar', 'The Loner', 'The Loner-part 2'."

Davies shook his head. "Nope. Never heard of 'im. But never mind that. What's he got to do with us?"

"He's going to direct our commercials," Bill said. "And trust me, anyone who goes to the movies very often will know who he is."

Davies' smile returned. He pushed his hat toward the back of his head and looked out at the expectant faces all around him. "Ladies and gentlemen, I've got some really exciting news!"

They all swarmed closer, but somehow he managed to shepherd them toward the door.

Bill admired the natural crowd control instincts of even this most parochial of politicians. He watched them squeeze through the door like Hamelin's rats chasing the Pied Piper.

"Alonzo Fernandez?"

Bill grinned at Mali. "Eavesdropper."

"It's but one of my many fine qualities."

And how I'd love to discover the others, Bill thought. "I meant it when I said I needed more information. I've only got the bare essentials. Could we get together and discuss it?"

"Why don't you come out to my house for lunch? I know Aunt Glynnis would like to see you again."

"I'd love to," he said. "But I don't want you to go to any trouble on my account. How 'bout I pick something up on the way?"

She chuckled. "I don't live that far."

"I don't mind, really."

"If there was someplace for you to stop, I'd take you up on your offer," Mali said. "My aunt told me she'd taken you to see the rock. Do you remember how to get there?"

He nodded.

"Just stay on that road a mile out. Look for a driveway on the left that isn't overgrown. That's us. Ignore the dogs when you get to the house; they'll bark but they won't hurt you."

"No problem," he said. "I'm looking forward to it."

Her long dark eyelashes lowered for just a moment. "Me, too," she said.

Chapter Four

Mali pulled her 1966 Mini Cooper into the long winding drive and coasted down the slight hill toward the house. No sense using more petrol than she had to. Besides, the little car had been operating on borrowed time for as long as she could remember. If spirits there were, surely they had a soft spot for Mali's car. It kept running when others would have given up entirely. She coasted to a stop in front of the cottage and set the parking brake.

"I'm home," she called as she approached the door. The dogs, Samson and Delilah, bounded from the garden and crowded around her feet all but tripping her in their eagerness to greet her. Mali laughed at their unreserved show of affection and eventually gave in to it. Sitting on the step, she gathered Samson, a one-eyed corgi into her left arm, and Delilah, a border collie with a permanent limp, into her right. They wiggled with delight and showered her with wet doggie kisses.

Glynnis opened the door. "Shoo," she said shaking her apron at the dogs. "Go on now, catch us a rabbit."

At the word "rabbit," the dogs bolted back into the garden where every wild creature, including the rabbits, were utterly safe. Mali gratefully regained her feet. "Thank you. Another greeting like that one and I'll need a proper bath." She slapped at the fabric of her blouse; golden corgi hairs clung to it, and she made a mental note to brush it off before the Yank arrived.

"You looked like you needed a rescue," Glynnis said, bustling Mali though the door. "Come inside and tell me how it went in town."

"With Dylan or William?"

"William, of course."

"Ah." She smiled. "That went well enough, though I did tease him a bit at first, last night. It was a novelty having someone who didn't actually know me; I couldn't resist having him on, just a little. Especially since Michael had a bit of fun at my expense. Our visitor paraphrased Michael's description of me. I think his words were 'bookish, tea-totaling historian.' In truth, it's not so far off the mark," Mali said, hanging her keys on an old wrought-iron hook near the front door.

Glynnis's eyes sparkled with mischief. "Then he'll be surprised to discover the real you."

Mali leaned back against the door and exhaled as if she'd just run all the way from the village. "That's not very likely..." She brushed a fall of dark hair from her forehead before continuing. "And the worst thing is that the Yank's going to start making commercials soon, and he wants to use some of the townsfolk in them."

"Really," Glynnis said, "I can imagine them vying to see who gets to stand closest to the Rock. I think Michael should get the honor as he has the biggest...."

"Aunt Glynnis!"

"I was going to say the biggest ego, but I can see that American has made you think along other lines."

"I can't believe you'd even think that, let alone say it!" Until this moment, she hadn't thought of the American in that way at all. It startled her to realize the notion was an appealing one.

"Well, no doubt this will give us all something to talk about for the next fifty years."

"Or more." Mali shifted away from the door and into the living room. "By the way, I invited him over for lunch today."

"Invited who?"

"William Thomas."

"The Yank? Here?"

"He was a perfect gentleman at the pub this morning," Mali said. The man was a good sport and had impressed her with his wit and charm. She couldn't help but notice he was also quite handsome. Tall and a bit on the lean side, there was nothing wrong with his looks, and from her observations, nothing wrong with his temperament, either. She tried to bury thoughts of what he might be like in more intimate ways.

"But the house is a shambles," Glynnis said.

Mali glanced around their tiny quarters. The only area which looked even the slightest bit unkempt was her "office," and she didn't anticipate letting her guest spend any time there. "It looks as neat and tidy as always. Besides, Caitlin swears men have a different approach to neatness because their value systems are usually crippled."

"Hmpf. A lot of nonsense, if you ask me. I suspect it's Caitlin Morgan is the one with crippled values. She never comes to church, you know."

Mali chuckled. "That doesn't mean anything. Besides, it's never bothered you before. You know Caitlin is a darling who'd never harm a flea. As for Mr. Thomas, we'll see what sort of values he has, I'm sure."

Values aside, he appealed to her, despite his insistence on going ahead with the disastrous adverts. Lord knew she could never mention to Aunt Glynnis that she found him attractive.

"It never hurts to have the upper hand in a relationship," Mali said.

"I see," Glynnis said knowingly on her way to the kitchen, "and is that based on your own extensive experience, or are you leaning on Caitlin again?"

Mali was convinced her aunt would condone her marriage to any male in the district. The chair by the fireplace beckoned, and she sank into it in gratitude, resting her feet on the cold hearth. The small fire they usually maintained in the winter was enough to warm the entire house. In the summer they rarely lit it. "He got comfy with Dylan and the others pretty quickly, but I confess he dealt with them much better than I dealt with the idea of making advertisements about Saint Owain."

Glynnis popped her head through the doorway

from the kitchen. "You're back at that, are you?"

"Don't you see? It's inviting disaster. The more people hear those ridiculous stories, the more likely it is someone will actually come to investigate, and before you know it they'll be after the letter, and the truth will be out." She shivered and leaned toward the fireplace wishing for a blaze.

"No one outside of us and Mr. Smythe-Webley from London even knows that silly letter exists. You worry too much." Glynnis handed Mali a cardigan. "By the way, do you remember that odd little man with the camera I told you about? The one I saw by the Rock?"

When Mali failed to react she went on. "Well, he's back and still poking about the same places. Do you think we should ask the constable to have a chat with him?"

"No need. I'll do it myself," Mali said. "You said he looks harmless."

"You be careful just the same. Maybe you could get that Yank of yours to go with you."

"Aunt Glynnis! He's no more 'my Yank' than he's yours."

Glynnis only laughed, and Mali fought hard to keep an embarrassed grin from creeping to her lips.

"There's soup and fresh bread in the kitchen, luv. That should do for your lunch. I won't be staying unless you want me to. We're having a bit of a sing at the church this afternoon. Mrs. Edwards' son, Sion, promised to start us in practices for the *gymanfa ganu*."

Glynnis lived and breathed the hymn fest and everyone in town who could sing usually joined. This year Mali guessed it would be bigger than ever. Sion Edwards lived in Betws-y-Coed and always brought a carload of middle-aged and elderly gentlemen singers with him. As a consequence, all the unattached middle-aged and elderly ladies in the area were keen to participate.

"You go along, and have a great time. Sing well. I'd hate for the *gymanfa* to start and discover no one was prepared to sing the hymns. I'll be fine."

"Ta, then." Glynnis said as she plucked the car keys from their perch and closed the front door behind her.

Mali checked her watch. William wasn't due for at least another hour, and the dogs would give her plenty of warning when he arrived. She stretched out on the sofa, listened to the chirps of the little wrens nesting nearby and let her mind wander. Soon the outside noises disappeared, and a whirl of modern faces appeared--overlaid with ancient writing. She drifted away seven centuries and a couple miles. A scene evolved, one she'd taken part in before....

Three village elders sat brooding and distraught under a broad oak looking as if they all had an appointment with the executioner. One especially dejected man--who looked remarkably like Dylan Davies--handed a drinking skin to one of his companions, a man whose resemblance to Dai Thomas was nothing short of uncanny. Dai took a long pull on the skin, swallowed several times and smacked his lips, as Dai always did after a long draught.

"What're we going to do?" Dylan wailed. "We can't just send his body back."

The third man--who could easily have passed for Michael Wells--muttered, "Why'd he have to up and die here?"

Dai shook the skin. Very little wine swished inside. "And in the arms of a harlot!"

Michael broke into a wide grin. "I can think of worse ways to go."

"Aye. You've a good point there," Dai said, passing the wine skin to Michael. "If I had the money, I'd be spending a lot more time over there m'self."

"I know they're supposed to be damned and all, but one has to admit they perform a valuable service," Dylan observed.

Michael nodded, drained the skin into his open mouth and passed it back. "Valuable indeed. I can't afford them."

"True enough," Dai said, "but worth every penny. Evidently, Owain y'Craig thought so, too. The fool. A man with a weak heart shouldn't tempt fate."

Mali walked close enough to smell them. She wrinkled her nose at the odor of medieval men who would benefit from a week-long soak in scented oils. "What's it to be, then?" she asked.

They showed no surprise she was there. "We don't know," Dylan said. "The Abbot sends us a saint--a man supposedly above reproach--to rid the area of sin and degradation--"

"A man you had no wish to see," Mali reminded him.

"That's not the point. The Abbot sent us a saint, and we killed him."

"We most certainly did not!" she said. "He killed himself. All that abstinence must've clogged his system.

An overdose of piety turned to poison."

Dylan shook his head. "We can't say that to the Abbot! He'll have us hanged and take everything we own for the Church."

"Why not just bury him and claim he never arrived?" Mali said. "Who's to know?"

"He had an escort," Dai said. He turned to face her, suddenly looking quite sober. "What happened to them?"

"They were in another part of the house," Mali said, "and well taken care of. They'll not be eager to call our hand if we alter the facts a bit to protect them, too. Wouldn't the Abbot rather hear how this saintly man successfully fought evil as he breathed his last?"

Dylan looked her straight in the eye. "You'd have us lie to the Abbot?"

"Aye, or would you rather hang?"

The man's words were lost in a cacophony of hounds barking though there were none to be seen. "Do you see any dogs?" she asked her companions, but they had disappeared.

Mali opened her eyes. Samson and Delilah were still barking.

She jumped up in alarm. He's here, she thought, and she hadn't even taken the time to tidy herself up. Looking down at the frumpy cardigan her aunt had given her, she slipped out of it and hurried to her room to find something with a bit more zing. She prayed Samson and Delilah would hold him at bay long enough for her to complete her transformation.

~*~

Instead of going directly to the Rhys' home, Bill

drove in the opposite direction intent on finding a florist, or at least some wildflowers. He had the time, and, despite Llansantowain's pastoral charm, he needed to get away from the confines of the hotel and pub. Easing down the single lane leading out of town and hemmed in by six-foot high walls of stacked slate, Bill quickly recalled why he'd been so happy to reach town in the first place--a healthy fear of narrow Welsh roads and the insane traffic circles used to intersect them.

Thankfully, he didn't run into any oncoming vehicles before he reached a road with nearly two whole lanes and the added bonus of a numbered highway sign. Though the pavement bore a freshly painted middle stripe, he wondered that trucks of any real size could fit in the width allotted. He remembered his first day behind the wheel in the UK, shifting gears wrong-handed and flipping the windshield wipers on every time he meant to signal a lane change. Whose bright idea was it to drive on the left anyway? He supposed it made sense to blame the medieval English rather than the Welsh. According to the tourist brochures, Wales had been forcibly joined with England a thousand years ago, and some locals still talked about Welsh independence. He chuckled.

"And folks say we Southerners are still fightin' the War of Northern Aggression." The thought made him warm to the Welsh even more, though not quite enough to forgive them for their Lilliputian roads.

After passing through two towns without finding a florist, Bill started paying more attention to the countryside. Wildflowers seemed to grow everywhere, and he was certain he'd seen some foxglove just like what grew in gardens all over Wetumpka when he was a child.

A bend in the road revealed a gap in the ever present slate walls, and Bill parked his car in the narrow opening. A field surrounded by oak trees played host to a dozen black-faced sheep, all of whom eyed him with undisguised suspicion.

Bill eased toward a stand of reddish-purple foxglove and helped himself to a half dozen tall, spiky plants in full bloom. He had neither vase nor tissue paper in which to wrap them so he bundled the stalks in one of his brochures.

Just as he pulled back out onto the highway a cement truck flew by in the oncoming lane. Bill swerved as close to the wall as he dared, hearing the slap of vines striking his outside mirror. Getting back on the road to Llansantowain became a top priority and the rest of the return trip proved uneventful.

Bill had no trouble finding the drive Mali had described earlier. He drove slowly to avoid hitting the two barking dogs racing around his car. So much for a subtle arrival. The corgi hung back, but the black and white border collie leaped and barked wildly, even trying to nip at the car's tires. Mali had claimed the dogs would only bark, but he wasn't so sure. Even a friendly dog can get the notion to protect its home from a stranger. He carefully opened the car door, and the dogs retreated to the small porch at the front of the stone cottage.

Both dogs kept him under intense scrutiny as he approached the house. With the flowers held behind his back, he muttered reassurances to them as he knocked on the door. He felt like a teenager on a first date. He thought he probably looked the part, too. He ran his fingers through the hair hanging over his forehead. Did he have time to comb it? Did he even bring a comb? And what was he doing with flowers, for cryin' out loud?

Suddenly, the flower idea seemed completely and irrevocably over the top. This was supposed to be a business meeting not a date. What had he been thinking?

He cast around for a trash can or some other place in which to stash the flowers. He leaned down to stuff the vibrantly colored foxgloves into a space behind a rhododendron growing next to the front door when it opened.

Caught in the act, Bill straightened slowly, hoping his face didn't betray his embarrassment.

"Can I help you there?" Mali asked.

"No, no. I'm fine. I..." He held the flowers out to her. "I saw these as I was driving over and thought you might like them."

"How thoughtful," she said, gathering the stems in both hands and rewarding him with a smile. "They're lovely."

The border collie wiggled itself between him and Mali, barked and began nipping at his feet as if to herd him away from the house. Bill wasn't sure what to do so he stood perfectly still. This had the unsettling effect of increasing the dog's efforts to get him to move. Suddenly he developed a great deal of sympathy for sheep.

"Delilah!" Mali scolded. "That's no way to treat a guest, especially one who brings me flowers."

The animal raised her head and stopped barking,

and with tail wagging, resumed her efforts at herding Bill.

Mali's laugh was buried in a mass of dark brown curls as she shook her head at the dog. "Off with you!" The dog looked up expectantly. "Rabbit," said Mali and the pair of dogs scampered away toward the back of the cottage.

"I imagine having dogs herd men *into* the house wouldn't be a good idea way out here."

"Aunt Glynnis would probably disagree," Mali said, her smile warming him. She held the bouquet in front of her like a torch. "Come in, please."

As soon as she opened the door, both dogs came barreling around the corner. Delilah and the corgi rushed for the door, but Mali blocked them and waved Bill in ahead of her. The dogs stood with tails sagging.

"Oh you," Mali chided. "Stay outside and play. If I let you in, all you'll want to do is go back out anyway." She let the door close behind her.

"Come with me while I put these flowers in water. My aunt made soup, so I hope you're hungry. You really don't want to miss it."

Bill followed her into a tiny kitchen where Mali dispatched him to a chair at a built-in table already set for two.

"Is there anything I can do to help?"

"Probably," Mali said, "but there isn't room for more than one cook in this kitchen. Bread and jam with your soup?"

"Sounds great," he said, watching her move about the cramped space with an ease born of familiarity. Nor did he mind the view. She wore tight-fitting jeans as she had the night before, though she'd exchanged a lightweight sweater for last night's heavy one. This one, in the same reddish tones as the foxglove blossoms, showed off her figure to better advantage. Seeing a woman allowing her natural curves to show without the fanfare or eye-popping seductiveness Rhia favored was refreshing. She set the flower vase in the center of the table against the wall then turned back for the soup.

She deposited two huge, steaming bowls of thick, cream-colored liquid on the table, and Bill let his gaze drift up to meet hers. As if locked together, neither spoke. Finally, Mali lowered her eyes and backed away.

"Want your bread toasted?"

"Don't go to any trouble on my account."

"Good." She grinned. "The toaster doesn't work all that well anyway."

He took a spoonful of soup and blew on it. Cooled, it went down smoothly. The taste of potato wasn't completely unexpected. It made him chuckle. He watched Mali spread butter on a slice of bread nearly the same color as the soup. "That wouldn't be potato bread, would it?"

She stared down at the thick slab in her hand. "I don't think so. Is there something wrong with it?"

"Oh, no," he assured her. "I've just gotten the impression that spuds are the national vegetable of Wales."

"We're more into beer and rugby." When he raised an eyebrow, she continued. "Beer being the vegetable of course."

The soup filled the damp coldness in his belly he'd felt more than once since his arrival in Wales. They didn't talk much during the meal. He was content to focus on the food, though from time to time, their eyes met. He wondered what kind of fight she'd put up to keep the project from proceeding.

They finished lunch, and Bill followed her into the main room. Rustic, with dark wood antiques and lace doilies. A woman's house. In the corner stood an antique oak desk cluttered with papers, books, and a small glass case. He moved closer. The sealed case contained a few ancient, hand-lettered pages.

"This looks interesting. What is it?"

Mildly flustered at first, Mali waved the document and the case into insignificance, then put a doily and the vase of foxgloves on top. "Just an old letter. It's been in the family for ages. The case keeps it safe from humidity."

"It must be valuable."

She shrugged. "Possibly."

The dogs resumed their barking at the door. "I'm sorry, those two just will not be put off. I'm going to let them in. Be prepared to have dogs in your lap." She walked to the door and opened it a crack. Instantly, the house seemed overfull with squirming canines desperately trying to be petted everywhere at once.

"Samson! Delilah! Calm down," Mali said, though the dogs ignored her. "They're hungry."

Bill pressed back against the desk as the dogs took up positions in front of him with considerable tail-wagging.

"I know I spoil them," she said.

Bill reached down to pet Delilah, but she leaped sideways unexpectedly, bumped the desk, and knocked a pile of loose papers to the floor.

"Delilah! Get in the kitchen," Mali said sternly. "You, too, Samson. Scoot!" Both dogs bounded out of the room.

Bill knelt to retrieve the papers.

"Don't bother," she said. "I'll get them later."

"It's no trouble. Besides I've already got most of them. You go ahead and feed those critters before they start chewing on me."

She paused a moment as if to argue with him, then followed the dogs into the kitchen while Bill straightened up the mess. What he first took for letters were in fact overdue bill notices. He was suddenly embarrassed for her and carefully rearranged the papers so the past due notices were on the bottom. Maybe she'd think he hadn't seen them. As Mali came through the doorway bearing two bowls of food for the dogs, he made a show of tidying the pile.

"You're giving 'em soup?" he asked.

"Just a bit. For flavor." She lifted both bowls high. "C'mon, it's a nice day. Let's talk outside."

He followed her to a gray slate patio that overlooked a neat garden resplendent with flowers and vegetables. A large building, looking long abandoned and with grounds overgrown, stood about a hundred yards away.

"What's that?" he asked. "An old school or something?"

"It's served many purposes, but I don't believe it was ever a school," she said. "It's the original family estate, and the original section there on the left dates back to a time even before King Edward dotted Wales with his bloody castles. No one's lived in it since my father was a child--it was his dream to restore it."

"Interesting," Bill said. His mind drifted back to his conversation with Michael that morning about Mali wanting to finish her father's renovations on the old manor house. "Michael said something about you wanting to open a hotel".

"Michael Wells talks too much," Mali said, but her eyes, soft with a longing he couldn't define, drifted toward the building in the distance.

"It's an empty dream, I'm afraid," she said, brusquely turning away. "I don't have the knowledge or skills to do the kind of work my father did. And hiring someone to do it for me is far too expensive."

Bill thought about the unpaid bills on her desk. He would tread lightly when it came to the topic of money. Nevertheless, something about the old place enchanted him. He'd love to see it completed, and maybe spend some time there himself.

"Y'know, if this ad campaign works out, you might be able to get a loan to finish the work. Lord knows, the town will need a hotel, and folks would jump at the chance to stay in a real live manor house."

His interest seemed to excite her. Perhaps this was what she'd been thinking all along--a small tourist trade to make a decent living and still retain her paternal heritage. It brought a flush to her cheeks he found captivating.

"My father did a lot of the work already," Mali said, "but there's so much more still to do. I just don't see..." She looked into his eyes and paused. "Forgive me. You didn't come here to chat about my woes. You're here to learn about Saint Owain."

"Right," Bill said. "By the way, the rock your aunt

took me to see, is it very far from here?"

"Not at all," she said, as if glad for a change in subject. "There's a path if you'd like to walk down there."

"Great idea," he said. "Maybe it'll help me get a better feel for the legend. Your aunt covered the basics pretty well, I think. The story's absolutely charming. I can't imagine why no one's made a big deal of it before now."

Mali looked at him with undisguised skepticism. "Because it's nonsense. It's a legend grown in the telling, and it's been told so many times it's now totally ridiculous. Who in their right mind would believe that a man could out-drink the devil?"

"He was drinking milk, after all," offered Bill. "People are always looking for stories of some good person defeating the devil at his own game."

"That may be, but turning mead into milk? Believe me, our Owain was no Jesus. It was more likely he'd want to turn milk into mead!"

The path meandered through a grove of willows. Cows, or more likely sheep, had eaten the grass as if it had been mowed. "Maybe not," Bill said, holding back a low branch until she passed out of whipping range. "But don't you think many such stories have a grain of truth to them somewhere? I mean, if you went back in time, isn't it just possible that you'd be able to see how the stories got started?"

In obvious agitation, Mali strode well ahead of him.

He hurried to catch up with her. "I'm sorry if I offended you. I--"

"You didn't offend me," Mali said, stopping

suddenly. "It's just... This whole fuss about Owain is preposterous. There's more to this than you understand." When he just stared at her in confusion she put both hands up as if to surrender. "You'll just have to trust me on that."

That made no sense and only intrigued him more. Of course legends grew, but it didn't change the fact the legend of Owain was a good one. One that could bring much needed income into the village. "Mali, I'd believe anything you told me. I'd like to know the real story, assuming there is one, but right now the only story I need is the one we're going to make into commercials. That's the story the whole world is going to see, and with any luck, it's the one that's going to impact Llansantowain."

She looked at him with real pain on her face. "As much as we need an economic boost around here, I'm just not sure that's a good idea."

For some unfathomable reason he wanted to take her in his arms and hold her, convince her everything was going to be all right. Instead, he took her hands. "I understand, and much of what you said in the pub needs to be considered. But the reality is that this little town is dying, and the only way to save it is to bring in some kind of sustainable enterprise. If all the rest of north Wales is swimming in tourists, why shouldn't Llansantowain join them?"

"You make a convincing argument, William Thomas," she said, pulling away from him. "But I'm still uncertain this is the right thing. I'm not sure we want or need to be swimming in tourists."

She folded her arms across her chest, and he could see this wasn't the moment to press the issue.

He'd give her some time.

"Speaking of swimming, I'm dying to see the hot springs your aunt told me about."

Mali pursed her lips, an unfathomable look settling on her smooth features. "Some other time perhaps."

He smiled in spite of wanting to swear. He'd pushed too hard and feared he'd lost what little support he had from her. The problem was he couldn't let it go. "Okay, but after talking to my boss back home, I'm certain we'll need to use it for one of the spots. So that's two locations we'll need your permission to use."

"It is, isn't it?" Mali pushed aside some low branches and pointed toward the faintest of trails through the woods that surrounded her property. "The rock's just over this way," she said.

"You really puzzle me," Bill said. "Convince me why I shouldn't put much stock in Saint Owain's tale."

"Saints!" she said, kicking at a pebble in the narrow path. "The story just isn't credible. The real Owain was a braggart; how saintly is that? Most people don't realize that back in those days, everyone in a position of authority at a local church could be called a saint. Most were probably good people, perhaps even exceptional, but saints? No. Rome's reluctance to canonize them makes perfect sense to me."

"Maybe so," Bill said, "but there's only one patron saint here, and he's the one I'm interested in. We just need to present him in a positive light, and based on what you've told me, that shouldn't be very hard to do at all." He needed her permission to film on her land,

and if he didn't do whatever it took to get that permission, Rhia would send someone else.

"I worry it'll get the Hollywood treatment," she said.

"I'm sure there will be a little of that. I don't like it much either. Our corporate schedule demands we start shooting soon. It's going to happen with or without either of us, and probably even without your help if the town has its way, but I'd much rather have your good will and cooperation."

"You make it sound like I'm the official keeper of the legend."

"Well, aren't you? Owain's Rock is on your land; the hot springs are on your land; we can't shoot either without your permission."

"You don't really intend to film the rock, do you?"

Bill couldn't see any reason to dummy something up for the spots when the real thing was sitting in plain view. "Eventually, everyone's going to see it anyway. What good would it do to show 'em one thing on television and something else when they get here?"

"It's in horribly bad taste. Why use it at all?" Mali's voice rose.

"Because that's where the most dramatic event took place!" He paused, casting around for the right thing to say. "That's part of the legend."

Mali covered her face with both hands and sighed heavily before looking up. "Yes, yes, but it's just a legend--a story! We can't be sure any such thing ever happened."

"True or not, legends draw tourists, and that rock is the highlight of the story. We've got to film it. All we need is your permission."

When she said nothing, he took a chance. While Rhia might find a lie to convince her, Bill preferred to use the truth.

"I don't want to manipulate you, or try to spin this as something for your own good, but it will benefit the village, and I need your permission to go forward."

"I'll think about it," she said, her expression softening. She slowed her walk as she approached a clearing Bill recognized from his earlier visit with Mali's aunt. The rock, in all its neolithic tumescence, lay just ahead.

"Hold on," Mali said, squinting at a little man sitting in the shadow of a tree with a pair of binoculars trained at the business end of the rock. "What's he doing?"

"You know him?"

"No, but my aunt mentioned him. She said she'd seen a stranger hanging about." She stepped away from Bill and into the clearing. "Pardon me, sir," she called, "but didn't you see the private property signs?"

"What? Oh, dear me," he said, struggling to his feet. Shorter than Mali by half a head and thin as a schoolboy's excuse, the man all but trembled in Mali's presence. "I didn't mean any harm, madam."

"Well, I didn't think so, but--"

"Gillet," he said, extending a distinctly birdlike hand to Mali. "Clive Gillet, first recording secretary, Greater London Ornithological Society. I'm birding you see, and I came across the most extraordinary find. Do you realize what you have here?" He nodded at the tip of Owain's Rock.

A giant penis? Bill thought.

"A bird's nest?" said Mali.

"Yes, of course, but what *kind* of bird is it? That's the thing you see. It's a very rare creature we have here, very rare indeed." He held up a hand as if he was stopping traffic and slowly crept to a nearby tripod supporting the largest camera lens Bill had ever seen. The thing was at least eight inches long, and trained on the nest. "Shh," whispered Gillet, "he's back." The steady click of the shutter was the only sound.

Bill squinted at the nondescript little man taking pictures of a nondescript little bird. "Looks like some kind of sparrow to me."

The birder chuckled.

"What's so funny?" Bill asked.

"Nothing, nothing at all. It just amazes me that people can't tell obvious differences between species. Sparrow, indeed. A passerine, of course, but what we have here is a *Cistothorus faciemuris*." He clicked another picture.

"A what?" Mali asked.

"Common name: rat-faced wren. Terribly silly, I know. Shows an appalling disregard for decorum, what? Yes. Well, according to my guidebook, they're all but extinct. The last known mating pair was seen in the Lake District six years ago. No one thought they'd come this far south, but just look at this one. A charming fellow, don't you think?"

"Quite charming," Bill said. "Have you been observing him very long?"

"Almost a week. The female's been sitting on the nest for two days now. I expect she'll not move much until the eggs hatch, except to feed a little herself, of course. That's when the male steps in, like now. You're lucky to see him at all. This behavior is rare in passerines. I wasn't quite sure what I'd stumbled onto at first, but now I'm certain." He turned slowly around as if inspecting the perimeter of the Rock until he came back to Mali. "I can't wait to break the news."

"What news?" Mali asked.

"The news of my discovery, of course! You'll be seeing my name in the *Journal* this quarter for sure."

Mali tipped her head in recognition. "Congratulations, Mr. Gillet."

"Gratified, I'm sure, and the Society will be in an uproar of excitement. You know, there really aren't too many good vantage points. I do hope there won't be a great deal of crowding."

"Crowding?" Bill asked.

"Sadly, yes. It can happen when word gets out that a rare specimen lives within driving distance of the city. A long drive to be sure, but our members are nothing if not dedicated."

"I must remind you, Mr. Gillet, this is private property."

"An excellent point, madam, and one I shall mention in my write-up. It certainly wouldn't do for a mob of enthusiasts to show up and scare the poor things off the nest."

"In the very near future," Bill said, "this whole area is going to be completely off-limits to the public."

Gillet stared at him over the top of his half lens spectacles. "What on Earth for?"

"We'll be filming some commercials."

"Possibly," Mali interjected.

"Out of the question!" Gillet said, his hands flapping at his sides in distress. "That would be a catastrophe, far worse than a smattering of birders."

He scribbled furiously in his notepad.

"Nothing's definite," Mali said.

"Yet," added Bill.

~*~

Bill tried mightily to be understanding about it, but Mali's reluctance to go along with the project threw him. It made absolutely no sense for her not to cooperate. Of all the people in the village, she had the most to gain. Why she persisted in making things difficult was a total mystery. And, he thought to himself, as if that weren't enough, suddenly this little sandpiper of a man shows up with a cross between a camera and an artillery piece muttering dire warnings about the consequences of disturbing his precious rat-bird.

"I need a tall one, Brenna," Bill said, following Clive Gillet into the Cock and Bull.

She looked the newcomer up and down, then turned to Bill. "Who's this, then?" she asked as she pulled a lager.

Bill leaned forward conspiratorially and whispered, "He's the official Chirp Checker of the Greater London Society for the Birds."

"Ha!" laughed Gillet. "That's a good one!" He turned to Brenna and bowed at the waist. "Clive Gillet, madam," he said, touching the brim of his sand-colored Tilly hat. "Greater London Ornithological Society."

"And what will you have, Mr. Gillet?"

"A glass of sherry, if you please. As I suggested to our American friend here, a celebratory libation is definitely in order."

Brenna removed a dusty bottle from beneath the

counter, pulled the cork, and sniffed at the open neck. "We don't get many requests for sherry," she said. "This is all I have and it may be a sight gamy. You sure I can't get you an ale?"

"No, no, thank you. It's sherry or nothing for me. Delicate constitution you know. Quite. Mustn't lose sight of that even if this is a banner day."

Brenna lowered a brow and looked at Bill. "What's he going on about, then?"

"Rat-bird," Bill said, keeping his voice low and his face straight. "A giant carnivorous creature living in the woods by Owain's Rock. It's been feeding on old ladies and little children. Mr. Gillet here has been taking pictures of the beast and its mate, but I think he may have angered it. Who knows? It could burst into town at any moment. I'd secure the taps if I were you."

Gillett's snorty laugh was infectious, and Bill grinned that his exaggeration fell on appreciative ears. Now if Gillet would only lighten up about the filming.

Brenna set a glass of amber liquid in front of the Londoner. "Can't say I've ever heard of a rat-bird."

Gillet cocked an eyebrow at her and winked at Bill. "It's a rat-faced bird, madam," he said, raising the thin-stemmed wine glass delicately and sipping from it. "In fact, a wren. Very rare. Very rare indeed. Your village is blessed to have a mating pair, and I'm twice blessed to have discovered them." He raised his glass to his hostess and dipped his head.

"Congratulations," she said.

"I tried to explain to Mr. Thomas and his lady friend why it would be utterly inappropriate for them to bring a movie crew into the area while my specimen is nesting."

"Your lady friend?" Brenna turned to Bill, all smiles and silent questions.

"Mali Rhys. We bumped into Mr. Gillet over at Owain's Rock. He and I got into a discussion about the pros and cons of commercial film making and, well, Miss Rhys took her dogs and walked home." In fact, she'd not taken very well to either Mr. Gillet or Bill at that moment. With a curt whistle, she recalled the dogs from their rabbit hunt in the pasture and marched back home without even a polite 'good day'. Gillet had driven him back to town. He slapped his forehead. "Damn!"

"What?" she asked.

"I left my car at Mali's house."

Brenna chuckled. "You're fitting in quite well. Folks walk nearly everywhere hereabout; most forget they even own cars. I can lend you a bicycle, or Dai can run you over there."

"I'll give you a lift, my good man," Gillet said. "I shall determine Miss Rhys' official address in the event papers need be served."

As congenial as Gillet was, Bill couldn't allow that to happen. "Surely nothing that drastic will be necessary."

"One can never be too careful. No, indeed. We in the Greater London Ornithological Society consider ourselves stewards of the feathered world. If we don't watch out for the birds, who will?"

"But no one's going to hurt them!" Bill said, unable to hide the exasperation in his tone. "They aren't being hunted! No one's going to show up with a net. All we want to do is shoot a few feet of film. They don't even have to move. I'll buy birdseed. What kind do they like?"

Gillet snorted as if Bill had just made another great joke. "You Americans are so earnest. Always a delight, always." He finished his sherry. "Now I've got to be off. I prefer to drive the country lanes with a good bit of sunlight, what? Much safer, don't you know. Besides, one can never tell when some glorious specimen will pop up, completely unannounced, and beckon to have its photo taken." He preened. "I've done some of my best work out a car window."

"I'll bet," Bill said.

"Ta," Gillet said. "Shall I drop you at Miss Rhys'?"

Bill shook his head. "It's okay. I've got a beer to finish. I'll get up there later." Besides, it'd give him a great excuse to go back out and see Mali without anyone looking over his shoulder.

"Cheerio, my dears," Gillet said bowing to Brenna as if she were royal and doffing his hat to Bill. "I shall return in a day or two to renew my investigations." With a wave he stepped carefully through the door.

"Caitlin would say he likely didn't get enough protein as a child," Brenna said. "She looked around the otherwise empty room. "Can I get you another beer before I step out back? I've dinner to prepare and it may be quite a while."

"Thanks." Bill accepted her offer and wandered over to an easy chair in the corner of the room near a cold fireplace. He settled down and stretched out his legs, still thinking about Clive Gillet, Mali Rhys, Rhia Jones, Owain y'Craig, and the other usual suspects. He closed his eyes and before long a scenario popped into his mind with all the pomp and bluster of Broadway....

The devil's own voice emanated from the mouth of a wild woman. My God, Bill thought, it's Rhia, and she looks pretty good in those skimpy rags.

"You, braggart saint," she creaked in a smoker's version of Clive Gillet's tenor, "you're a fine one to claim piety. You're no better than me. Prove that your faith is stronger than the contents of a cask. Meet me in the mead house, and match me drink for drink."

Bill wasn't sure it was appropriate for him to enter a drinking contest with the devil. A refusal seemed in order when from somewhere the three pub regulars appeared at his elbow, all dressed in tights and jerkins, with little Robin Hood plumed hats.

"You can do it, Owain," Dai said, patting Bill on the back.

"We're counting on you, Owain," Dylan Davies said, his arms folded across his pot belly. The tights weren't working for him, Bill thought.

Michael Wells shrugged and adjusted the longbow draped over his shoulder. "It's only mead. What can it hurt? Be a man."

Bill, suddenly quite thirsty, acquiesced, and they set out in the direction of the tavern, drawing onlookers at each step of the way. By the time they arrived at the inn, an even larger crowd met them. By its size, Bill guessed every person in the village was there. They'd left a clear wide circle outside in which the devil waited for him, looking very much like Clive Gillet, only much, much bigger. He no longer spoke through Rhia, who hung on his arm. The devil, his nose grown larger and distinctly beakish, stood, cup in hand as Bill and his entourage approached.

"Owain y'Craig," the devil cried, "you have more

nerve than I thought!"

"'Tis nothing, I assure you," Bill said to the amusement of his companions. He grabbed a drinking cup of his own from one of several offered by Dai, then ambled to the waiting cask. He poured off a ration and without any fuss at all tossed it down.

The devil laughed and did the same. Bill felt nothing and the devil showed no ill effects. Not likely that he would, thought Bill.

"Another!" cried the throng.

When that round went down as smoothly as the first, Dai called for a third and then a fourth. The drinkers continued in that fashion until the onlookers grew weary, and the sun hovered low on the horizon.

"Tomorrow's a work day," Michael said, yawning. "I don't suppose you lads would want to take this up again later?"

Bill hushed him.

Staggering ever so slightly, the devil belched. "I admit, Owain, ye've lasted far longer than I thought you would. Not that it matters. I can last all night. Can you?"

Bill laughed back at him, comfortable in his role. "I can last all night if I must, demon. Stand aside, vile fiend, and I'll fill my cup yet again."

As the devil watched, Bill turned the tap, filled his cup, put it to his mouth and drained it in a single draught. Still smiling, he offered to pour one for the devil. The Dark One handed him his cup, and it burned Bill's hand--the wood hot as coals. Ignoring the pain, Bill filled it, avoided the steam as the contents warmed, and handed it back.

The devil tipped it up and poured it all into his

mouth at once. Instantly, he began to cough and gag. He foamed at the mouth. His face turned red, then yellow, then green. He clutched his distended belly with taloned fingers, groaned, and moaned and rolled on the ground before he finally spewed a substance from his mouth in a great, white, foamy arc.

"What treachery is this?" he cried, spitting and gasping. "That was no mead in my cup!"

"Aye, 'tis true," Bill said, a superior smile etched on his lips. "T'is mead in the cask and mead in the tap, but whenever I try to pour some out, it turns to milk."

"Cheat!" the devil screamed. "Scoundrel! Rogue! Deceiver!"

"I'm none of those," Bill said, his arms folded comfortably across his chest. "The Lord watches over me. I gave you wholesome milk, yet you act as if I'd poisoned you."

"That's exactly what you've done--I'm lactose intolerant!" Still groaning, the devil crawled to the edge of the circle then stopped and faced Bill again. "Don't think you've proven yourself yet, foolish mortal. Your trickery has but earned you another trial." He gestured at Rhia, who stepped forward. "The wild woman will explain." Pushing through the crowd of watchers, he hurried away into the growing dark.

"William! William, wake up!"

Bill opened one groggy eye toward the voice. "Hm?"

"You were dreaming," Brenna said. She nodded toward the bar at a pair of smiling farm workers. "You kept calling for more milk. They'd begun to wonder about you."

"Right," Bill said, sitting up and stretching.
Concern filled her eyes. "Are you all right?"

He smiled. "Fine. Just a dream. A very weird dream."

With the episode fresh in his mind he decided to give Rhia a call. It might be a good jumping off point in the commercials. Besides, he needed to make sure they could get something filmed before Gillet and his bird brigade made trouble.

~*~

Just like a man, Mali thought, to have a testosterone spike over something as innocuous as a sparrow, or a wren, or whatever it was. The dogs, unaffected by her mood, rolled over each other as they half ran, half tumbled through the thick weeds on either side of the path. How had she lost control of the situation? What had started as a pleasant walk had somehow turned into a contest of wills--which neither of them had won--and then deteriorated into a shouting match between an ad man and a bird man. She grinned in spite of her anger. They bloody well deserved each other, and William should be heartily ashamed for letting her walk home all alone. Not that she hadn't done it a thousand times before, of course. He was so involved in his tête-à-tête with the bird watcher, he didn't even see her leave. That rankled more than their argument.

When she reached the cottage, she discovered Aunt Glynnis was still at choir rehearsal and so wouldn't be able to press her for details of Mali's afternoon with the Yank. She glanced over at the bouquet of stately foxglove she'd left on top of the glass display case. Once she'd positioned it over the letter, Bill had been gentleman enough not to disturb it, and she almost regretted it. She was getting very tired of covering up the truth. But, there was absolutely no denying the flowers were lovely. How long had it been since a man had brought flowers into the house? She frowned in concentration. Surely these weren't the only flowers a man had ever given her. Were they?

Kicking off her shoes she flopped down on the sofa. Well, no matter. He had brought her these, and that was that. She slowly returned her gaze to the blooms. Was he just trying to make amends for that first night at the pub when he hadn't known who she was, or did he have something more in mind? That appealed to her, in spite of all his arguing. He certainly hadn't hesitated to accept her invitation to lunch, nor did he appear to have any complaints about her company. Of course, Aunt Glynnis could have all the credit for the soup. The memory of catching him staring at her, once when she casually looked over her shoulder and again when she saw his reflection in the polished chrome of the toaster lingered warmly. The look of approval on his face pleased her far more than she imagined it could.

Still, how could she know if he was truly interested in her, or merely in getting her to allow him to film his stupid commercials? She desperately wanted to believe he wasn't trying to manipulate her, but she'd heard advertising people could fake sincerity at the drop of hat. She just didn't want to be taken for a simple rustic. Of course, she admitted, that's precisely what she was. Perhaps Caitlin could whip up a truth serum. She winced. No, that wouldn't work; it would surely taste as revolting as her other concoctions. It might be entertaining to have Dai and some of the other lads pound it out of him. Not very practical, she decided, especially if she had truly caught his fancy. Beating up prospective beaus was not a good way to win their hearts.

Blast! Why did such things always have to get so complicated? Why couldn't she just have him over for dinner and arrange it so that she could collect a kiss from him on his way out? If he was a good kisser, she could always arrange for another. Just to be sure, of course. And no denying she wanted more than one.

She'd ask him over for dinner. Who would object? It's not like there was any impropriety involved. Thousands of people shared innocent meals together every day without jumping into bed with each other. Anyway, if Aunt Glynnis thought Mali wanted to jump into bed with him, she'd probably volunteer to pour the wine, dim the lights, and turn down the covers!

The thought left her smiling broadly. She wiped her hand across her forehead. She had to get her mind off the subject.

How would Meleri, her long dead ancestor, have handled such a challenge? Of course, for a woman like her, it'd hardly even be a challenge. Now there was someone with courage, damned though she may have been.

With most of the menfolk away crusading, the women worked the fields, tended the livestock, and still struggled to make ends meet until Lady Meleri had taken the hard course and opened her own home as a tavern. Girls who needed a few extra coins were safe to ply their trade upstairs. What was the loss of a bit of virtue when the survival of her people was at stake?

Without the missive, Mali would never have had the chance to know anything about Meleri. What amazing nerve she'd had to record what really happened when Owain y'Craig came calling. The truth of that encounter was far less magical than the pictures on the bedroom walls in the pub, but no less shocking. Wouldn't the Yank find that a lovely film to make! She allowed herself to daydream....

Owain y'Craig emerged from the mists of her imagination. He leaned piously against a wooden table in the common room of an inn while his men dallied upstairs with a handful of girls working there. He looked remarkably like Bill, though more sullen-faced and deceitful.

"Yes, I have seen the devil," the saint said to Dylan, Dai, and Michael, the three most worthless men to ever work the valley--assuming they ever had.

"You can't be serious," Dylan said with undisguised awe in his tone.

"Oh, aye. 'Tis true. I met him on the road. I saw him inside hordes of sinners--his serpent eyes flickering in the depths of the depraved. It's not just the old crones you have to worry about, lads. Nay." He made a great show of looking down into his empty drinking cup.

Mali, nearly tripping over her floor length skirt, went to fill the cup from a pitcher of mead at the end of the table. Dylan, Dai, and Michael held their cups out as well.

"Get away with you," she said, knocking their hands aside. "If you want more, you'll have to work for it. Lord

knows you never pay for it."

"You're a cruel, cruel woman, Meleri, and that's a fact," Dylan said. "How d'ye expect a man to walk home in this weather without a drop in his veins to keep him warm?"

"Perhaps ye should've worn an extra layer of clothing, then," Mali said. "Men who work can usually afford a cloak."

"A pious man needn't worry about such things," Owain observed when Mali refreshed his drink. "The Lord watches over him."

"He surely watches over the idiots," Mali muttered. Owain was about as pious as a rooster in a hen house, only more canny when it came to drinking without paying. "And he doesn't expect free drinks."

"What's that, Meleri?" Dai asked. "Did you say 'drinks'?"

"No. Go back to your snoring."

"Dylan's right," Michael said, moving closer to her. "It's a dreadful cold night. Why not spend it with me, Meleri? I'll keep you warm." He reached for her with both hands.

Mali wanted to hit him with the pitcher of mead, then thought better of spilling it. She slapped him across the cheek instead.

Michael recoiled, a hand to his face while Mali rubbed her stinging palm on her apron. Next time maybe she would hit him with the pitcher. Right after dumping its contents over his head.

Owain ignored them completely. "It takes a special sort of purity to be able to open yourself to the Lord and accept his protection," he said.

"And you've got it?"

Owain lowered his head, spoke a few silent words, then looked up at her as if suddenly beatified. "I am thus blessed." He took a long drink from his replenished cup.

Mali had had enough. His piety was only outdone by his avariciousness. "Prove it."

"Here?"

"Why not? A tavern is as good a place as any, and with all the sinning going on upstairs, surely the Lord would be here in a heartbeat to help you! You claim the Lord looks after you, and that's all well and good for you, but what about the rest of us? What about me? What about my girls upstairs? We're struggling to stay fed in the absence of most of the able-bodied men hereabouts. And some folks, naming no names, are slow to pay."

Owain straightened with wounded pride. "You suggest we won't pay our debts?"

"I haven't seen a single coin since you came in, and all I've heard is how you let the Lord set things straight." Mali pushed the hair back from her face. "That doesn't leave me overly confident you have any money at all."

"You're a feisty one, then," Owain said, a slow smile forming across his lips.

"It helps."

He produced a leather pouch which hung from a strip of hide around his neck beneath his tunic. He patted the plump bag which resulted in a satisfying clatter of coins. "I'm good for it."

"Ought to be ashamed of yourself, Meleri," Dylan said. "If you can't trust a saint, you've no heart a'tall."

"I'm chary of any man who claims righteousness for

a surname." She reached for the pouch, but Owain pulled it away and slipped it back under his shirt. There was only one way that man would part with any of his money, and she was certain it wouldn't be for services provided by her tavern. She looked him in the eye for a moment, then spoke. "If you're willing to put your trust in the Lord, I'm willing to put mine in myself."

Owain belly-laughed. "Then you give yourself no chance!"

"I'll bring out more mead. One pitcher for each of us. We'll take turns draining them--a cup for you, then a cup for me. Whichever of us can stay awake the longest keeps the purse. The whole purse."

The smile on Owain's face hovered between amusement and condescension, but Mali didn't care. She knew if she didn't drink the pious fraud under the table and claim his purse, neither she nor any of the girls toiling upstairs would see a penny. Fortunately, he was already a few cups ahead of her. "Well, what say you, Owain?"

The saint squinted at her with a sly grin. "What if we need more than two pitchers of mead?"

Mali nodded at Dai. "He knows where it's kept. He's slept under that cask more times than I can count."

Dai frowned. "Never. I was merely guarding it, Meleri."

"Ah, yes. I forgot. Your snoring kept the wolves at bay and the dead awake all night." She turned to Owain. "Well? That pouch and all the English coin in it. We need three new milk cows."

"You're willing to suffer the consequences of competing with Almighty God? Understand I fully intend to open my person and let him act through me to

the fullest."

She kept a straight face. "I'm ready." She raised her eyes to Heaven. *If You'll come for a drink, perhaps You'll take a little from my pitcher?* She fancied she heard Him laugh.

"Bring on your mead, then," Owain said.

Dylan clapped him on the back and earned a scowl for his trouble.

"I'll stand by you, Meleri," Michael said, nuzzling close to her.

His aroma testified he'd likely not changed his clothes yet this year. Mali pinched her nose. "I'd rather you stood beside Dai."

She left the common room and refilled the pitcher Owain had been drinking from. A second pitcher she filled half full then topped off with water. "Coming, coming!" she sang as she wove her way through the benches and tables to the waiting men.

Owain's eyes bored into her when she returned as if searching for someone else within her skin. No shred of good humor remained on his face.

"Such a sober look for such unsober business." Smiling, she set the pitcher of undiluted mead beside him and gestured for him to begin. Instead of filling his cup, he brought his hands together and prayed. "Oh Lord, let us drink all the mead this sinner can provide." He appeared ready to continue praying.

"Very well, then," Mali said, "I'll go first." She poured herself a cup and drained it in a single draught. Dylan, Michael, and Dai nodded at her in admiration. "If I should win," she said to them, "I'll need you to carry our guest to a room where he can sleep it off."

"As delightful as your rooms above are, I'm sure

that won't be necessary," Owain said, dripping condescension. "Besides, it would hardly be fitting for me to spend the night here." He looked around the room as if it bore some taint, then he closed his eyes and drank a full cup of mead. He slapped the empty vessel on the rough table and drew his sleeve across his mouth. "Your turn, I believe."

The scoundrel drinks for free, and insults me while doing it, she thought. Mali wasted no time chugging down her watered, still honey-sweet, mead. She had but one prayer, that it would be a long time before she had to find the privy.

With every draught Owain prayed, and soon he slurred nearly every word. Twice he slid off his chair and needed Dylan to help prop him up.

Mali retrieved two more pitchers, though she used even less mead in hers the second time. She almost felt sorry for Owain knowing what a head he'd have in the morning.

"Come, come, Meleri, I don't have all night," Owain groused.

Almost sorry? No, she decided, she didn't feel sorry for him at all. In fact, if his head was anything less than huge, she'd be very disappointed in the quality of her brew! She poured a cup from his pitcher and handed it to him. "This won't take much longer," she said.

He made gurgling noises as he drained the cup, though a significant portion of the mead ran down his chin and soaked his tunic. Mali handed him a cloth, which he had trouble closing his fingers around, then drank her own quite neatly.

Owain cast a bleary eye her way and belched. Breathing heavily, he began to tilt until Dylan propped *him back up. "Witch," he breathed.*

If he only knew the half of it, she thought. Cheat and harlot, too, they'd call her. And all because she felt responsible for her people.

"Here, let me help you," Mali said, pouring him yet another. She held her own cup high and offered a toast.

Owain held his cup in two hands, wobbled a little, and stared down into it with eyebrows knit together as if to discover some secret.

"Cheers," Mali said and raised the cup to her lips.

Unable to raise his cup to his mouth, Owain slumped over onto Dai, the cup falling from his leaden fingers.

She'd won.

"Thank God that's over," she said. "I've got to pee." She opened Owain's shirt to extract the pouch from around his neck and caught sight of an ornate gold crucifix under it. After removing the pouch, she quickly refastened his shirt to hide the cross. Such a rich item was an easy target for thieves, and she'd not have him accuse anyone in her house should it mysteriously disappear while he slept.

"Take our saint upstairs, if you please, and put him to bed."

Dylan's mouth twisted as he thought through her request. "All the rooms upstairs are taken, except Bett's."

"You can't leave him with Black Tooth Bett," exclaimed Dai. "He's a man of the cloth, and she's--"

"She's just as hard a worker as anyone else here, and a damn sight more reliable than you three."

"But she's a harlot!" burst Michael. "You'd put him in her bed?"

Mali crossed her arms in exasperation. "All the women upstairs are harlots. What difference does that make?"

Dylan chewed his lower lip for a moment then nodded. "Aye. There's that. I'd not find it unpleasant to wake up in a lady's chambers myself. C'mon lads, give me a hand."

Mali watched them half-drag, half-carry the saint, then rushed out the door toward the privy.

Chapter Five

Bill sprawled in a chair near the back of the Cock and Bull with a notepad in front of him and dozens of tourist brochures from all over North Wales arrayed like a rainbow just beyond it. Brightly colored glossies proclaimed the can't-miss values of castles, gardens, manor houses, and former slate mines. Something for everyone--from the curious Italianate village of Portmerion, to narrow gauge railways chugging up Mount Snowdon. It made a jigsaw puzzle of North Wales. Where would tiny Llansantowain, with little beyond rustic charm and a giant stone penis, fit into the mosaic?

He was so lost in thought that when his cell phone rang he merely stared at it for a moment in dumb fascination before his urban instincts took over, and he grabbed it off the table.

"Bill Thomas."

"Great news," Rhia said, her voice bursting out of the phone with cheerleader exuberance. "The copy writers have come up with five spots based on those tall tales of yours. Great stuff. I know you'll like 'em, especially the last one."

"You mean the one where Owain dies under the rock? I've been thinking about that, and I'm certain that if we work the camera angles right the audience may not even be aware of the rock's shape."

"That's exactly what Chuck said. Told me not to worry about it. If there was a problem, the art department could take care of it."

"Good ol' Chuck."

"But you haven't heard the best part."

Bill closed his eyes. "I can't wait."

"Stay with me," Rhia said. "Knowing Alonzo, he'll have audiences weeping when poor Omar sacrifices himself for the villagers."

"That'd be Owain, not Omar."

"Whatever. Now, after we've aired that spot enough to saturate the market, we move into phase two."

He idly wondered if she ever bothered listening to anyone. "Is that when we, as you so delicately suggested, 'go after the Pope'?"

"That's later, and only if you're able to come up with some real proof that the saint and I are related."

Bill stared at the dart board, imagining Rhia as one of the brown blobs of possessed virtue being exorcised by the saint in his bedroom. Rhia related to Owain? Right. David, maybe. "I may not be the right person to--"

"You want me to send someone else? Dammit, Bill,

what's the matter with you?"

He wanted to tell her it was a stupid idea, and he had no time for more stupid ideas. He felt his stomach knot, but he forced a positive note into his voice. "I'll work it into my spare time."

"Good. Now, pay attention. You're gonna love this. It's the best idea I've had in years!"

Bill tried to remain hopeful. If it was her best idea in years, maybe it wouldn't completely suck.

"Remember when I asked you if anyone had ever looked under the rock?"

"When you--" What a convenient memory she had.

"I'll go slower if it'll help you keep up," she said, her voice syrupy.

"I'm with you."

She continued. "Well, I've been thinking of little else since you told me no one had ever done anything like that. In fact, I've been talking to one of the networks, and they're interested in doing a live broadcast. They want to have a crane lift the stone so experts can zip in and dig around underneath it. If there's anything left of ol' saint Orville, they'll find it, and when they do, the cameras'll be right there. Is that brilliant or what?"

Just thinking of how Mali and Clive Gillet would react to such news unknotted Bill's stomach. He'd pay a week's salary to see Rhia deliver that announcement in person.

"What the network is offering will cover our production costs for the commercials, though this isn't carte blanche to overdo your expense account. They've even agreed to kick in some money for some sort of marker. We'll head up the memorial fund raiser, of course. It shouldn't be too hard to round up enough for something suitable. Anything would be better than that big brick boner."

"It's granite, I think."

From across the room Michael informed Dai that Bill was talking about Owain's wang. That elicited guffaws from several of the men assembled. Michael waved.

"I was waxing poetic," Rhia said.

"Right." He steeled himself for her reaction to his news. "I've gotta tell you, Rhia, I think we might run into a little trouble with the network idea."

"You don't like it?" The sudden ice in her voice was unmistakable.

"I didn't say that. The problem is getting the land owner's permission to shoot at Owain's Rock, though I think she's warming to the idea." More like succumbing to public pressure, he thought, but he'd take his luck where he could get it. "I still haven't seen the hot springs location, by the way, but I'm hoping to get by there in the next day or two."

"How thoughtful," Rhia said glacially. "It's not like we're in a hurry or anything."

Bill's jaw muscles tightened, and he consciously fought to unclench them. "I might be able to talk Miss Rhys into letting us shoot at the rock, but there's no way she'll go for the whole network production thing. Besides, there's an organization sniffing around which may raise some objections to the filming altogether."

In a voice as dark as slate, and about as soft, she said, "What organization?"

Bill was glad the Atlantic Ocean separated them.

He felt sorry for Stacey or anyone else within a hundred miles of her office. "The Greater London Ornithological Society. When she didn't respond, he added, "They're bird watchers."

There was a long silence from Rhia's end. Then, "Bird watchers?"

"Yes. There's a rare bird nesting on the rock."

Another long pause. "Bill?" Her calm and quiet voice chilled him like no tirade ever had.

"Uh huh?"

"Fix it."

"Right."

"We're doing those spots and the network special. It's a done deal. Letterman is going to interview me, for Christ's sake."

"For Christ's sake?"

"Don't even try to be cute."

"Right."

"Do not disappoint me, Bill. If it takes a miracle, work one. And don't forget about the genealogical stuff."

"But--"

"Look for the film crew this week. They'll need a place to stay."

"How many will--"

Bill looked at the dead receiver in his hand. Did Rhia hang up on everyone?

Suddenly the phone rang again, and Bill stabbed his thumb at the talk button. "No problem, I'll just take one impossible task at a time, starting with the damned Rock."

"What about the damned Rock?" Mali asked.

Bill squeezed his eyes shut. Had he said enough to

prove himself a complete ass? "Mali."

"Hi."

"I'm sorry," he said, lamely. "I thought you were someone else."

She chuckled. "You're good at that."

He pounded his forehead with the heel of his hand. *Idiot!* "Uhm. I--"

"I thought if you could join us for dinner tonight, we could talk over this business of filming at the Rock. What do you say?"

Bill briefly considered proposing marriage to her instead and somewhere in the back of his mind, it didn't seem preposterous. "Sounds great. What can I bring?"

~*~

"I still think using the silver is too much," Mali said as she watched her aunt give a final buff to a candelabra which took up entirely too much space on the little built-in table in the kitchen.

"Nonsense, dear," Glynnis said. "We don't want William to think we're of reduced means."

"But, we are of reduced means."

"That's got nothing to do with it." She gripped Mali by the shoulders as if to straighten her. Mali obliged by stretching her spine and displaying her brightest, most parent-appealing, primary school smile.

Glynnis fastened an additional button on Mali's blouse near her neck then chucked her lightly on the chin. "My, but you're a beauty. Your mother all over again, only better."

"Thank you," Mali said. She didn't usually think of herself that way, but with William coming for dinner, she very much wanted to look her best.

They both started at a knock on the door.

"What happened to the dogs?" Mali asked.

"I'm wondering the same thing."

Mali hurried to the door, heard the dogs' happy whines, and opened it.

Bill, flanked by Samson and Delilah, knelt at the threshold, patting both dogs. His winning manner and their complete acceptance of him warmed her. She didn't know which was more comical--the dogs struggling to keep their heads up under the weight of the enormous butcher bones he'd brought for them, or his self-effacing grin while caught in the act of bribing them. She couldn't keep her own smile from spreading past her cheeks. She was beginning to like this man very much.

"I think the dogs and I are friends now," he said.

"For life," Mali added, "at the very least."

The dogs tried to sneak past Mali's knees into the house with their new treasures.

"Oh no, you don't! You two stay out here with those things." She moved forward to let Bill in and keep the dogs at bay. He squeezed through the narrow gap, and she felt herself flush as he brushed past her. He smelled of a man's cologne she couldn't name, but which filled her with an overwhelming desire to inhale deeply. Instead, she held her breath, afraid to move until he'd stepped away from the door.

"Come in, William!" Glynnis said, warm welcome in her voice. She took his jacket and laid it over the comfy chair in front of the fireplace and settled herself on the arm of the settee. "You've a grand way with those dogs."

"I like them," he said. "A family isn't quite complete without a dog around the place."

"You've one at home, then?" she asked.

He gave her a wistful look. "Not now. My last dog was a big, flop-eared mutt named Hammurabi."

"I'll bet you called him 'Ham' for short."

"Abi. She was a real sweetheart."

His easy way with Glynnis as well as the dogs impressed Mali, but also bothered her. From the very beginning he'd done the right things in the right ways, and had always been charming and engaging. She desperately wanted to trust him, but she trusted her natural skepticism more. She wondered if this was a trick of all advertising people. Was William really as good-natured as he appeared?

"Shall we?" Mali guided him into the kitchen and aimed him at the chair in the middle. She sat her aunt beside him.

"Cozy," he said.

"Small," she amended.

He gave her a smile that sent her heart racing. "No, I meant cozy. It feels homey and comfortable. I like it." He gestured to the candelabra. "That's pretty."

Glynnis cast Mali an I-told-you-so look. "Thank you."

"We're having chicken," said Mali. "I hope that's all right."

"Wonderful," he said, then slapped his forehead. "I left the wine in the car."

"You didn't have to do that," she said.

"I know; it just happened." He winked at Glynnis. "I'll be right back." He slipped out from behind the table and hurried from the room.

When they heard the front door close, Glynnis whispered to Mali, "You're crazy if you don't drag that man to the altar!"

"Aunt Glynnis!" Mali said in horror. "You make it sound positively sacrificial! If--no *when*--the time comes, I'd prefer my future husband to make it to the altar on his own two feet."

"Just the same--"

The front door opened. "Got it!" Bill called.

Mali wrinkled her nose at Glynnis. "Shh!" As he walked into the kitchen, she turned to him. "White or red?"

"Brown, I think." He held one of the two containers up to the light. "It's kind of hard to tell, but I couldn't resist the bottles. Look, they've got little cows on them."

"I'd guess red," Glynnis said playfully.

"It looks lovely." Mali handed him a corkscrew. "Would you? I'll get some glasses."

"The good ones are in--" Glynnis started.

"The sideboard," Mali said. She retrieved three glasses and passed them around.

Bill filled them and offered a toast. "To new friends."

"And romance," Glynnis added.

Something caught in Bill's throat, and Mali glared at her aunt before turning to him.

He pointed to his neck. "Frog." He raised his glass again. "And romance," he said, gently clinking his glass into theirs.

"You're not married, are you, William?"

"Aunt Glynnis!"

"There's no harm in asking, Mali. That's how we

village folk are, always curious, always asking. Where are you from? Who are your kinfolk? You know the sort of thing."

"I do. Unfortunately, I've never been terribly lucky in love. Maybe I've just been too busy."

Glynnis persisted. "Traveling all over the world as you do, I should think you'd have plenty of opportunity."

Mali locked eyes with her aunt and bared her teeth. "Why don't you see if the chicken's ready."

"Oh, I'm sure it is, luv." Glynnis rose from the table and drifted toward the oven. After a flurry of activity involving pot holders, platters, and pans, she produced a feast of plump, steaming chicken breasts, green peas, sautéed mushrooms, carrots, and more of the thick slabs of bread they'd had at lunch the day before.

"No potatoes," Mali said, smiling. "Hope you don't mind."

"Not at all. It'll do my system good."

"So," Glynnis asked as she heaped vegetables onto his plate, "what would you look for in the ideal woman?"

Mali kicked her under the table.

Bill didn't seem to have noticed--he kept his eyes firmly on his food and chewed as if contemplating an answer. Glynnis acted as if her leg were made of wood.

When he finally stopped chewing, his face took on a solemn expression. "I think she'd be a woman with a dream she's willing to share; someone who fires my imagination simply by being; someone who can laugh at adversity and success with the same gusto." He slowly raised his eyes from his plate and looked directly into Mali's.

His gaze electrified her. Mali was certain she'd begun to melt and would soon be dripping onto the floor. "More bread?" she asked, dragging her cuff through the butter.

"My niece is a gifted historian," Glynnis said. "She graduated from Cambridge, you know, and has quite a successful little translation business going. I--"

Mali struggled to find her tongue. Would Glynnis never stop? "I doubt William cares very much about all that. I'm sure he'd much prefer to discuss the adverts he's been sent here to film."

"In fact," he said, wiping his mouth with his napkin, "I'm interested in the commercials and Welsh history, and I'm going to need your help with both. My boss, David Jones, made some preliminary investigations before his doctor grounded him. I promised to try and verify some of the things he's come up with."

"There are extensive records in Cardiff, but that's a long way from here," Mali said, "and I know of some local churches which also have a great wealth of material dating back to Arthurian times."

"Arthur, as in King Arthur?"

"Yes." Glynnis and Mali responded in unison. "Was there another?"

"As in Camelot and the knights of the round table?"

"The very same."

Bill looked sheepish. "I thought he was, you know, a legend."

Mali felt relieved to be back on home turf.

Perhaps it would keep Glynnis from making premature wedding plans. "Most of what you've heard is legend. The same as with Saint Owain."

"Except we've got proof Saint Owain lived," Glynnis said brightly.

Mali's relief evaporated. Of all the people to say that to! She aimed a flinty glance at Glynnis, who suddenly became intensely interested in the fibers of her napkin.

Bill leaned forward, completely focused on Mali. "Proof? Really? That's excellent!"

"We don't really have proof-proof," Mali stammered, struggling to think of a way out of telling him about the letter. "I don't have his family tree or anything like that, but if he came from a prominent enough lineage, there may be some documentation. Perhaps in the old church records. Of course, finding out anything useful will take a great deal of time." More than you or your boss has to spare, she hoped.

"Would you be willing to help me? I've no idea where to even begin."

The earnestness of his expression charmed her. She needed to say no. She wanted to say no, but she couldn't just let him fail when she had some means to prevent it. Perhaps she could do both--keep the letter safe and lend him the help he needed. "Maybe, if my schedule's not too busy."

"That'll be the day," Glynnis said with a snort. When Mali gave her another icy stare, she added, "I'll get dessert. D'ye fancy cheesecake, William?"

Bill, apparently oblivious to the glances between aunt and niece nodded with enthusiasm. "Sounds wonderful. More wine?"

Mali pushed both her glass and her aunt's toward him, though the way Glynnis had been going on Mali suspected she'd had quite enough already. Mali'd already had two glasses and feared she'd passed her limit with the first.

Glynnis delivered the desserts, and Bill helped himself to a taste of the sinfully rich cheesecake. It had cost Glynnis a small fortune at the bakery in Betws-y-Coed, but she insisted she couldn't make one as good. They'd argued over it in front of shop. Mali pointed out how ridiculous it was for them to spend so much when William was the one on an expense account; he should've taken them out. Now she was glad they'd bought it. He took another bite, closed his eyes, and smiled.

"Divine," he said, then looked up suddenly, concern darkening his features. "Do real men say 'divine'?"

They laughed, and he cleared his throat as if he wanted to say something. Mali nodded for him to go on. "I was talking to my office earlier today. They're eager to start shooting, and they say it's critical we use Owain's Rock."

Mali was resigned to allow it. So much was at stake for the entire village. She couldn't justify denying the town a chance to prosper more than it had for the last hundred years. "All right."

He looked at her in surprise, obviously expecting more resistance. "Then you'll let us film there?"

"Only if you promise me it can be done without any harm to Mr. Gillet's wrens."

"Mr. Who's whats?" Glynnis asked.

"Clive Gillet is that gentleman you saw at the rock

the other day. He's a London birdwatcher and has discovered a rare bird nesting there. He'll make quite a fuss if the nesting is interrupted.

Bill listened attentively, but seemed uncomfortable about something.

"Are you all right?" she asked.

"There's one more thing I need to mention." He hesitated, and Mali fancied she saw doubt and confusion in his expression. Whatever it was, he certainly was taking care in how he worded it.

"The hot springs?" Glynnis asked. When Bill looked at her in surprise, she turned to Mali. "Oh, go ahead, dear. Let them shoot there, too. What can it harm?"

Mali felt like a tennis ball batted back and forth between the two of them. She raised her glass and took a sip of wine.

"I want to talk about that, too," Bill said, "but what really concerns me now is something else." He took a deep breath. "Y'see, Rhia, my boss, made a deal with ABC--"

"The American BBC, right?" Glynnis asked.

"Yes, sort of," he said. "Anyway, they'd like to hoist the stone to its original position. They'll bring in experts to search under it for Owain's remains."

Mali inhaled wine. Coughing and choking, eyes watering, she struggled for breath.

Glynnis patted her vigorously on the back, and when Mali waved a hand to show she wasn't dying, Glynnis sank back into her chair and fanned herself as if she were about to faint. "Oh dear! Are you all right?"

Mali nodded, but she certainly wasn't all right. The thought someone might really want to look under the rock had never occurred to her, nor to anyone. She coughed again.

"I told them you wouldn't like the idea," Bill said as he offered her a glass of water.

Mali carefully sipped the water and avoided eye contact with either of them. This was dreadful. The legend of Saint Owain was nonsense, but the letter wasn't clear on the actual disposition of his body. He might very well have been buried beneath the rock. But if he wasn't there, it could prove the legend even more bogus and destroy the village's hope for a decent tourist trade. Or, she realized with horror, it might fuel a belief that he'd been bodily transported to heaven. The trouble finding a body would cause was nothing compared to the trouble that might arise if they found nothing at all. She drained her wine glass. Either way, it was going to be bad.

"I'm not crazy about the idea myself." Bill had been holding his fork poised over the dessert, and when Mali still said nothing, he took a large bite.

"Great cheesecake." He shoveled another forkful into his mouth and chewed lustily. "Truly awesome!"

Glynnis sat, still fanning herself, a worried frown wrinkling her forehead. "Oh my! Raise Owain's Rock?"

"There's liable to be a lot of money in it for the village," he said, obviously aware of how lame the statement sounded. "Archaeologists would assess the site."

At last, Mali found her voice. "That's certainly something to think about. Rather forces one to re-think the request to film, doesn't it?"

"Like I said, it's a zany idea. But I promised I'd run it past you, and now I have."

Glynnis looked from Bill to Mali and back to Bill, then exclaimed, "I can't believe they want to dig up Owain's grave!"

"Yes. I mean, no! They'll look under the rock, that's all. Anyway, just think about it, okay?"

Mali clung to his voice as something tangible to focus on. All she needed was a few minutes to clear her head. Raising the rock put a whole new twist on the legend of Owain and what she'd do about the letter. She definitely preferred to keep everything exactly the way it was, guard the legend as a myth, and keep as little attention on the whole thing as possible. For a moment she imagined what would happen if this was picked up as a novelty by the BBC. The village's fifteen minutes of fame would turn into a nightmare. But now, with the urgency of Bill's film crew arriving, she wasn't sure what to do.

"We don't need an answer right away," he added. "Besides, there's probably some sort of historical authority somewhere whose permission we'd have to get."

"Indeed," she said slowly, "there are always bureaucratic hoops to jump through. This is expedited only if someone on your end knows someone on our end who needs a favor. You'd be amazed at how political the search for antiquities can get."

"I'll take your word for it, but it sounds like politicking everywhere." He smiled weakly and leaned forward. "Now, how about telling me a little more about your mysterious hot springs?"

If his goal was to keep her off balance, he was doing a fine job of it. No one outside the family had been to the spring in years, and it held bittersweet memories. For those reasons alone she wasn't sure she wanted strangers trampling through that rare and lovely place, to say nothing of making one more fine mess of the Legend of Saint Owain. If Meleri was to be believed, Owain would have needed to bathe in it before any of the girls would go near him. She forced herself to think about the public version.

"According to legend, he baptized all the women of the village there," she said, "converting any who had fallen to evil back to the path of righteousness."

"And you've been there?"

"Heavens, yes!" Glynnis said with sudden vigor. "We all have. Mali practically lived in there while her father installed lights."

"*In there?* In the water?"

Glynnis chuckled. "Yes. Even with the cavern illuminated, the water looked dark and forbidding. The underwater lights changed all that."

Bill's look of astonishment spread across his face and settled into an expression of delight. "I'd love to see it."

Glynnis looked at Mali. "Why don't you take him there, dear? It's easier to show than describe."

The thought of walking alone with Bill across the pastures to the hot pool made her face burn. She'd been to the pools many times, though not in years. It had always been a place of romantic fantasy for her, and as a girl she'd dreamed of taking her future husband there. She'd never wanted to take anyone else. The thought of being alone there with Bill both excited and frightened her. "You'll come along, won't you, Aunt Glynnis?"

Glynnis gave her the same expression she used

when forcing Mali to swallow homemade cough remedies. "Nonsense. It's a nice hike for young couple. I'll stay here and do the dishes."

Mali glanced at Bill, who was studying the candelabra. Judging by the half smile lurking on his lips, he wasn't going to object. Maybe Glynnis was right, a walk would do them good. What harm could come from a simple stroll?

Glynnis bustled out of the room and quickly returned with a lantern and a pair of bath towels.

Mali eyed the towels with suspicion.

The older woman grinned as she loaded Bill with the lantern and towels and gave him a firm shove outside. "Just in case the water invites you to soak your feet. I wouldn't want either of you to catch a chill now, would I?"

~*~

The antique camp lantern Mali held in front of her cast a sphere of yellowish light on the overgrown path meandering through a grove of oaks. The tree limbs, like elongated fingers, seemed to wave in slow mystical movements that cast spells on the innocents passing below. Bill saw Mali shiver. It had turned cool, and a hint of mist rose to mingle with the trees.

It made him feel welcome in spite of the chill. How could a place so foreign be so familiar? He paused for a moment to drink it all in--the stars, the still air, the smell of damp grass, and the closeness of the trees. Surrounded by the night in a way he'd never known, he hadn't realized Mali had continued to walk. He hurried to catch up to her.

"I apologize for Aunt Glynnis's interrogation of you," Mali said as he stepped closer to her side. "She's been a mother to me, and she's eager to see me involved in a romance. If she had her way, I'd have married long ago and provided her with a house full of great-nephews and nieces. She doesn't seem to understand how embarrassing it is when she puts people on the spot like that."

"Like who? Me?"

Mali looked at him over her shoulder. "No, the other Yank at the dinner table."

"She didn't embarrass me." It was the truth, though the sudden idea of Mali surrounded by a host of kids--all with his eyes--did. What was going on? He should be thinking about Rhia and filming and bringing the Legend of Saint Owain to life, not familial bliss with a woman he barely knew.

Mali stopped and turned the light fully on him, studying his face. Her hazel eyes flashed, but the lantern light showed the blush creeping up her cheek at dinner hadn't retreated very far. He wanted very much to kiss her.

"She didn't embarrass you at all? Not even with that nonsense about what you'd look for in the ideal woman? Don't be silly."

He put on his best cat-grin. "I didn't mind the question. I hope you didn't mind the answer."

Her eyes widened just a little, and she started to say something, then changed her mind. She turned back to the path and didn't look at him when she finally spoke. "I was too busy being angry at Aunt Glynnis to notice. And then, as if that wasn't enough, she practically assaulted you with the towels. I couldn't believe it."

Bill draped the towels over his arm like a waiter.

"Don't you think we'll need them?"

She laughed. "Not the way you might think."

He tried to read her suddenly amused expression but failed. "You aren't going to tell me what that's supposed to mean?"

"Heavens, no! It would spoil the surprise. Come on, you'll see for yourself soon enough."

The path ended in a cluster of car-sized, moss-covered boulders at the base of a steep hill. Mali held the lamp higher, but he couldn't see any trace of an opening.

"My father never got around to working on the entrance; we'll have to squeeze in between these rocks. It's a good idea to look first; there could be almost anything crawling on them."

"Wonderful."

"Don't worry," she said with a chuckle. "We hardly have anything poisonous to worry about around here. More as like we'll startle a hare or two.

"Here we are." Mali ducked low and wiggled between two slabs of gray stone that formed an inverted V, the top of which reached Bill's forehead. She thrust the lantern ahead of her and blocked most of the light with her body as she went through. Once she'd disappeared inside, the light seemed to burst from the opening. "All clear!"

He eyed the small opening with dismay. Getting through would be interesting. "I won't get stuck, will I?"

"I hope not." When Bill didn't answer, she laughed. "You're a wee bit larger than my dad, but you'll make it if you squat a bit."

It was wide enough at the bottom, but narrowed

quickly a few feet from the ground. Rather than waddle like a duck through the opening, he opted for the more decorous hands and knees approach.

He wondered about moving a film crew through, but the notion of seeing Rhia on her knees trying to get into the cave pleased him. Even if she could squeeze through as Mali did, she'd still likely soil her expensive Bloomingdale's outfit of the hour.

The entrance opened into a roomy cavern, the air ripe with the odor of sulfur. Mali waited for him on a rock about eight feet from the cave entrance with the lamp on the stone floor. She stood as he entered. "The ceiling is a little low here; mind your head." Promptly ignoring her own advice, she walked away, her hair barely missing the tunnel roof.

The smell got stronger as they proceeded further into the depths, and with each step he took, the air became warmer and more humid.

"Another twenty feet," Mali said as she came to a halt. "I'd forgotten how hot it was in here." She put the lamp on the cave floor, removed her cardigan, and tied it around her waist.

Something landed on Bill's cheek, and he jerked sideways swatting at his face.

"Relax." Mali chuckled. "It's just condensation from the steam. The hot pool is right around the corner."

Bill wiped at his face, already starting to drip from perspiration. "So that's what the towels are for?"

She gave him a wicked grin, picked up the lamp, and resumed her steady pace. "Of course."

Bill hurried to catch up.

A few more paces led them into a much wider

chamber, the center of which was filled with a dark pool. Steam wafted upward and dissipated, but he figured the humidity was pretty close to a hundred percent. A ledge surrounded the pool and varied in width from several inches to a few feet. A pair of derelict beach chairs with gaily striped fabric hanging in tatters from white wooden frames cluttered the wider parts of the ledge. Mali set the lamp inside a niche cut into the rock wall then walked around the pool lighting thick candles sitting on similar shelves. In the flickering steamy light, the wooden chair frames looked like the skeletons of long dead animals. He'd never seen anything like it.

With the addition of each candle, the light level improved, and Bill marveled at the rest of the grotto. The high ceiling sloped down to the sides, making the entire chamber tear-dropped shaped. Most of the condensed steam slipped down the walls and away from the pool. Spindles of lumpy rock pointed down from the ceiling and up from the floor like teeth. The steam diffused the candlelight, and Mali whistled lightly as she worked her way back around to his side.

"What do you think?" she asked, pride evident in her wide smile and open arms.

"It's stunning, and much bigger than I thought it'd be. I've only seen pictures of such places, but it does surprise me. I thought stalactites and such were more colorful."

"Not really. They're mainly whitish gray minerals. Dad's underwater lighting and color filters solved that problem, but I doubt if it works any more. I thought about getting Michael Wells to take a look at it."

"So, why don't you?"

She turned to him with a wistful expression. "I didn't want to share it with him. With anyone really. It's too special to me."

He definitely wanted to kiss her. "Then I'm doubly honored you'd allow me to see it." He knelt down and reached toward the pool, then stopped. "Is the water safe to touch?"

"Safe, but hot." She dried her neck with one of the towels and hung it from a black metal hook in the wall. "Dad took great pains to locate the spots where water doesn't drip and put towel hooks there."

"Clever man," Bill said, hanging his own towel beside hers. The hooks were wrought iron and in spite of the dampness, had not a sign of rust. He wondered if they were done locally, or even if Mali's father had made them. He admired the craftsmanship used to improve on the grotto without overdoing it. Too many "fixes" and the area would have quickly lost its charm, though the decrepit lounge chairs had to go. "This is such an amazing place, I can't believe it's not in regular use. You could retire on the income from parking fees alone."

"I doubt it'd be that popular." One eyebrow arched royally, and she gave him a quirky look of disbelief.

"I'm serious, Mali. This is a gold mine. There's only one other hot spring in the entire UK," Bill said, thinking back to his brochures. "And the folks who run it aren't going to like hearing about this place." He chuckled. "Not one little bit."

"I'm not sure I'd want hordes of people traipsing through here."

Bill scratched his head. "I just can't understand

that. This is a natural. It's--"

"Dad had good reason to shut it down when I was a child."

"Why?"

She paused and let the pool drag her eyes away from his face for a moment. Solemn and sad, she turned back to him. "My older brother came in here to do some work. We think he intended to surprise Dad. Anyway, he was alone and had an accident."

She captured his gaze and held it as if looking at him could blot out something painful. Bill feared what would come next and took her hand. "Go on."

"He fell, hit his head, and drowned. After that, Dad lost all interest in the project. He'd already lost Mum and said he didn't want to take a chance on losing me, too."

"I'm so sorry," Bill said. "I had no idea." It pained him to see the sorrow in her face. He and Mali had a lot in common--both of them were alone in the world. No, that wasn't quite right. She had Glynnis.

"It's not the cheeriest topic of conversation. I still miss them, of course, but it was a long time ago." She gave him a soft smile and squeezed his hand. "I haven't seen the colored pool lights in all these years. I wish now I'd made the effort to keep them working."

Bill jumped at a chance to bring the conversation back to the present. Besides, his natural curiosity was aroused. Growing up in his grandfather's house had made him a pretty handy guy once, he thought. Maybe he could figure this one out. "Do you have any idea what's wrong with them?"

"Not really." She pointed at a painted metal cabinet mounted on a far wall. Heavy conduit ran to it from a little hole in the ceiling, and an open padlock hung from the latch. "That's the switch box," she said. "You're welcome to take a look inside if you'd like, but be careful. The power's still running out here."

Bill retrieved the lantern and walked over to the box. He slipped the padlock from the latch, and the front of the box swung open. "Have you ever looked in here?"

She shook her head. "I don't pretend to know anything about wiring." She clenched her fists in frustration. "I know damn little about any of the building trades, and that's made this whole process doubly difficult. It takes me forever to figure out how to do something. I have more fix-it books, repair manuals, and videos than a trade school!"

Bill looked at the antique fuse bar inside the box. All four fuses in the little service panel had been unscrewed and lay inside the box waiting for someone to put them back in. He held them up to the light to be sure they were still good. "I think this might do the trick," he said, and threaded them back into the panel.

Nothing happened.

Mali pursed her lips and frowned. "I thought it'd be too good to be true."

"Hold on." Bill reached for a large paddle switch on the side of the box. "Let's try this." When he pressed the switch, it closed with a loud snap, and suddenly the pool was flooded with pastel lights.

"You did it!" Mali shrieked and clapped her hands in delight.

Bill puffed out his chest with a sense of well-earned pride. "How 'bout that?"

"It's beautiful," she said, settling on the nearest

ledge. "I'd forgotten just how much."

"And hot." Bill slipped his own sweater off and hung it from one of the hooks.

Mali ran her hand through the water. "Mmm. I remember soaking in here as a child. I was always afraid to go in the water until Dad put in the lights."

Bill stuck his hand in, too. "Feels like a hot tub. I sat in one once at a ski resort. It was posh, but nothing like this."

Mali slipped off her shoes and socks and rolled her pants legs over her knees, swung around to face the pool, and immersed her feet in the water.

"Feel good?" he asked.

"Wonderful." She patted the ledge. "Join me?"

In moments, Bill parked his shoes and socks beside Mali's and had his bare feet in the water, too.

They sat quietly for a while listening to drops of condensing steam plopping on the ledge and occasionally blipping into the water.

"What're you thinking?" Mali asked after a while.

Her voice reminded him he'd been daydreaming. "I'm imagining what this place would've looked like filled with Saint Owain and a mob of village women."

Mali laughed. "You certainly have a one track mind."

"True," he said. More than she could possibly know. Torn between wanting to stay here forever and Rhia's pushing him to get Mali's permission to film, he needed to find the balance. He feared that balance was in Rhia's favor. "Just think about it." He gestured to a spot in the middle of the pool. "Can't you see him standing there, with the women lined up all around the edge? He'd dip one in the water, help her up, and reach for the next."

Mali pointed to a shelf in the pool wall that could easily serve as a bench. "If they were smart, they'd have sat along the wall waiting their turn."

"I don't suppose folks bathed all that often back then."

She splashed water with her feet. "Some did; most didn't."

"This setting is dramatic enough that I think I can convince Rhia to shoot here entirely instead of at the Rock. Would you be agreeable to that?" Maybe he could convince Rhia. That woman was unpredictable enough to go for almost anything.

"I'm not wild about the idea, but all right. You've worn me down."

The comment startled him. "I'm sorry. I--"

"Don't worry about it, William. You're just doing your job." She stood up.

Disappointment flooded him. "Time to leave already?"

She chuckled. "Not unless you want to. I had another idea."

Bill stood, too. "I'm listening."

"Wait here," she said, walking back toward the corridor they'd used to reach the grotto. She collected a short, fat candle along the way.

"Where are you going?"

"You'll see."

He watched her step into a side corridor and disappear. "Mali?" His voice echoed in the empty cavern. When she didn't answer, he followed the route she had taken, the warm yellow glow of the candle small in the darkness ahead. Shortly after he turned the corner he came upon a pair of curtained chambers. Candle light flickered beneath the fabric of one; the other stood empty.

"Mali?" He could hear her, but standing there by himself in the warm dark made him feel lonely. He needed to know she was there.

"I'll be out in a moment. I have to make some adjustments."

That intrigued him. "To what?"

She pushed the curtain aside with a flourish. "To my bathing suit."

He stepped back in surprise and surveyed her up and down. She looked wonderful, though the Sixties era, one-piece suit left nearly everything to the imagination.

"It's not very stylish, I'm afraid," she said, wrapping a towel around her torso. "My aunt must've worn it ages ago."

Bill whistled appreciatively. "You do wonderful things for it."

She blushed. "Look in the other changing area. You should find a couple men's swim suits. They're old, like this one, but it's better than going naked."

"Who says?"

"I do!" She handed him the candle and slipped past him into the short corridor. "Don't take too long. I'm eager to get in, and it's not a good idea to stay in the water more than fifteen or twenty minutes."

Bill found four pairs of trunks in the changing room, but only one that looked like it would fit. He quickly stripped out of his clothes and pulled on the swim suit. Thin and baggy, it had a drawstring at the top that broke when he pulled it tight.

"Are you coming?" Mali called from somewhere down the corridor.

"Yes," he said, trying to make do with the shortened string. He finally gave up on it, determined not to dive in and risk leaving the borrowed suit behind. The route back, with the well-lit cavern in front of him, proved easy.

Mali was already in the water when he returned to the grotto. Standing by the edge of the pool, she looked up into his face and beckoned him in.

He sat on the edge and slipped into the water beside her. Though he knew it would be hot, it still came as a surprise, and he inhaled sharply.

Mali laughed at him. "You'll get used to it pretty fast."

He sank down beside her to sit on the underwater shelf, his chin just above the water. "You're shorter than I am. How can you sit there with your head completely out of the water?"

She grinned. "I know where the rocks are. I'm sitting on one."

"I've another question."

"It's a regular quiz show this evening."

Bill pointed at the tattered fabric of the deck chairs. "How is it that the material on those chairs is in such bad shape, but these swim suits have held up so well?"

She shrugged and wouldn't look at him. "It's a mystery," she said lightly.

"And how come you knew there would be candles in each of the niches around the wall?"

"Good memory?" Her face was a perfect deadpan.

"And how likely is it that matches could sit in this

damp cavern for twenty years and still work?"

Mali looked into his eyes as a smile grew wider and eventually connected her dimpled cheeks. "Do I look like Agatha Christie?"

"Not in the least," he said. "But...."

"But?"

He grinned back. "But I suspect you're a fair hand at coming up with a plot."

"Are you accusing me of something, William Thomas?"

"Not at all, but I think you know more than you're telling. Now those towels Glynnis gave us make complete sense."

She looked away. "It was all her idea. She said she'd been in here to tidy up in case we wanted to use it sometime. I suspected that if we came here, I'd be very keen to give the springs a go myself, and I couldn't very well get in without inviting you. I hope you don't mind."

Bill's one track mind kicked in. "What I had in mind was more of a thank you." He leaned closer to her and raised her chin with his hand. She closed her eyes as their lips met.

Mali's mouth was warm and soft, and the kiss was chaste by Hollywood standards, yet Bill felt a thrill that ran down his arms and legs and curled his toes. "Oh yes," he said softly, "a thank you is definitely in order."

~*~

For the third time, Clive Gillet checked his reflected image in the plate glass entrance of the "Bird House," the official home of the Greater London Ornithological Society. He squared his shoulders, drew his envelope of photos high up under his arm like Monty with a swagger stick, and eased open the heavy door.

Sound died in the plush foyer of the Society. The cream colored walls were accented in shades of forest green and mauve; the furniture trended to stout mahogany with thick brocades and brass accents, and everywhere he looked were birds--painted, photographed, sculpted, stuffed and even worshipped as suggested by the hieroglyph of a raven taken from an Egyptian tomb--all byproducts of two centuries of dues collected from loyal subscribers. He knew every piece, and had procured a third of them himself during the forty years he'd maintained full membership. That tenure earned him the right to serve on dozens of standing committees, including his current post on the Executive Board. Such a *curriculum vitae* should guarantee that his discovery would not be ignored. At least not by the membership. The Society's *Journal* was another matter.

Editorial control of the quarterly rested entirely in the hands of Eleanor Pynchon, as it had for as long as Clive could remember. And, as anyone who knew anything about the Society and its premier members was well aware, Mrs. Pynchon, the society's resident expert on waterfowl, held small, unobtrusive Passeriformes like his wren in very low esteem.

Clive stood before a vast and orderly reception desk and waited for the slender, fifty-ish woman sitting behind it to finish her telephone conversation. Constance smiled at him while she spoke which helped to put him at ease. She'd been the receptionist at the *Journal* for nearly as long as Mrs. Pynchon had been editor.

"Now then, Mr. Gillet," she said as she cradled the receiver, "how may I serve you?"

Clive patted the envelope under his arm. "I have photos of a rat-faced wren." He stood a little straighter. *"Cistothorus faciemuris."*

"How lovely," she said, her smile unwavering.

"I'm sure Mrs. Pynchon will be thrilled to see them," he added.

"I'm sure she will," echoed Constance. "If you'll just put your name and number on the envelope, I'll see she gets them."

He took a step back. "You don't understand. I--"

"I'm sure you know how dreadfully busy Mrs. Pynchon is and how often many of our enthusiastic members come by to share their discoveries. Hence the procedure. Surely you realize if she dropped everything whenever someone came calling, the *Journal* would go from a quarterly to a semi-annual." She smiled wider at her own humor.

Clive wasn't amused. "Ah, but this is--"

"Different?" She batted extraordinarily long eyelashes at him.

"Yes."

"I see."

"You do?" He exhaled. "Thank God. You had me worried."

"Nevertheless, I'm afraid I must insist you follow the same protocol as everyone else." She reached for his photos.

It was too much. "See here, Constance," Clive said, drawing himself to his full height, "this is no way to treat a member of the Executive Board. I'm the

Recording Secretary! I demand to see Mrs. Pynchon immediately."

"What seems to be the trouble?" Eleanor Pynchon stood in the doorway of her office. Her expression never changed as she rotated her head from the receptionist to the supplicant. "Why Clive, how nice to see you."

Her stone face belied the sentiment. Nevertheless, he decided to thrust aside their decades of differences.

"I've exciting news, Eleanor," Clive said, holding up his envelope. "A discovery in north Wales and photos to prove it."

He knew her well enough to recognize the hint of interest her raised eyebrow suggested. "What kind of discovery?"

"*Cistothorus faciemuris*. It's the find of the season, perhaps even the decade! Why, it could be a completely unknown subspecies. If that proves to be the case, I thought we might name it Gillet's Wren."

Mrs. Pynchon puffed out her cheeks as she did an about face and marched back into her office. "Come," she said as she walked away.

Clive stole a glance at the receptionist. Constance had already returned to her primary task--preparing to fend off the next Society member to come through the door. He hurried to catch up with Mrs. Pynchon.

She had seated herself behind her own massive desk, this one as cluttered as the receptionist's was barren. "Let's have a look then, shall we?"

Clive handed her the photos and took a seat across from her.

She held the first at a slight angle, squinting as if the image of the bird occupied a corner of the print

instead of stretching from one edge to the other.
"Mmm," she said. "Yes." Dropping the rest of the
photos on her desk, she retrieved an already well
worn copy of Hume and *Hayman's Complete Guide to
the Birdlife in Britain and Europe* and flipped through
it until she came to a color plate which she compared
with Clive's photo. She stared from one to the other
for several moments.

"Well?" he asked.

"It certainly appears to be a rat-faced wren," she
said. "Last seen, as I recall, in the Lake District."

"Six years ago," Clive said, struggling to mask his
excitement.

"Of course, there's no way to tell where, or even
when, this photograph was taken."

Clive forced himself to breathe. "What are you
suggesting?"

She reached for the other photos. "You would be
amazed at the nonsense we're subjected to--
retouched photos, photos of stuffed and mounted
birds, photos copied from older photos--people are
devious, Clive."

He was horrified at the innuendo. "For God's sake,
Eleanor, we've known each other for thirty-five years!
You know I'd never do such a thing!"

Unruffled, she continued. "Then you know, Clive, I
must remain constantly vigilant to avoid the taint of
fraud. I pride myself on my ability to do that. I am a
guardian of the public trust."

He knew defeat when he heard it. No one in the
Society ever had a comeback for her guardian line. He
resigned himself to letting her make her own decision,
and in her own good time. He sank into the chair

facing her desk to wait. Even if it meant weeks.

She flipped through several more photos before she came to a sudden stop, the color draining from her face. "My God in Heaven! What's that?"

On his feet in a flash, Clive leaned across the desk to see what had upset her. She turned the photo for his benefit. Owain's Rock filled the entire thing, the tiny wren, all but invisible, nestled in the tip of it.

"Oh, that!" he said, relieved. "That's just an old standing stone that's been toppled over. They're everywhere."

"Didn't you notice its shape?"

When he looked at her blankly, she waved the photo in front of his face. "I can't believe you'd bring photos of such a nasty thing into my office!"

He focused on the photo and concentrated on the shape. Ah, he thought, I see the problem. "It's probably five thousand years old. The ancients obviously had a different outlook on such things."

She fixed him with a stare that lowered the temperature of his blood. "Which perhaps explains why they died out as a race, don't you think?"

"I'm not an anthropologist, Eleanor, I wouldn't have an opinion on that."

"You, Recording Secretary and lifelong upstanding member of our Society, wouldn't even have an opinion on that disgusting statue?"

"It's a standing stone, like Long Meg or those at Stonehenge, or any of a thousand others littering the continent."

Mrs. Pynchon's breath continued to come in short gasps and her face had worked its way through progressively darker shades of pink until it approached crimson. "As I recall, none of those rocks had been carved into a shape like this!"

"It's coincidence, a mere freak of nature."

"I must disagree, Clive. It's an abomination! And you say it's in plain view?"

He shook his head. "Not entirely, no, but that's really not the issue here, is it? What about my wren?"

She rose to her full height of five feet. "What about the greater good? If I print news of your discovery--"

He perked up, smiling.

"--in the *Journal*, you must know people will go there to see the bird for themselves. People of all ages. Children." She turned flinty eyes toward him. "Do you think little children should be subjected to such filth?"

This wasn't going at all as he'd planned. "Well, I--"

"Certainly not!" She stabbed a button on her intercom and barked, "Constance, ring Mr. Pynchon immediately."

She stared down at the offending image. "You've done your country a noble service, Clive. It won't go unrecognized."

That was what he wanted to hear! "I'd be delighted to write the accompanying article," he said. "How long--"

She looked up in surprise. "What accompanying article?"

"To go with the pictures in the *Journal*."

She looked at him as if he had suddenly split in two. "I can't print these!"

"But the stone is only visible in one or two of them. The others--"

"Would merely lure the unsuspecting into the wilds where they'd have to look at... at... that thing!"

She shook her head. "No. It's utterly out of the question."

"But--" He felt the energy drain from him with the same speed she shook her head. He had to do something!

"I have multiple obligations, Clive. In addition to my invaluable work for the Society, I'm also president of the All-UK Anti-smut League. I can assure you, this topic will soon be on the very top of the League's agenda."

Seeing his first real chance for ornithological fame slipping away, Clive seized upon the only alternative argument he could think of. "There's more to this story than you realize. I met an American while investigating the wren and learned that he intends to film that stone as part of a commercial broadcast."

Mrs. Pynchon struggled for air. Her mouth formed a circle, and her cheeks puffed out like a bellows. "Broadcast?" she croaked.

"Yes. If you think printing my photos would cause harm, what about splashing that image on the telly night and day? At least if our membership knows about the bird, they can be rallied to protect it."

"You have a point."

The phone rang, and she punched the speaker button. "Alister?"

"Of course, my dear. You called?"

"We're going to Wales."

"Of course, my dear," her husband said with obviously practiced patience. "When?"

"Today," she added.

"I'm terribly sorry, my dear, but I'll be in meetings all day. The tunnel project, you know."

She squeezed her eyes tight. "Your meetings couldn't possibly be as important as my need to conduct an investigation for the League."

"I'm sure that's true, but--"

"Are you coming with me or not?"

"Now Eleanor--"

"Say no more; I'll go alone." She punched the line dead and looked straight ahead at Clive. "Not a syllable over two thousand words and concentrate on the destruction of habitat. Is that clear?"

"Crystal. When would you like it?"

"Tomorrow will suffice, assuming I've returned from Wales." She reached into a cavernous drawer in her desk and extracted a Michelin road map. "Would you kindly show me where this abomination is located?"

Chapter Six

Bill waited for Rhia's call in his room over the pub. Brenna had moved her television set to the front of the building to make it as quiet for Bill as possible, and the handful of regulars had been forced to choose between England's Idol, a BBC trek through east Africa, and a rebroadcast of a sheep dog competition from Australia. Only occasionally could Bill hear one of the dogs barking.

He'd put in a call as soon as he got back from his evening with Mali, but Rhia was too busy to talk to him. Typical. Even if she was in her office doing nothing more than sitting with her feet up and staring out the window, she'd make him wait. Stacey had told him to call back in an hour or so. "Any luck finding me a Welshman?" she'd asked.

A lone bark had wafted through the floorboards from below as he contemplated his answer. "Not yet," he'd told her, "but I'm still looking."

He reached for the double scotch he'd brought up from the bar and took a sip. It worked its warm way down his gullet. With any luck, the beverage would calm him. The last two hours he'd spent with Mali, including twenty astonishing minutes in the hot pool, had left him unexpectedly tense, tightly focused, and definitely wanting more.

She had finally given in to his harassment about shooting in the cavern, and done so gracefully, making him feel only a little guilty. He smiled. Whether Mali or her aunt had set everything up, including the inoperative fuse panel, the effect was the same.

Closing his eyes, he tried to relive their kiss. That, he knew for certain, was what had left him wanting more. A great deal more. But she had moved gracefully away, not actually rebuffing his advances, but always finding something to discuss whenever they reached one of those conversational lulls which cries out for non-verbal communication.

"Careful now," he told himself. "That gal could be trouble. Rule number 1: Never fall for a client."

He swirled his drink purely out of habit, since it had neither ice nor anything else to dilute it, and took another sip. As a precaution, he set his alarm clock for an hour hence, then stretched out on the bed to let his mind wander.

He had to quit thinking about Mali and focus on the project, or Rhia would hand him his head on a plate. The grotto scene seemed like a good place to start getting back on track. The narrow opening posed some logistical problems, though not insurmountable. The real challenge would be to get all those people in the small cavern. He'd have his hands full juggling a camera crew, Alonzo Fernandez, and a couple dozen Welsh women of assorted ages, shapes and sizes, sprinkled around the steaming pool. No, he decided, it shouldn't start there. He needed someplace else, somewhere outdoors, to give the viewer a sense of the crowd, and then fade into a closer shot in the grotto. He closed his eyes. A dirt road perhaps....

The woman standing in front of him with her hands perched defiantly on her hips looked very much like Rhia, but sounded like someone else entirely. Her voice came out as scratchy as the woolen rags that hung from her tight, gym-chiseled body.

"Not so fast, Owain y'Craig," she crowed. The voice was gritty and had the condescending tone that marked nearly all of Rhia's remarks, but it definitely wasn't hers. Something was speaking through her. "You've another challenge to meet if you expect to prove yourself."

"I needn't prove myself to anyone but God," he said, noticing for the first time the crowd of well-wishers surrounding him. Must've followed me here from the tavern, he thought.

"That may be," said the demon inhabiting Rhia's body, "but if you want to save any souls in this village, you'll have to get the devil out of the way first."

He eyed her with suspicion. "And you're going to tell me how to do that?"

Rhia shuddered; her voice ranged from a cricket chirp to a predacious growl, and her eyes bulged out like a frog's. "You must recognize virtue to be virtuous."

"I do, and I am!" he cried.

She twirled great lengths of stinking, knotted hair around her fingers. "Saying it is one thing; proving it is quite another."

He waved her off with a laugh. "My life is proof enough."

"Not proof enough for the devil," she said. "You must assemble all the women in the village and separate the virtuous from those who've given themselves over to evil."

"That shouldn't be difficult."

"Oh?" She cackled. "There's a catch. You must do it without benefit of their testimony, for none of those women will be able to utter a word until you've finished."

That worried him a little, but he wasn't about to let her see it. He shrugged for her benefit. "No matter."

"We'll see, Owain. We'll see!" And then she was gone, along with everything else--the rutted dirt road, the trees, the people--all of it, replaced in a twinkling by the grotto.

Sitting next to him with her feet in the hot water sat Mali, her clothing distinctly medieval, her dark hair piled on top of her head and held in place with carved wooden pins.

Bill removed his sandals, hiked up the hem of his robe, and put his feet in the water, too. "This feels so good it's positively sinful."

Giggling, she pushed lightly against him. "What would a saint such as yourself know about sin?"

"Fair question, but what if I told you I'm just a regular guy?"

She reached out and fingered the ornate cross hanging from his neck. A look of concentration darkened her features as she considered his words. At length she shook her head. "No. I can't believe you."

He stretched his arms out one at a time and pulled back the sleeves of his robe. "Trust me, I'm no saint!"

"What about your cross and your clothes?"

"This comes off," he said, slipping the cross over his head and placing it beside the sandals. "There. Better?"

She gave him a slow smile. "A little."

The water rippled around their feet in shades of pink, yellow, and orange. The warmth was delicious, and Bill stretched his toes, remembering how it felt to be in the water beside her. "You know what would feel even better than soaking our feet?" he asked softly.

"What?" Her response held only warmth and a willingness to contemplate conspiracy.

It encouraged him, and he took a chance. "Getting completely in."

She laughed. "That's not possible. My clothes would be ruined."

Bill gave her a long look and spoke slowly, hardly believing he was suggesting it. "Then perhaps we shouldn't wear any."

Broad grins grew simultaneously on their faces.

"It's out of the question." Her demeanor and tone belied her words.

"We can take a dip in a pool if we want. It's no one's business but ours. Besides, who's going to find out?"

"Well, the villagers--"

"Aren't here, and we are," he said, reveling in the growing look of anticipation on her face.

She balled her fist and playfully threatened him. "Swear you won't breathe a word of this to anyone!"

"Absolutely." He drew an imaginary zipper across his mouth, sealing it.

"All right, then." She giggled playfully. "But you must go first."

He stood up, stepped a few feet away, and pulled the thin robe over his head and tossed it aside. Underneath he wore slacks and a shirt. He started unbuttoning the shirt.

Mali watched him for a moment then yelped, "Wait!" and scrambled to her feet. "If we're going to do this, I'd rather we did it at the same time. Otherwise, you'll be watching me, and, well...."

"Would you feel better if we turned our backs to each other?"

"Yes." She scribed a circle in the air with her forefinger. "Turn around, then."

"My pleasure," he said as he pivoted away and finished unfastening the last few buttons on his shirt. He heard the rustle of her clothing, and though he desperately wanted to turn and watch her disrobe, he didn't. He slipped off his pants and hung them on a hook in the cavern wall with his shirt.

"Okay," she said, "I'm getting in."

"Did you, uhm... Did you--"

A wave of hot water splashed up out of the pool on his legs. "Did you leave anything on?" He turned to look at her standing in the water below, facing him, her chest pressed against the ledge.

She stared up at him wickedly. "Not a stitch."

"I see."

"Not as clearly as I can."

He laughed, knowing he'd been swindled and not caring in the least. "Cheater."

She shrugged. "I'm just a simple country girl. I'm trusting you not to take advantage of me."

"Ah. Right." He slipped his thumbs inside the waistband of his boxers and stretched the elastic. Mali, resting her forearms on the ledge, smiled up at him. "Not a stitch?" he asked.

She blinked ever so slowly. "None."

After taking a deep breath, he ran his thumbs down the sides of his legs pulling his shorts with them. In a single motion he stepped free, tossed his underwear aside, and jumped in beside her.

She flowed into his arms, her breasts pressed softly against his chest, and he closed his arms around behind her just as his cell phone rang.

Mali and the exotic cavern evaporated, replaced by the mundane walls and ceiling of his room. He gave life to his disappointment with a savage stab at the phone's TALK button. "What?"

"My, my. Aren't we testy today?" Rhia said.

Damn, he thought. From the dream of a lifetime to this nightmare. He rubbed his eyes, desperately trying to shake off the sense of loss, and the loathing with which Rhia's voice replaced it. "It's been a long evening, Rhia. Besides, I thought I was supposed to call you."

"You were, but I'm in a hurry to leave, and I didn't want to have to wait."

How nice for you, he thought.

"Stacey said you had some good news."

"Good news?" He remained fuzzy, still attached to Mali and the pool. "Oh, right. Mali, I mean Miss Rhys, has agreed to let us shoot a segment in the hot springs."

"If we need it, then fine."

"*If* we need it? We'd be crazy to pass it up. This location is straight out of a fairy tale. Picture a massive, rock-lined hot tub in a cavern complete with stalactites and colored lights. In the water!"

"Sounds nice," she said dismissively, "but the network is really keen on looking *under* that big rock." She emphasized it just enough to remind him the rock idea was her baby. "They want to work a side deal with Alonzo. They're talking about interviewing me, too."

"You mentioned that before."

"No, not the Letterman thing, that's extra. They want me in the program as the living descendant of a saint!"

"Whoa!" Bill gasped. "Slow down." This wasn't happening, he told himself. Couldn't happen. "I see at least two problems here. First, we have no proof that you're related to Saint Owain. And second, we still don't have permission from the Rhys family to shoot the rock in the first place, let alone lift the damn thing."

"Then what in God's name have you been doing over there all this time?"

Bill gripped the phone as if to crush it. What had he been doing? In his eagerness to win Mali over, had he put aside his primary purpose? It didn't matter. Mali would agree, albeit reluctantly. The town was counting on her. He forced himself to relax and take a deep breath before he spoke. "I've been working on the locals, trying to pave the way for the filming."

"You don't have much time left," she said

brusquely. "The film crew arrives tomorrow. I was going to make you the producer, but if you can't do something as simple as get a land owner to cooperate, I'll have to come out there myself. And if I do that, there won't be any need for you to stick around--here or there."

"Now wait just a damn minute, Rhia--"

"Come to think of it, I might enjoy working with Alonzo. He might need my help directing."

Bill instantly recognized her trademark management style: threats in bare steel followed by silken words of justification.

"Do you also intend to do your own genealogy research? How 'bout housing arrangements for the crew? And... Rhia?" He looked down at the unresponsive phone in disgust. She'd hung up on him again.

~*~

"Well?" Glynnis asked, her voice rising.

Mali looked at her aunt in surprise. "Pardon me?"

"Do you want more eggs or not? Though I'm sure they've gone cold as Christmas since I asked you the first time."

"Eggs?"

"Yes dear, they come from chickens. Sort of ovally round they are; perfectly lovely with bacon and toast."

Her aunt stood next to the little built-in kitchen table with the bowl of scrambled eggs. Mali grinned up at her, grateful for anything which momentarily pulled her mind away from the thoughts which had occupied her all morning and most of the night. "No thanks. I've had enough."

"If you'd told me that when they were still warm, I

might've eaten them m'self."

"Sorry, Aunt Glynnis, I'm a bit distracted this morning."

"I should say." She separated the eggs into two yellowish lumps and dumped them in with the dog food. "At least Samson and Delilah still love me. When they smell this they'll worship me."

"Mm hmm," Mali said, her gaze returning to the kitchen window and the garden visible beyond.

"What's the matter, dear?" Glynnis put her hand on Mali's shoulder. "That Yank didn't do anything last night he shouldn't have, did he?" A worried look clouded her features. "I'd never forgive myself if he did. After all the work getting the pool ready, I didn't think you'd go unless I gave you the towels and a good excuse."

"Everything was fine last night. William behaved like a true gentleman." Mali patted her aunt's hand and smiled deeply enough to convince Glynnis her hard work at the pool wasn't wasted. "We had a lovely time. And it was wonderful to see the old place lit up the way Dad intended. Thank you."

"That's a relief, I suppose," Glynnis said as she returned to the sink to do the dishes.

"You 'suppose'?"

"Well, yes, since it was a different kind of worry."

"What are you talking about now?" Mali asked. If she lived to be a hundred, she'd never understand Glynnis's thinking. She rubbed her face with both hands.

"I usually worry that you don't spend enough time socializing with men. It occurred to me that I might have gone overboard and that last night you might've socialized too much."

Mali shook her head. "You're sweet to be concerned, but I'm fine. Just... worried."

Glynnis washed the dishes one by one and set them in a rack to dry. "That makes two of us, then. As for William, I've done what I can to hurry him along, but you can't dally too much--he may not be here much longer. If he leaves before you've got his heart in your hand--"

"Oh Aunt Glynnis!" Mali said. "The way I feel about William isn't the problem."

With a dish towel clutched in one hand and a wet plate in the other, Glynnis sat down beside Mali. "Then what is? Why are you so gloomy after having a wonderful evening?"

"I'm just tired of lying to him. He makes me want to be completely honest. I'm desperately sick of having to pretend there's some niggly bit of truth behind the legend of Saint Owain." She looked up at her aunt, suddenly full of resolve. "In fact, I've made up my mind. I'm going to tell him the truth."

Glynnis dropped the plate. The tinkle of shattering china was the only sound for a span of moments. She bent over to pick up the pieces, but her hands were shaking. "You can't be serious, Mali. What will he think? We're descended from... from..."

Time to say it aloud. "A madam? The keeper of a bawdy house? A--"

"Yes! On top of that, the entire neighborhood will know we're all nothing but frauds. And it won't just be you and me the world sneers at; the whole village will be ridiculed." Glynnis pushed Mali aside and picked up the fractured pieces, dropped them into the trash bin, and leaned back against the sink. "It will all come to naught. As for William, you realize what will happen when you tell him, don't you?"

Mali's worst fear was that he'd never speak to her again, and any chance for them would vanish the second he knew the ad campaign would fail. "I'll sleep better."

"You'll sleep alone."

"Aunt Glynnis!" Mali's cheeks burned, but the words rang true. A fortnight ago she wouldn't have given such a notion a second thought. Now, after the encounter in the hot pool, she'd thought about little else. "I haven't--"

"Nor will you if he learns the truth. We'll be ruined--the laughingstocks of Wales. My Gymanfa days will be over, and you'll be marked. Do you want the likes of Michael Wells to think he can lay hands on you whenever he wants--if he's got money enough?" Glynnis tried to blink back tears, but they spilled down her cheeks. She brushed them away, then untied her apron and hung it on a hook beside the refrigerator. "Don't spoil a good thing."

"I wouldn't harm our reputations for the world. It's the lie that's spoiling things, not the truth." And the town would get over it. She hoped. "William must accept me the way I am, complete with history, or it's no good. We can't build a relationship on deceit." She bit back her own tears burning in her throat.

Glynnis stepped closer and put her arms around Mali's shoulders. "You really do like him, don't you?"

Mali leaned into her aunt's embrace and nodded, and Glynnis patted her gently on the back the way she used to when Mali was a little girl. But now, she was all grown up and had to face living an honorable life. The truth had been hidden too long, and she was tired of covering up sins hundreds of years old. After a while, Mali gently pushed her aunt away. "I'm determined, Aunt Glynnis."

The older woman nodded with a look of resigned sorrow. "Y'know, your William is likely the only one who'll understand; everyone else believes in Owain." She stood quietly for a few moments.

"It's ancient history," Mali said. "No one's going to say or think anything."

"I hope you're right. If not, I have a friend in Cardiff I could stay with until the furor dies down. In, say, twenty or thirty years."

Outside, the dogs started barking. If volume meant anything, then the cottage was being invaded by aliens from outer space, or possibly the Rastafarian bill collector from Bedgelert and his wretched little companion which drove the dogs crazy. The sound of tire treads on the gravel drive soon followed. "I'll see who it is." Mali grabbed Samson and Delilah's food on her way out. She'd just passed out of the kitchen on the way to the front door when the dogs went silent.

Mali hurried. Only one person could silence the dogs like that. Juggling the food dishes, she opened the front door and stepped through. Samson and Delilah, the fiercely loyal guardians of the Rhys estate, were both on their backs, tails awag and legs kicking, as William rubbed their stomachs.

Mali whistled for the dogs and set their dishes on the front stoop. Both flipped over and raced to her. William trailed them, smiling.

"You've won their hearts," she said. "I've never

seen them do that for anyone but Aunt Glynnis and me."

"It seems they've enlarged their inner circle to include me. And believe me, I'm honored!" He sniffed his hand and made a face. "But in all honesty, at least one of them needs a bath." He straightened his arm, his hand turned away. "Desperately."

She laughed. "Members of the inner circle are required to assist in the bathing. Are you up to it?"

He paused as if weighing his decision. "Sure. But not right now."

The look on his face and the odd lull in their conversation put Mali on alert. "What's wrong?"

He extended his hands, palms up in supplication. "Please don't hate me for bringing this up."

The filming. The bloody rock and the bloody pool. If she told him everything, there would be no reason to prevent it. The idea of moving to Cardiff with Aunt Glynnis grew more appealing. Damn it. "I can't very well hate you unless I know what you want to discuss, can I? Come in." She held the door open for him. "Tea?"

He nodded and sat in the chair in front of the cold and dark hearth. "We need to talk about the Rock."

Mali's hope dissolved.

Bill went on in a rush, "We've got to shoot there, both the commercials and the special. My boss is locked into the idea, and she's got the network brass keen on it, too. I have no choice but to ask you again."

"I suppose I could give in on the commercials," Mali said slowly. Bill's eyes brightened and he rose, taking a step toward her. She waved him away. "But it's pointless to move the Rock. There's nothing under it."

He stared at her in disbelief. "How can you know that? Your aunt said no one's ever moved it."

"No one has--ever! The whole story about Saint Owain wrestling the devil and urging the villagers to crush them both under the rock is utter nonsense."

"But--" Eyes wide in confusion, Bill just stared at her.

"I can prove it if I must." She made straight for her desk. A few of the flowers he had given her still sat in the vase on top of the glass case where she kept Meleri's letter. She picked up the vase and pointed to the letter. "That tells the real story, and it's not very pretty."

He leaned over the case and looked at the letter with renewed interest. "I can't read it, but whatever it says must be grim." He glanced up, his face reflecting worry. "What's in it, and if it's all that bad, can you be sure it's authentic?"

"It's genuine. It's been in my family for centuries. Sit down--it's a long story."

He sank back into the chair, and Mali lit a fire. Somehow, keeping her hands busy helped her. She didn't think she'd have the courage to look him straight in the eye and tell him.

"During one of the Crusades, when most of the men of this region were away, times were hard. Women left alone handled day-to-day affairs as best they could, but few could manage as well as they had with their men. So, my ancestor, Lady Meleri, provided a way for the women to survive."

Bill listened attentively. "That doesn't sound bad at all. What did she do?"

"She opened up the manor house as an inn. The main road to the coast once went straight through the village and many men came along that route. The inn had both a tavern and a few rooms upstairs in which ladies of the village stayed." She couldn't find the words to explain exactly what they were doing. Bill looked at her, comprehension absent from his face.

"Go on."

She cleared her throat. "To keep themselves from starving, Meleri turned the family estate into a bordello."

"A bordello?"

"That's a polite term for it, and Owain's Rock served as a sign post, no doubt an effective one."

She gazed solemnly at Bill. His eyes twinkled, and she felt the flush of embarrassment rise to her cheeks.

"Owain was sent by the Abbot to put the fear of God back into the village, but all they did was try to profit from his corruption. He drank himself into a stupor and died in the bed of a prostitute. The people of Llansantowain didn't bury a saint--and Owain certainly never acted like one--but they pretended he was in order to avoid the Abbot's wrath. They made up the tales to dignify his death. Over the years we kept telling the lies until eventually we all believed them. No one knows the truth anymore, except Aunt Glynnis and me, because we have the letter. I can't say that I blame them, really, for forgetting. Most of the townfolk are descended from the women who worked for Meleri."

Bill was chuckling by the time she finished. "That's wonderful," he said. "I couldn't have come up with a better angle if I tried."

"I can't understand why you're laughing! This is quite a serious matter for us. It's hardly 'an angle,'" she said. "And when Dylan Davies and the others find out, they're not going to be pleased."

"Why? What does it matter? If anything, it'll just add more flavor to the story." Bill's smile grew as broad as she'd ever seen it.

"It's not a laughing matter! This has been a source of dismay and horror for my family. If word of this gets out, my poor aunt may have to move away--she's convinced she'd never live down the humiliation!"

"Put it in perspective," he said. "No one cares about such things anymore. It all happened a long time ago. Besides, who would expect Owain's remains to survive that long anyway? Oh, Mali, this is too rich. But, we've still got to dig there."

"No," she said. "I can't allow it. All my aunt and I have left is our dignity, and that goes for most of the people around here as well. If the truth about Owain came out, we'd lose that, too. I'll not have my village become a laughing stock. It's my responsibility."

No longer smiling, and gnawing on his lower lip, Bill looked deep into her eyes. "This is more important than you realize."

"I was going to say the same thing to you."

"Don't you think you might be over-reacting just a bit?"

She crossed her arms. "Are you saying our dignity is worth less than your convenience?"

"Of course not."

"It just seems like every time we've been together, the only topic you're interested in is filming adverts in front of that stupid stone. What else am I supposed to think?"

"It's my job. It's the job your town hired me to do, and I'll be damned if I don't do the best work I can for them."

His words, coming fast and harsh, took her by surprise. They hurt more than she'd imagined possible. "Yes. I see now it's all part of the job, and you have to do whatever it takes to get it done. That includes me, too, doesn't it?"

"You know that isn't true."

"Do I?" She'd allowed herself to be romanced into doing just exactly what he wanted. Her throat burned with unshed tears, but she locked her eyes on his in defiance.

His mouth twisted to one side as he began to speak, then rejected the effort. Instead, he turned around and walked to the door. "I'm sorry you feel that way," he said on his way out.

Mali watched him swing his vehicle around and drive away. As he pulled out of sight, she let go the tears she'd been holding back.

Glynnis stepped up from behind and embraced her and Mali cried for a long time. "You gave him the whole story, didn't you?" said Glynnis softly.

Mali sniffed and dragged her sleeve across her eyes. "Yes."

"I told you it'd only drive him away."

"I had no choice!" She faced Glynnis and buried her head again in the older woman's shoulder. "It wasn't the truth that hurt him, it was the truth that hurt me. He was only interested in me to get permission to raise Owain's rock. I wouldn't let him."

"Nonsense. I saw how he looked at you. Men can't

pretend that look. He may have been doing his job, but he was enjoying himself, too. I could practically hear his heart beating every time you went near him."

Mali paused. Could it be true? She didn't have enough experience with men to know he felt the same way about her as she did about him.

"Are you suggesting he wasn't pretending to like me just to get my permission for the filming?"

"Heaven's no, dear. He was too conscious of you when you weren't looking. It reminded me of the way your father looked at your mother."

Mali's knees wobbled, and she had to sit. "That means not only did I just reject him, but I insulted him as well?"

"I suspect so, dear."

"That's just bloody lovely," Mali said, unable to keep the sarcasm at bay. "All I wanted was to protect us and the town. What am I going to do now?"

Glynnis dragged a handkerchief from her pocket and pressed it into Mali's fingers. "That depends on whether or not you really want to see him again."

Mali blew her nose. "I think I do."

Glynnis laughed. "Either you know or you don't. If you aren't sure, then don't worry about it. You'll get over him, and we can go back to living our lives as we always have."

"What are you suggesting? That after all this, you've changed your mind about the letter? No moving in shame to Cardiff for a few decades?"

The older woman sighed. "No, not really, but I've come to think some things are best brought out into the open. Like how you feel about William."

Mali blinked in surprise. "You think I should go

after him? Chase him?"

Glynnis retrieved the hanky and wiped a tear from Mali's face. "Though I'll live to regret saying it, yes. Go after him. Love doesn't come along every day. Accept it when it does."

"But--"

"If you want him, go. Now. The car keys are in my pocket."

Hope rekindled, Mali smiled. "I'll probably have to give him permission to shoot his silly commercials at the Rock. And lift the bloody thing."

"I know. Don't worry about that; we'll deal with it when the time comes."

Mali kissed her aunt on the cheek. "Have I told you how much I love you?"

"Not lately," Glynnis said, pressing the keys to the Mini into Mali's palm and then pushing her through the door. "Now get going!"

"Well, I do!" Mali yelled as she ran to the little car and jumped in.

She fumbled with the keys until she got the right one and stabbed it into the ignition. Mumbling a prayer to the automotive god, she turned the key.

Something in the motor protested with a grinding whirr and then clicked once before going completely silent.

~*~

Bill drove for an hour with no objective other than clearing his head. He needed to release his anger, his frustration, and above all, his confusion. Mali'd agreed to filming in the hot pool grotto and had said she'd likely permit shots at the Rock, too. But then she refused to allow the excavation. Once again, the woman didn't make sense. He still thought the news about Owain not being very saintly was hilarious; it served Rhia right--her being related to an unsaintly Owain would be poetic justice. When word got out, there'd be no way she could exploit that relationship and still be taken seriously. On the other hand, good dramatic tension could be built around an excavation. It was the sort of thing which would intrigue people for days. The value to the town, the network, and the agency was astounding. How could Mali refuse?

He slowed the car, then rolled to a stop. A flock of sheep taking up the entire road approached. They slid past him like river water around a mid-stream boulder, and their unmistakable aroma permeated the air.

He tapped the steering wheel impatiently. The whole situation stank. He was no closer to solving the filming dilemma, and his problems with Rhia only added to his frustration. Going head to head with Rhia would leave him bleeding from the ears at best.

The shepherd finally passed, two young dogs at his heel while two others nipped and ran around the entire flock ensuring no stragglers.

He wondered what had set Mali off. Especially after last night when everything had been so different, when he'd let himself believe....

Damn rock. Yes, he'd pushed the issue of shooting there, but it wasn't as if he had much of a choice: either lose his job or lose his girl. Even if she wasn't exactly his girl. Yet. Mali was a treasure he had no desire to lose.

He accelerated a little, then coasted to another stop. The valley spread green before him--as it surely had for hundreds of years. Some of the oak trees may have been alive when Owain and Meleri walked there.

The Owain legend being a fairy tale only made things more interesting. Certainly there were people in the world who would take offense at the idea of an unsavory saint in a house of ill repute, but what point was there in anyone getting upset? All the principal players had been dead for centuries!

Still, if it meant that much to her, how could he justify turning her world upside-down? He liked her world, and he liked it better than the one he was going back to. Spending more time with someone like Mali, that would be worth working for.

He shook his head. What was he working for? He had a job in the States, if Rhia didn't can him. Which, she would almost certainly do. After tonight, she was unlikely to relent now. Without her cooperation, there was nothing he could do, and there was nothing to film.

He dreaded the thought of talking to Rhia, but he had to let her know how things stood.

He whipped out his phone to tell her they might as well forget the whole thing. The worst of it was there'd be no reason for him to stay in Wales; he'd lose his excuse to spend any more time with Mali.

Whoever answered the phone at the agency was new to Bill. "May I speak with Rhia Jones, please?"

"I'm sorry, but she's not available," the mystery voice said.

"Do you know where she can be reached?"

"I'm not at liberty to say."

Bill tried to keep the growing impatience from his voice. "How 'bout Ms. Jones' secretary? May I speak with Stacey?"

"I'm sorry sir, but she's not available either."

"Is anybody working today?" he asked. "How 'bout Grady? Grady Banyon."

"One moment please, I'll see if he's taking any calls."

"Tell him it's Bill Thomas, and if he doesn't want me to hand him his ass on a platter, he'll answer the damned phone!"

After a moment's pause, Grady came on the line. "Bill! I'm glad you called."

"Yeah, it's great to hear your voice, too," Bill said, "but I've got to talk to Rhia."

"She isn't here. She left a few hours ago." He paused. "For Wales."

Bill's stomach did a back flip. "Why? Has David taken a turn for the worse?"

"Just the opposite," Grady said. "He's out of the hospital and says he's ready to come back to the office. Maybe as early as next week."

"But that's great news! He can come over here and clean up this mess all by himself."

"You don't understand." Grady gave a low whistle. "David's improvement is the problem. Rhia wanted to have the project finished before he came back to work."

His stomach did another loop-de-loop. "She's coming here to take charge, isn't she?"

"I'm afraid so."

"But that's stupid!"

"I agree. Unfortunately, that's not the worst of it."

Bill groaned. "Don't keep me in suspense."

"You have no idea how much I hate being the

herald for that woman, but she told me that if you called, I was to tell you she'd cover your travel expenses for one more day. After that, you're no longer an employee of Jones and Associates. It's time to pack your bags and shag it home, my friend. Maybe you can find another job before she gets back and puts an anchor on your career."

Bill was too stunned, then too angry to say anything. If it did come down to a head-to-head confrontation with Rhia, one of them would walk away bloodied, and he didn't aim for it to be him. The project, David's project, had become a proving ground for Rhia's ego. He couldn't allow that. She'd drag Mali, Glynnis, and the entire village down before she'd admit defeat. He didn't want to leave, but to make sure that didn't happen, he needed to talk to David. In person.

"Bill? You okay?" Grady asked.

"Yeah."

"What're you going to do?"

He decided. "There's an afternoon flight out of Manchester." He checked his watch. "If I hurry, I can get back to Llansantowain, pack my stuff, and still make it."

"Well, good luck, amigo. Whatever you do, just make sure you aren't there when Rhia arrives. She's already pissed; don't give her a reason to kill you."

~*~

"When I suggested you go after him, dear, I didn't mean on foot," Glynnis said when Mali quit threatening to have the traitorous Mini hauled to a landfill.

Mali scowled and turned her back on the car. "I've

walked to the village a million times. Once more won't hurt me."

"And what if he's not there?"

"Where else could he be?" Mali smiled knowingly. "I'll bet he's at Brenna's right now nursing a beer."

"Why not call her and find out? If he's there you can have her bolt him to the bar until you arrive."

Good idea, Mali thought. Losing William just when she thought she'd found him shouldn't preclude her common sense; there was no point in walking all the way to the pub if he wasn't there. Instead, she walked into the cottage to make the call. Brenna answered on the first ring.

"Bren? Mali here; I'm trying to reach our favorite Yank. Can you call him to the phone, please?"

"Sorry, luv," the pub owner said. "Dylan, Michael, and Dai are the only ones here. The last time I saw William, he was headed your way."

Mali squeezed her eyes shut in frustration. "When he comes back, will you tell him I called, please?"

"Certainly. Will you be dropping by this evenin'? Darts night y'know."

Darts? How could she begin to think about darts when she faced losing her pride, the lock on the family secret, and the man she was falling in love with? "I'll think about it." She looked through the open door of the cottage at her forlorn little Mini. An idea struck her. "Does Dai know anything about motor cars?"

"Cars, sex, and football are the only things he ever talks about."

Mali chuckled. "You sound like Caitlin, except she says that about all men."

"She'd be close to right then, I 'spect."

"My car's given up," Mali said. "I was hoping maybe Dai would take a look at it."

"Hold on, I'll ask him."

Mali could hear muffled conversations, punctuated by laughter and the occasional guffaw as some thrower missed his target. She fidgeted until Brenna came back on the line.

"Dai wants to know what's wrong with it," she said.

"It won't bloody start! I turn the key and nothing happens. No lights, no sound, nothing."

"Cars and blokes," Brenna said, *sotto voce*, "always let a girl down, but I'll pass that along as soon as Dai finishes his turn."

Mali endured a brief but high level background discussion of ignitions, electrical systems, and weather before Brenna spoke again. "Dai says it sounds like a dead battery."

Mali heard laughter in the background and then Michael's voice rose above the others: "I'll jump start ya, Mali girl!"

"Bren dear, trot over and slap Michael a good one for me, will you, please? And tell him the next time he comes near me I'll set my dogs on him."

"Happy to oblige, Mali. Anythin' else, then?"

Disgruntled that William hadn't returned to the pub yet, Mali decided to walk to the village anyway. He'd likely arrive by the time she got there, and at the very least, they could sit in a corner and discuss what needed to be done. It pleased her to think what his expression would be when she told him they'd be allowed full access to the Rock. "I suppose not. It looks like I'll just have to pop over on foot and wait 'til he gets back."

She hung up and started toward the door; her aunt was waiting for her with an umbrella and a coat. "The sky's black with rain threatening. I thought you might need these. Are you going to cut through the woods?"

Mali slipped into the coat and retrieved a scarf from a pocket which she tied over her head. "No, I'll take the road in case he drives by."

Glynnis gave her a hug. "You're doing the right thing, dear."

"I hope so." She stepped into a pair of wellies and whistled for the dogs to come inside so they wouldn't follow her, then set off for the village. Halfway there, the rains came. Mali held the umbrella low and trudged down the suddenly muddy road. The rain amplified her misery. Just as she'd met someone she took a real fancy to, life conspired to snatch him away again. She wasn't getting any younger, but the thought of having to settle for the likes of Michael Wells if she wanted children was enough to spur her on to greater effort. She had to find her man.

The road was never busy, even on nice Sunday afternoons when folks with cars would travel up and down just for the sake of it. Now, not a single vehicle passed her en route, and she reached the Cock and Bull winded and wet at the cuffs. William's rental car wasn't in the lot; she saw only Michael's old lorrie and Dai's even older Ford Escort. She took the time to shake out the umbrella, and her disappointment, and went inside.

Brenna greeted her with a wave, as did Dylan and Dai. Michael, his eyes locked onto a Manchester

United soccer match on the Beeb, didn't notice her, which suited Mali just fine.

"Looks like it's going to be a wet one tonight," Mali said as she settled in at the bar and accepted a cup of tea from Brenna.

"It's good for business. The lads can't abide sitting in the house doing nothing but listen to the rain on the roof or watch the telly."

Mali grinned. "Nice to hear it's good for something. It rains so often I sometimes fear I'm going to break out in a layer of moss."

She settled herself on a stool close to Brenna and exchanged pleasantries. Every ten minutes, or when the door was opened by some fellow with rain hard on his heels and a thirst for both ale and darts, she stared at the door and willed it to open to Bill. When the soccer match eventually wound down, she doubted he'd ever return. Damn it, she thought, if she had to wait all night, she would. After the game, Dai brought his empty glass to the bar.

"Another?" Brenna asked.

"No thanks, Brennie m'love. I've got to slip over to Bedgelert and pick up some new sheep shears."

"This late in the year," Brenna said. "Whatever for?"

"They've been on order forever, seems like, and knowin' my luck, if I don't fetch 'em now, someone else'll have off with 'em before I get there. Better to go now, while I'm thinkin' of it, and have 'em come spring. The old ones were givin' my darlins a rash." He smiled warmly at Mali. "You're welcome to come along and pick up a battery for your car."

"Go on," Brenna said. "You're just wastin' your

time here. I'll tell William you're lookin' for him when he comes in."

After a moment of hesitation, Mali agreed. She thanked Brenna and followed Dai. He held the car door open for her as she slid into his rusted sedan, then he clambered into the driver's seat. His door shrieked an unearthly wail when he opened it and again when he pulled it shut. Mali managed to cover her ears for the second one. She wished she could roll down a window to thin out the odor of stale cigarettes. Though the rain had picked up, she was tempted to do it anyway.

She cast a wary eye at a large, dark stain on the front seat and a crack which ran the length of the windshield. "Are you sure this car can make it there and back?"

Dai laughed. "This old bucket's as reliable as me."

"That's comforting," Mali said. He completely missed her sarcasm. In a few moments, however, she wondered if she'd be able to survive the trip. Dai's driving was worse than her aunt's. At least Glynnis looked before she made a turn; Dai maintained a sloth's pace, crept through traffic circles and around corners as if he was plowing an open field and had nothing more to contend with than rabbits.

Hunched over the wheel of a vehicle a good half size too small, Dai concentrated on the narrow road ahead as if it might suddenly jump out from under his car and scamper away.

"Have you ever wondered why there are always more cars behind you than ahead of you?" she finally asked when the pace became excruciating.

"Now how could you know that, Mali Rhys? I can't

remember the last time you rode anywhere with me."

Mali eyed the line of vehicles queued up behind them waiting for a chance to pass. "I'm just guessing."

"My first wife was always in a hurry," he said. "She used to nag me constantly about taking my time. On and on she went, like a water wheel--all that noise and motion goin' nowhere. Wore me out she did."

"Imagine that," Mali said as the first of a dozen cars pulled out and sped around them. They drove for nearly an hour, but to Mali it felt like a week.

Just outside Bedgelert, she spotted William's car at a stop sign. She squinted through the rain and an arc of dirty windshield which the wiper on her side faithfully missed at every pass, but it was him. She waved both arms at him, and when he didn't respond, she reached over and pushed the car horn. It responded with a low, sheep-like blat.

"What's got into you?" demanded Dai.

The Yank's car accelerated, the driver intent on the road ahead. Mali tried to roll the window down, but the crank refused to turn. "What's wrong with the window?"

"I dunno," Dai said, "I never sit on that side."

Mali yanked open the car door as the red Peugeot sped past them, kicking up a low wall of spray that coated Mali's jeans from the knees down. "Damn it!" she cried, pulling the door shut. "You've got to turn around!"

"I haven't got me shears!"

"It doesn't matter. I've got to catch up with William."

"The Yank?"

"Yes, of course, the Yank. Do you know any

others?"

Dai's lower lip protruded as he pondered the question. "Aye. There's William Jones over in--"

Mali groaned. "Please, Dai! Turn around and go after him. He's getting away!"

"All right, all right. Ye can't say I'm not the sort to offer a hand to someone in distress." He slowly turned the wheel and accelerated, the maneuver causing two cars in the oncoming lane to apply a liberal helping of both horn and brake. Dai remained implacable while Mali sank lower into the seat and wished she had a place to hide.

"I didn't think you'd turn without looking first," she said.

"I used the blinker, didn't I? It should've been obvious what I was about."

Mali leaned forward, peering through the grime-streaked window. "Can you see him?"

"The Yank? No. He drives like a mad man."

Mali wished a little of William's speed-related dementia would rub off on Dai. It didn't, no matter how much she prevailed on him to go faster. If anything, because of the rain, he drove slower.

"Life's too short to rush through it," he advised as they finally pulled back into Llansantowain, and he squished to a stop outside the Cock and Bull. The parking area was no longer deserted. Darts night, Mali remembered.

Out the door before Dai could set the hand brake, Mali raced inside the building and slid to a halt on the slate floor. Brenna stood behind the bar drying a glass.

"Where is he?" Mali asked.

"Gone."

"You said you'd tell him I needed to talk to him."

A look of embarrassment crossed Brenna's gentle features. "I never got the chance, luv. According to Michael, he came racing in like someone was after him. I was in the back fixing stew. Tonight is darts--"

"Yes, yes, I know. Go on."

"If it hadn't been for Michael, I wouldn't even have known he came back."

At the sound of his name, the electrician paused at the throwing line. "'E looked to be in a terrible hurry."

"Why didn't you tell him to wait for me?"

He shrugged. "Could be 'cause I didn't know you wanted him to. I'm no Caitlin; I don't read tea leaves." He threw a dart. "Or minds."

Dylan Davies set his glass on the bar. "He didn't give us much time to even say cheers. He was digging in his wallet for money to pay his bill, but I told him we'd cover it. He said he was in a hurry to get to Manchester and catch a flight back to the States."

"No!" Her heart sank.

"Aye."

"Just like that? No warning?"

"I thought that a little odd m'self, since there's still a great deal of work to do on the adverts and all. But he said he already discussed that with you."

Mali slumped into a chair, crossed her arms on the table and rested her forehead on them.

"He did, didn't he?" Dylan asked.

"Yes," Mali said, numbly. "We discussed it. Several times." She covered her head with her hands. She'd waited too long, and now he was gone. "Bloody hell."

Brenna stepped around the bar and shooed Dylan away. She put her arm around Mali, leaned close to her ear and whispered, "You didn't go and let him steal your heart now, did you?"

Mali couldn't respond; something dark and wet and heavy and final had settled over her. Suddenly, all she wanted to do was get away. She wanted to sit at home in front of a fire with the dogs beside her.

"I'm terribly sorry," Brenna said. "Can I get you anything?"

Mali shook her head. She'd find something at home. Tea, maybe, or brandy. Lots of brandy. It didn't matter. She stood up and faced the door. It was a long walk home in the rain and with any luck, maybe she'd be struck by lightning on the way.

Just then a crowd of noisy people pushed the door wide and poured through in a jostling mob of dripping hats and flapping umbrellas. The villagers fell silent as the invasion progressed. Brenna moved back behind the bar.

Near the middle of the pack strode a young woman clad in something that shined like plastic and hugged her body like paint. Mali didn't need to look around to know that every local male's eyes were zeroed in on the woman.

She sauntered to the middle of the room, her high heeled boots sounding like gunshots. "I'm looking for Bill Thomas," she announced.

"William?" Mali asked.

"The Yank?" echoed Brenna.

"That's the one," she said, unzipping her form-fitting top and peeling it off.

Braless breasts swayed under the woman's thin blouse and Michael Wells nearly fell over his own feet trying to offer her a chair.

"He left about a half hour ago," Brenna said.

"In that case I need to speak to whoever owns the land under Orvan's Rock." She flipped her jacket over her shoulder and adopted a stance Mali had last seen on the cover of a fashion magazine in Caitlin's shop.

Brenna nodded towards Mali. "That'd be her."

The woman looked at Mali, her eyes cold above a fixed smile. Mali felt like the entree at a cobra dinner party.

"I'm Rhia Jones," the woman said, extending a bony hand. "We need to talk."

~*~

The only seat open on the flight back to Atlanta was in first class, and Bill took savage pleasure in charging the outrageous, last-minute fare to the company. It served Rhia right. Unfortunately, neither the food, the movies, nor the free drinks did much to dispel his doleful mood. The alcohol did, however, mask the hurt, and after several high altitude highballs, he fell into a dreamless sleep.

A solicitous flight attendant helped him off the airplane, and the sudden heat in the ramp walkway nearly toppled him. He stopped to lean against the wall and chastised himself for not taking it a little easier with the drinks. Wales had been cold when he first arrived there, and now "Hotlanta" was living up to its nickname. He waved off a helping hand from the flight attendant and caught his breath. Hoisting the strap to his laptop over his shoulder, he made his way through customs to the baggage claim area. He'd grab a few hours of real sleep at home before he had to finish figuring out just what he must do to save Mali's little town.

Grady Banyon stepped beside him. "Welcome home, stranger," he said, his hand extended. "You look like hell."

Bill, glad to see a friendly face, took the offered hand and shook it. "You have no idea how good it is to see you. I figured I was *persona non grata*."

"Naw. Besides, with Rhia gone, I figured nobody'd have to know I came here to pick you up," Grady said.

"Thanks. It means a lot."

"So tell me what happened," Grady said as he wheeled Bill's bag to the car. "Then we can try to figure out your next move."

Grady tossed the luggage in the trunk of his Intrepid, and the two climbed into the car. In minutes they were headed north on Interstate 85 to downtown. On the way, Bill gave his friend a quick recap of his trip including Mali's revelation that the stories about Saint Owain were lies made up to spare the village from the vengeance of Owain's Abbot.

"That's hysterical," Grady said. "So, instead of David and Rhia being descended from a saint, their family tree was planted by a drunken john."

"A *cheap*, drunken john," Bill said. "Yeah, that's pretty much it."

"Wouldn't you love to see *that* story told in a series of 60-second spots!"

Bill chuckled. "I somehow doubt that David would." He fell silent as they drove past the Ted, home of the Atlanta Braves. He felt a momentary regret; losing his job would also mean losing his season tickets--one of the very few perks Rhia hadn't yet stripped from senior staff.

"I just don't know what to do now," he said.

"There's a woman there--"

Grady raised an eyebrow. "Mali? The one who turned saint into ain't?"

"Yep, she's the one. I like her. A lot. She's so down-to-earth, so... I dunno. I can't explain it. All I know is, I'd like to spend more time with her. A helluva lot more time."

Grady took his eyes from the road for a moment and assessed his friend. "So, what's the problem?"

"She's stubborn. In fact, she's probably the most stubborn woman I've ever met."

"Worse than Rhia?"

No one was worse than Rhia. "Rhia's not stubborn; she's possessed. There's a difference."

Grady made a smacking sound with his mouth. "Right." They rode in silence as he exited the expressway and swept through the wooded hills of Vinings to reach Bill's suburban apartment complex. Grady parked in a shaded spot in front of the building. "I hate to break this to ya, buddy, but all women are stubborn. I don't know why; they just are. I think it goes back to Eden and the whole apple thing. We're being punished."

"Could be," Bill said. "But every now and then it's possible to talk sense into one of them. I was gettin' there with Mali. She'd already caved on filming the spots, she just couldn't get past the idea of anyone moving the damn rock."

He remembered the fresh innocent smile she'd given him after their kiss. No guile, just pure simple pleasure. He realized suddenly that her concession to allow filming had everything to do with him and precious little to do with being sensible. Maybe she'd retract her offer once Rhia had shown off her people skills. "If Rhia thinks she can talk Miss Mali Rhys into anything, she's dead wrong. No one's going to get her to do anything she doesn't want to do."

"That may be true," Grady said, "but you and I both know Rhia doesn't work that way. I doubt she'd fly over there unless she knew she could get exactly what she wants."

Grady popped the trunk, and Bill retrieved his bag. "Want to come up for a beer?"

"Nah. It's still way too early for me," Grady said, "and besides, you're bleary-eyed as it is. You probably could use some sleep."

Bill nodded. He shook his friend's hand and started up the walk to his apartment. Halfway there he stopped and turned around. "Yo, Grady!"

Grady rolled the window down and stuck his head out. "What?"

"You know more than you're telling me, don't you?"

Grady gave Bill a sheepish grin. "I'm not trying to keep any secrets from you, if that's what you mean, but Rhia told me point blank I wasn't to volunteer any information about her trip. You might be able to pry it out of me, though."

Bill squatted beside the car, so he'd be head to head with Grady. "You said something about Rhia not going to see Mali unless she knew she could get her way. And you're right, that's the way she works. But, how does it apply here?"

"She made a comment about how stuffy British bankers were," Grady said. "She complained they wouldn't tell her anything, so she contacted a banker friend of hers in Manhattan and got him to dig up some information on property in Wales."

Bill thought back to the pile of overdue bills on Mali's desk. "What kind of information?"

"I don't know the specifics, and Stacey wouldn't tell me the whole thing, but she mentioned something about mortgages or liens--some kinda loan. All I know is, Rhia was smiling from ear to ear when they left yesterday."

Bill's heart began to race. Of course--and how like Rhia! She wouldn't have to *talk* Mali into cooperating. She'd merely threaten to foreclose if Mali didn't, and once Rhia owned the property, she could do anything she damn well pleased with it. "Hold on," he said. "Don't go anywhere!"

Grady's brows dropped as he stared at Bill. "Huh?"

Bill opened his apartment door just wide enough to shove his bag inside then relocked it, sprinted back down the walk, and jumped in Grady's car. "I need you to do me one more favor. Can you take me to David's house? I don't think I should be driving just yet."

"David's house? Are you nuts?"

"You said on the phone yesterday he was out of the hospital."

Grady stared at him in surprise. "Well, yeah, but--"

"So what's he gonna do, fire me?" Bill laughed. "Rhia already did that. Besides, I've got some information he might be interested in."

"You aren't going to tell him the truth about that saint, are you?"

Bill smiled. "Only if it'll force David to yank Rhia out of Wales."

~*~

"So," Rhia said to Mali, "you're the one."

Until Rhia showed up, Mali's thoughts had been completely focused on Bill. She had no desire to deal with this harridan. "Do I know you?"

"Bill worked for me," she said pointedly, "or used to. I've heard all about you."

"Really." She began to appreciate Bill's dilemma with his boss.

"Any information he didn't supply, I got from other sources. I have extensive banking connections in London."

"Bully for you," Mali said. "I'm sure they find you quite... entertaining."

Rhia sniffed. "You really should do something about your hair. The wet look went out with double knits."

Mali resisted reaching for her hair, still damp from the rain. "I'd love to stay and chat, but--"

"Sit," Rhia commanded. "I didn't come all this way to waste time."

"Good. I'm sure Brenna can use the business. I'm going home." She eased past the woman toward the door.

"Enjoy it," Rhia said. "You won't have it much longer."

Mali spun around, her fists clenched. "What're you talking about?"

Rhia lounged against the dark bar, clearly enjoying the moment. She casually scanned the room and acknowledged the men watching her. When Brenna approached behind the counter, Rhia motioned her closer. "Chablis," she said.

"Sorry," Brenna responded. "We're fresh out. How 'bout an ale?" She produced a bottle of Caitlyn's latest brew and set it gently on the bar. "It's named after our very own saint, y'know."

Rhia pushed it away with the tip of a perfectly manicured finger. "Make it scotch. Neat." She looked up at Mali. "Oh, you're still here? I thought you'd gone home to bed. I guess you decided to hear what I have to say after all."

Mali crossed her arms in silence.

Rhia continued, "My sources tell me you owe money to a lot of people around here."

"So?"

"It seems odd to me that you'd stand in the way of a project that would allow you to pay them all back."

"You have no right to pry into my personal business. What are you insinuating?"

"Before we discuss your house, I thought it might be good to go over your other debts. So I've arranged for an expert."

"You what?"

"Mr. Goldfarb will be here soon, along with the... the constable. Such a quaint title."

The noise level in the Cock and Bull had been so high Mali had strained to hear Rhia, but when the door opened and the Rastafarian sauntered in, nearly everyone quit talking. Many stared at the scaly creature clinging to his shoulder.

Mali began smiling as the rastaman made his way through the crowded room.

The smile on Rhia's face, however, faded. "*You're* Goldfarb?"

"Yeah, mon," he said offering his hand. "I'm

Samuel Goldfarb, Lion of Judah Account Services and herb shoppe."

"You don't look much like a Goldfarb," Rhia said.

"It be my professional name," he said. "My friends call me Ganja Bob." His mouth was home to an enormous grin punctuated by two gold-capped teeth.

"Where's the constable?"

"He busy with an accident. Weather be bad. Rain. Mud. The cars, dey slide aroun'."

Rhia's eyes grew wide as the lizard on his shoulder stepped toward her. "What the hell is that?"

"This be Winston, my iguana. Be careful wid him. He thinks he's de Lion of Judah."

Rhia slid a stool between them and pointed at Mali. "Tell her."

"She heard me. I know Miss Rhys. Nice lady, but her dogs don' like Winston."

"Tell her about our arrangement," Rhia said, her voice thin and strained.

"Oh yeah, mon. Dat. I sold your account, Miz Mali. You don't owe me nuting. I'm gonna miss comin' to see you."

"There," Rhia said. "You owe me, not him."

"You can't do that!" Mali looked quickly at Goldfarb. "Can she?"

"I already have." Rhia laughed in triumph. "And I demand payment in full." She held out her hand. "Now."

Goldfarb laughed with her, then his pleasant expression faded. "No, missy. You can't go so fast." He stroked Winston's head but gazed at Rhia. "I 'spect you be one fast lady, but not dis time. You gotta wait on de paperwork."

"What paperwork? What are you talking about?"

"I'm going on vacation to Jamaica, mon! It's too cold here. I'll do all de paperwork when I get back."

"And when is that?" Rhia cried.

"April maybe," he said. "We'll see." He winked at Mali before he left, shaking hands and exchanging greetings all the way to the door.

Rhia stood at the bar, fuming. She gripped her scotch and gulped it down in one swallow."

Was there anything else?" Mali asked as sweetly as she could.

Rhia took deep breaths. "Don't think you're off the hook yet. I still have bankers in my pocket."

Mali made a show of examining Rhia's body-hugging outfit. "I can't imagine where you'd hide a pocket in that get-up."

Rhia produced a letter from her handbag. "If you don't believe I can make things difficult for you, read this."

Chapter Seven

Mali sat near the bar in the Cock and Bull, her half pint ale glass untouched in front of her. The American woman had come on strong and bullied her into accepting the whole advert project. Mali wasn't sure if she was madder at herself for allowing it to happen, at Bill for setting it up and then abandoning her to the wolves, or at Rhia Jones, whose dirty tactics left more than a bad taste in Mali's mouth.

Brenna's pub had never been loud, even at the annual Darts Championship, but now--crowded with Yanks and locals alike--the din was spectacular. Clive Gillet, the bird watcher, sat with a cannon ball of a woman at a nearby table. Whenever Mali looked at them, they looked away. Everyone else seemed to be talking at once, except for Dylan Davies who sat on the bench beside her.

She watched the Spanish actor, Fernandez, in rapt

conversation with Rhia. She took some small satisfaction in the woman's claim to being a descendent of the errant saint. Rhia certainly dressed herself in the same come-hither fashion as the unsavory women Owain allegedly came to save. Yes, Mali thought sourly, there could indeed be a connection between the two.

She shouted so Dylan could hear her and pointed to Rhia. "The rest of her film crew is either upstairs or busy getting drunk down here," she said. "They want to start shooting first thing in the morning."

"Splendid. All this is happening much faster than I'd ever dreamed." Dylan patted Mali's hand. "I want you to know how much I appreciate your cooperation."

Mali snorted. She picked up her ale and held it so that she could look through it at Rhia hanging all over the Spanish actor. "My cooperation was guaranteed with a little blackmail."

"What?" He leaned forward, his hand cupped behind his ear. "I didn't quite catch that."

"The Queen Bee there talked to my bank. She offered to bring my mortgage up to date if I let her use the property, otherwise they'll foreclose." She took a sip of her drink. "It was all spelled out in a one-page letter. Isn't it amazing how little one's integrity is worth?"

He made a nervous clucking sound. "Now Mali, you know it's all for the best."

"That's easy for you to say." She took a large mouthful of beer, made a face, and pushed the glass away. "Is it just me, or is this batch flat?"

Dylan picked up her glass and took one sip, then

another. "Tastes fine to me."

Mali shivered. "You drink it, then. It seems my tastes are changing."

He took a long draught, drained the glass, and smacked his lips. "If so, it's a great shame."

A cooling breeze on the back of her neck announced the open pub door behind them. Caitlin Morgan, like the fresh air that accompanied her, entered the room. Despite her pink and green hair, no one but Mali seemed to notice. Caitlin looked about the jammed room for a moment or two before she spotted Mali, then walked straight to her. The crowd parted for her like the Red Sea parted for Moses.

Mali waved a greeting.

"I saw Bobby Goldfarb drive off as I came in," Caitlin said. "I worry 'bout him. That car of his is a sight--dents held together by rust. Winston's a cutie, though isn't he?"

Mali shuddered.

"Good afternoon, Cait'," Dylan said, gesturing to a small empty place on the bench.

Caitlin snugged in close. "What's this I'm hearin' about bulldozers and Owain's Rock?"

Mali exhaled wearily. "It's true. The day after tomorrow they're bringing in a crane to stand the Rock on its end. They've got experts who'll muck about in the dust looking for Owain's bones. When they're done, the gang in here plans to film a recreation of the scene where Owain wrestles the devil. God only knows what they'll use for a saint when they topple the Rock again."

Caitlin's nostrils flared as Mali spoke. Her hands circled into tight balls, and she began to shake with anger. "You can't allow it, Mali. You've got to stop them."

Mali shrugged helplessly. "I can't. I tried. I really did. There's nothing more I can do."

"Where's that Yank? Can't you get him to stop them?"

The crushing realization she was alone again hit Mali hard. It took all her willpower to keep her voice from trembling against the burning in her throat. In the past, she'd not minded being alone--her life was full enough and satisfying, she'd thought. Now it seemed unbearable. "William's gone," she said.

Caitlin's green-tinted eyebrows raised. "Gone where?"

"Back to America. I doubt we'll ever see him again." William had edged himself into her awareness so smoothly she hadn't recognized it until now. The thought of facing this without him hurt.

Caitlin seemed to look through her. "Don't give up just yet, luv," she said. "I know it'll work out."

Mali squinted at her. "What--"

Caitlin waved a hand as if summoning invisible forces and then leaned forward conspiratorially. "I don't know anything; I'm just saying that the heart can be a powerful motivator. One shouldn't assume the end has come as long as there's still breath in the body."

A smile played on Mali's lips at Caitlin's unique cheerfulness. "You've an odd way of putting things," she said.

"I thought it rather poetic, actually. But that's neither here nor there. We've got to stop this nonsense once and for all."

"What nonsense?" Dylan asked loudly. "There's no fuss, really. It's a rock that's been lying about for centuries. None but us ever cared about it, or even gave it a second thought. Now it's about to put our town on the map, increase revenue, and improve the economy, and you want it stopped? I say bring on the crane--full speed ahead!" He swept his arm in a wide gesture to include the full pub. "Look around. Our Brenna's not had a night this good, ever. I'll wager she brings in more this week alone than in the whole of last year."

Staring him straight in the eyes, Caitlin bore down on him as she spoke. "Money isn't everything, Dylan Davies. Moving the Rock would be a disaster--it'll disturb the spirits, cause warts to sprout on innocent babies, and dry up every cow for miles around. Do you want to be held responsible for that?"

"Of course not," Dylan said, without trying to hide his condescension. "Besides, that's all nonsense, Caitlin. No one really believes those things anymore, and we all know it takes more than disgruntled ghosts to dry cows and cause warts."

Caitlin drew herself upright and leaned away so she could focus on him even without her glasses. "Oh really?" she asked, her tone scolding. "And when did you become an expert on the spirit world?"

Dylan puffed out his chest. "I--"

"Honestly," Mali interrupted. "Spirits or no, I'd do anything to stop it. Anything legal, anyway. But there's not a damn thing I can do, and if I try, the bank will foreclose. We'll lose the manor house entirely."

Caitlin bit at her lip and narrowed her eyes as she surveyed the room. "Well, somebody ought to do something. Can't have spirits evicted just so some silly Yanks can make movies!"

"They aren't movies, exactly," Dylan said. "They're adverts."

Caitlin turned on him fiercely. "Even worse!"

Mali looked past her two friends and noticed Clive Gillet and his companion who appeared to have been intent on the conversation at Mali's table. He nodded to her, then stood and guided the woman toward them.

"Miss Rhys, allow me to introduce Mrs. Eleanor Pynchon, editor of the Society's Quarterly *Journal.*"

"How do you do?" Mali asked, and with no small curiosity, for the woman appeared to be struggling for breath. Mali decided it was most likely a glandular condition that caused her eyes to be so froglike.

Mrs. Pynchon wasted little time on formalities. "Are these wretched Americans really going to shoot adverts using that dreadful stone?"

"I took the liberty of showing her the nesting site," Gillet said. "I hope you don't mind."

"Of course not," Mali said before turning back to Mrs. Pynchon. "Shooting begins tomorrow, unless there's been some change in the plan." She pointed to Rhia and Alonzo inside a circle of village fans content to bask in the film star's glow. "That woman can give you all the details, but don't get your hopes up. I'm afraid all the good parts have already been cast."

~*~

Traffic was light and Bill and Grady made good time along the Mount Vernon Highway in north Atlanta, as they searched for David Jones' residence.

Grady patted the GPS unit built into the dash. "I've

only been here once before," he said. "A few years back, when David threw that Christmas party for clients and invited the office staff, too."

"I remember," Bill said, with a rueful smile. "Everything was rocking along fine until David found his wife in the guest bedroom doing the horizontal mambo with a VP from Happy's Hamburgers."

Grady chuckled. "Proof positive those fast food guys have no taste."

"You think that's what led to their divorce?"

"I think it was the last straw. Poor David was crushed that night," Grady said, "when he discovered she'd diddled her way through half the client list. Getting dumped would've been better if she hadn't taken so many customers with her to New York."

"Yeah, I know. It's how Rhia got her start. Well, no one can say she didn't learn from a pro."

Grady shrugged. "The apple doesn't fall far from the tree, they say." He pulled to a stop at the crest of a steep drive leading into a heavily wooded estate. The luxurious contemporary house was barely visible in the distance. "This is it. There oughta be a park ranger out any minute to guide us in."

"I 'spect you'll be okay if you stay on the pavement," Bill said. "Now, let's get moving."

Grady remained immobile. "Maybe we should've called first. I really hate to bust in on him cold."

"You don't have to bust in on him at all. Just drop me off; I'll call a cab when I'm done."

"I'm not leaving you here to face the music alone. I'm your friend; I gotta go in with you."

"No, you don't. This is my fight. Besides, I don't have much to lose. You still work for him."

Grady nodded reluctantly. "All right. But I'll wait for you on the road. Call when you're done."

"Go home," Bill said as he opened the door and got out. "I'll be fine."

"Then good luck. Let me know how it goes." Grady waved to him as he drove around the circular drive and back out to the main road.

"I'm better off doing this by myself anyway," Bill mumbled to the immense azaleas flanking the double walnut doors in the flagstone entryway.

He studied the entrance just briefly before deciding that genuine Welsh slate would have been a better choice than flagstone. He straightened as his thoughts shifted to Mali. That's why he was here--to protect her and her slate-ridden village. He punched the doorbell and heard a set of chimes go off somewhere inside. Moments later the door opened. Bill had been expecting a butler or housekeeper, and the sight of David Jones in the doorway caught him off guard.

"Bill! It's good to see you again," David said warmly, ushering him inside.

Bill shook his hand, pleased to note good color in David's face and no lack of strength in his grip. "You look great, David. We were sure relieved to find out you were gonna be fine. I hope you don't mind that I dropped by unannounced."

"Not at all. I have too little to do; I've been watching television. You're arrival is just what I needed to drag me away from the damn box. God awful invention, TV." He waved Bill into a broad sofa in his living room and took a seat in an easy chair beside him. "What can I do for you?"

Bill resisted the temptation to gaze in awe at his surroundings. A massive painting covered one entire wall and seemed to explode with red, orange, and purple splashes amid sharply angled blades of black. Buried somehow within stood the image of a cardinal, or perhaps a priest in some sort of ceremonial garb, arms spread wide. The painting dominated the room, though the two-story high ceiling, gigantic windows, and massive fireplace balanced the art well.

It took a few moments before Bill realized what was missing from the room--a sense of the owner, though it smacked heavily of David's ex-wife. There didn't appear to be a scrap of David's personality reflected anywhere. No photos, no knick-knacks or souvenirs, no papers or other hint of who dwelt there cluttered the huge room.

"Bill?"

Startled, Bill responded with a nervous laugh. "Sorry. I couldn't help but admire your painting."

David turned and stared at it. "Hideous, isn't it?"

Hagr. Bill remembered Brenna's word for the mural in his room over the pub. "I don't know...."

"I thought for the longest time Sandra would come back and get it. She loved it. Now I wonder if she just loved the way it affected me."

"Why not take it down then, or sell it, or give it to a museum?"

"I'd love to, but Rhia says she likes it. I tried to give it to her, but she insisted I leave it right where it is."

"Does she visit often?"

David shook his head. "Can I get you a drink or anything?"

Bill forced his eyes open wide. "No, thank you, I already had too many on the plane."

"Ah, that's right," David's eyes grew bright. "You were in North Wales. You actually saw Llansantowain."

His pronunciation of the tongue twisting village name sounded as if it had been spoken by a native, including the dose of saliva that popped out the sides of his lips when he said "Llan." Bill was impressed at David's versatility. "Yes, and that's what I want to talk to you about. I s'pose Rhia told you she fired me."

David's mouth fell open. "You're kidding! What for?"

"She wasn't too happy with the way I handled the Wales assignment." He sat as straight as he could manage on the body-swallowing sofa.

David regarded him patiently. "And?"

"I found two superb locations for shooting the spots the agency's in-house writers provided, but I was only able to get the owner's permission for using one of them."

"While little my daughter does surprises me anymore, I can't believe she let someone like you go simply for that. What aren't you telling me?" He leaned back and waited.

Bill had come all the way out here for Mali and the village's sake. No way would he back off the whole truth. "In a nutshell, she didn't like the fact that I found out the real story about Saint Owain. You're not going to like this, David, but you need to know, and she's not planning on telling you. The whole legend is a fraud."

"A fraud?" David remained attentive but relaxed.

Bill nodded. "I've seen the proof. Mali Rhys has a letter written during Owain's lifetime which completely spells out what really happened to him and how the legend of his miracles arose. The people in the village made up the stories about him." He paused, both to compose himself and to assess just how badly David was reacting to the news.

Rather than even frown, David sat comfortably in his chair with an amused look on his face.

David's reaction didn't quite sit with what Bill had imagined he was looking for, and so he plunged on. "How familiar are you with the Owain legend?"

"I know the basics," David acknowledged. "It's a fun story, but I never put much faith in it. Perhaps I just don't have enough religious zeal, but tales of the devil presenting beer-drinking obstacles for mortals to overcome has never struck me as very likely. Perhaps if I bump into the devil one day, and he offers me a challenge, I'll think differently."

That David already had an inkling of the truth stunned Bill. And with Rhia for a daughter, devilish challenges were probably commonplace. "Since you already know the story, I won't bother to rehash it. Suffice it to say, what *really* happened is a far cry from the public reports. Owain, it seems, was something of a drinker, a womanizer, and a cheapskate."

David grinned hard enough to cause himself pain, and Bill couldn't understand it.

"You say this indictment of Owain is contained in a letter?" David asked.

"Yes. A fairly lengthy document."

"I presume you read the original."

Bill frowned. "Well, no, not personally, of course.

Mali--Miss Rhys--read it to me. She owns it and keeps it in a special display case so it won't deteriorate."

"I've always admired your ability, Bill, but I'm not sure how much I can rely on your friend's interpretation of an ancient Welsh manuscript."

"She translates Welsh to English for a living," Bill said, trying not to sound defensive. "I believe in my source."

"Of course you do, but that doesn't make her right." David stood and walked to a pair of large cabinet doors. He opened them to reveal a well-stocked bar. "You're sure I can't get you anything to drink? How 'bout a ginger ale?"

Bill accepted his offer and waited while David poured two glasses and brought them back to the center of the room. "Any idea when this document was written? Did it have a date?"

"I don't recall seeing one."

"That's a good sign. Not many people dated letters back then, unless they were some sort of official decree. There wasn't really much need as letters were pretty rare. I imagine most people who were capable of writing--and there were damn few of those--would likely remember when they wrote something. Especially if it was important."

"I got the impression this one was intended to be kept secret."

"That's a bit of a surprise," David said. "How much do you know about Welsh history?"

Bill shrugged. "A bit. I read the tourist guides; they usually had a blurb or two."

David nodded. "About halfway through the first millennium--in the time of King Arthur actually--great hordes of Angles and Saxons crossed the North Sea into Britain. The Romans, after some 500 years of occupation, found their empire crumbling and so they left. That's when the tribes from Northern Europe invaded."

"This must've been much earlier than the time of Owain," Bill said.

"I'm sure it was, but bear with me. I don't often get to show off my knowledge of history." He smiled. "So, enter these fierce bands of warriors, hungry for conquest, for land and slaves. They found essentially two kinds of people: those who went along with them, and those who didn't. They absorbed the former, and what do you suppose happened to the latter?"

Bill shrugged.

"They were driven into modern day Wales, Scotland and Ireland. The new residents of Britain described the former residents as *wealisc*, or 'foreign.' Can you imagine? Anyway, that's where the word 'welsh' comes from. Many of the newcomers referred to themselves as Angles, their new country as Angle-land, and their speech as Angle-ish. I'm sure I've made a hash of the pronunciation, but it's not difficult to see what became of those words."

"That's all quite fascinating," Bill said, "but I don't really see what it has to do with Owain."

"A great deal, actually. You see, the barbarians weren't the only ones flocking to Britain. There were Christian missionaries as well."

"But Owain *was* a Christian."

"Owain was a *Celtic* Christian," David said. "It took quite some effort to convert the heathen, but the missionaries did it, and pretty fast, too. Only there was a problem for the Angle-Christians; the folks in Wales, Scotland, and Ireland practiced a version of Christianity tempered by thousands of years of their own religion, the religion of the druids. Some of the Christians among the Angle-ish took it upon themselves to discredit the *wealisc* Christians."

Suddenly, Bill realized where David was heading. "So you think the letter is a fake?"

"No, I'm quite sure it's a real letter, as you say. And it's likely terribly old. I'm just having a difficult time understanding the motivation of the person who wrote it. It certainly wouldn't be the first time someone tried to discredit a Celtic saint."

"But--"

"You've piqued my interest, Bill, and I'll certainly look into that more thoroughly. And I know you're only trying to be honest. I can appreciate that. But let's face it, unless you've spent a great deal of time studying this stuff--and I'm talking about a whole lot more time than you just spent over there--I'm going to rely on my own knowledge and intuition.

Bill bristled at the hand slap, but tried not to let it show. "Does that go for Rhia's decision as well?"

"To let you go?" David rubbed his jaw. "I always hoped you two would get along, and I deeply regret it hasn't worked out that way. You must realize that I put her completely in charge of the agency while I was gone. I can't go behind her back and reverse her decisions, or question her authority."

"I can't see her taking well to that."

David chuckled. "That's an understatement. She's family, after all; but more than that, she is the boss now. I can try to persuade her, but as long as she's in charge, her decisions will stand. The only other option would be for me to step back in and take over, and I'm not about to do that, yet. I decided to make the most of the time I'm off, and I've told Rhia she's got another two weeks on her own. But, damn, I'm sorry it turned out this way for both of you, and I'll be glad to give you a glowing recommendation. I still know most everyone in the business. If you'd like, I can float your name among them."

"Thanks," Bill said, disappointed David couldn't see the harm Rhia would do to the agency. Parental blinders. "But listen, I didn't come here to whine about my job; I came here to see if there was some way to stop the dig at Owain's Rock. You see--"

"Sorry, Bill, but Rhia's calling the shots now. I can't sabotage her efforts."

He nodded and stood. "I understand. I'd better be going. Thanks for the drink."

As David walked him to the door, he began to wonder where he might scrape up enough cash to get back to Wales. There was no way he wanted Mali to face the debacle alone. And no way he wanted to be anywhere else.

~*~

"Looks like a good day to keep the dogs inside," Glynnis said as she turned away from the lone window in the cottage's front room. "There'll be a storm today, that's for certain."

"It's cloudy all right," Mali said, "but I'd rather leave them out as long as possible. They're not exactly fragrant." She remembered it was William who'd called her attention to it. Wishing he had stayed to correct the problem only reminded her of how much she regretted his leaving. She wished she'd been more reasonable with him--she'd rather have given her permission to him freely than submit to Rhia's blackmail.

Glynnis pinched her nose. "Those dogs'll be a sight more fragrant if we leave them out until they get wet."

Further discussion was halted by the telephone. Mali answered it and was immediately forced to hold the receiver an arm's length away from her ear.

"I thought you agreed to cooperate!" Rhia shrieked.

Not only did her voice reach a frenzied pitch, it bore a condemnatory tone that made Mali boil with righteous anger.

"If you raise your voice to me again like that, Miss Jones, I guarantee enough Welsh curses to raise boils on your backside. You won't be able to enjoy your first class flight back to New York or whichever hellhole spawned your appalling lack of courtesy. For your information, I did agree to cooperate, though your tactics are underhanded and vile. I signed your bloody papers, and you can now shoot all the pictures you want. You can move the Rock, roll it over, stand it upside down, or haul it back to the States for all I care. There can be nothing more you want from me."

Rhia's response came just as bitter and just as fast, though her shrieks seemed reined in. "Come out here and see for yourself what I mean, Miss Rhys. You may think you're pretty damned clever, but you're not. Just because you turned Bill Thomas' head, don't think you can pull stunts like this on me. I am not one to fall for sentimental spinsters with their oh-so-genteel manners and poor-me shenanigans."

"What on Earth are you talking about?"

"Don't play coy with me. You know exactly what I'm talking about," Rhia barked. "Now get out here and fix it, or so help me God, I'll make sure the bank has your crummy little cottage bulldozed!"

The phone clicked off into blissful silence. "Damn!" Mali looked at Glynnis in disgust. "She hung up on me."

"I could hear her all the way over here. What a vexatious person. What'd she want?"

"I've no idea, really, but there's something going on out at the Rock, and she thinks I'm responsible for it."

Glynnis dipped one eyebrow. "You're clever enough to have a back-up plan. Are you responsible?"

"Of course not!" Mali frowned. "I haven't done anything except cravenly give in to that dreadful woman's demands. I've hardly been out of the house in two days." She drew her shoulders back, raised her chin, and strode to the closet to get her raincoat.

"Where are you going?" Glynnis asked.

"To the Rock. I want to see just what it is I'm being accused of doing."

"Better wear boots, then, and take an umbrella. It's likely to get messy."

In more ways than one, Mali thought. "I'd better get the dogs in after all. I don't want them following me. Who knows? William's boss might bite one of them, and we can't afford any vet bills just now."

Glynnis's smile was short-lived and replaced with worry. "Do you think it's a good idea to take an attitude like that with you?"

"Probably not," Mali said, "but it's the worst I can come up with on such short notice. With any luck, by the time I get to the Rock, I'll really be angry."

"Well, be careful, dear," Glynnis said. "But don't let her bully you. Remember, we can still move to Cardiff if we must and Gwen will give us temporary lodging if the bulldozers come for us."

The woman's faith that everything would work out comforted Mali. She kissed her aunt's cheek. "Don't worry, darling. I won't do anything completely stupid." She called the dogs and held the door open for them as they sauntered through, then she left the cottage behind. Her little Mini, complete with new battery, looked forlorn at the end of the drive, but Mali opted to walk. Not only would it take her slightly longer to get there, which served Rhia right, but she wouldn't have to worry about getting stuck in the mud since parking places anywhere near the Rock were nonexistent.

The sky grew darker as she trudged through the woods. The last time she'd come this way, William had accompanied her. The trees seemed morose now rather than magical. She wondered what William was doing as she walked under the leaden sky. The east coast of the States was about five hours later, so she fancied he was still sleeping, probably. In fact, she imagined he would be doing anything but thinking about her or worrying about Rhia's precious commercials. She used the umbrella to push aside a low branch and kept moving. The air felt heavy with the threat of rain, and she zipped her jacket a little higher. She wished she'd taken the time to tuck a scarf around her neck.

In the distance, a variety of excited voices clattered, competed and ultimately collapsed in confusion. Mali strained to hear what was being said, but other than a few random curses, very little came through intelligibly except anger. She hurried her steps and soon passed beyond the ring of trees which surrounded Owain's Rock. Once clear of the trees she came to an absolute standstill.

The scene which greeted her was like nothing she'd ever imagined. At least four distinct groups were on the verge of war with one another. On the inside, ringing the great stone with their arms locked and multicolored hair hanging down over long, sun-bleached white druid robes, stood a phalanx of Caitlin's New Age friends. Their faces all bore the determined looks of zealots prepared to defend the huge stone penis to the bitter end.

A second group was even more vocal, though they carried signs bearing phrases such as "Down With Smut!" and "Clean Up England's Act!" in case anyone failed to understand their chants. Mrs. Pynchon, the short, rotund woman Mali had seen with Clive Gillet two nights before seemed to be leading them. Mali feared she was exhorting them to make a charge at Caitlin and the latter day druids.

Beyond them, and occupying the fringes, came several dozen angry ornithologists, most of whom had brought their own placards demanding that everyone else "Spare The Wren!" or "Give Nature A Chance!" Clive flitted among this coterie, though his expression was anything but fierce. His attention seemed divided, and he spent his time staring above everyone else's heads, presumably looking for his rat-faced wren.

Commingled among the various protesters were Dylan, Dai, Michael, a dozen members of the network camera crew, Rhia, and the Spanish actor whose name Mali couldn't remember. The huge steel arm of a crane rose above the trees from the enormous lorry which consumed what little parking there had been. Mali could only imagine how the road into and out of Llansantowain must look with all these out-of-towners on foot, their vehicles left God alone knew where.

The entire scene was preposterous, but she clearly saw the reason for Rhia's fury. At first she merely smiled, but soon broke out in laughter. She didn't bother to hide it even when Rhia's enraged gaze locked on to her. The American broke from the pack of people crowding around her and steamed toward Mali like an icebreaker. Anyone who got in her way was either pushed aside or plowed under. Mali took a deep breath before she arrived.

"You did this, you--"

"Now, now," Mali said, "you've no call to start making accusations. I had nothing to do with any of this."

"Don't lie to me!" Rhia fumed. She turned and pointed at the woman leading the anti-smut brigade. "I saw you talking to her in the bar the other night." She swept her arm to the side until her accusatory digit was aimed at Clive Gillet. "He was there with her, and so was that weirdo." The arm swept back the other way and came to a stop as if ready to skewer Caitlin.

"You're right," Mali said. "I did speak to all three of them that night. But I never suggested they do anything like this." She swept her own arm in the direction of the massed protesters. "You give me far too much credit. Which isn't to say I wouldn't have done this if I'd thought of it."

Rhia fixed her with a hate-filled glare, her nostrils flaring like a winded horse. "I expect you to get every last one of these idiots out of here. Now!"

"And just how am I supposed to do that? Do I look like a constable?"

"I don't care how you do it! This is your land. All I know is we've got a shooting schedule to adhere to, and there's no way in hell we can do anything with this mob hanging around."

Suddenly, the shouting, chanting, and sign-waving picked up both in volume and tempo. Mali soon figured out why--a camera crew from the BBC had just arrived, and the various factions were all clamoring for face time.

Rhia turned as pale as the tight, ivory leathers she was wearing. Mali merely chuckled. The whole thing was out of her hands. Worrying about Owain, or the Rock, or its wren dimmed when confronted with media coverage. More people streamed into the clearing by the minute as reinforcements arrived for each of the competing groups. Mali guessed two thirds of the village had turned out to see the excitement. Soon, Rhia's people were pushed from the middle to the outside.

"Do something!" Rhia screamed.

People closed in behind Rhia as she rammed her way through the crowd back to the Spaniard's side. One of the BBC's cameras turned in her direction as she bowled over from behind an elderly woman half her size. The victim's sign, which read "Wrens Have Rights!" went sailing. Rhia didn't even slow down. Instead, she changed course, angling away from the Spaniard and toward the BBC crew. Arms flailing, she pushed aside anyone unfortunate enough to get in her way. Her voice rose above the general tumult, and soon there was a microphone in front of her mouth.

Dylan waved at Mali as he struggled to make his way toward her. She obliged him by weaving through the mob to reach him. Somewhere near the middle, they met. "This is insane," Mali said, shouting to be heard.

"Aye. She's threatening to sue you, me, the town, and the birdwatchers if she doesn't get her way. Worse, she thinks you set it up. I told her that was nonsense." He gave her a suspicious look. "You didn't set it up, did you?"

"No, but I wish I had. This is immensely funny." In fact, she hadn't been this amused in years.

"It won't be so funny if the Yanks pull out, and we lose our advertising campaign."

Mali hugged him. "Dylan, with all this fuss, that might be the best thing for everyone after all."

Suddenly, the sky brightened as if someone had thrown the switch on a great celestial flood light. Moments later the accompanying crack of thunder sent many of the protesters running for cover.

"I was going to ask you how we might break up the crowd," Mali said, "but it looks like a higher authority has assumed command."

Great fat raindrops began to pelt them, and Dylan pulled his hat lower. "I think you're right. And it's a good thing. I doubt there are enough police in all of

North Wales to break up this mob." He trudged away, bent into the wind.

Mali thrust her umbrella overhead and opened it. "I wish William was here," she said, shivering in the cold wind. "I'll bet he'd know what to do." He'd probably put his arms around me and make sure I stayed warm.

The crowds dispersed in fairly short order as the rain came down in torrents, though Mali knew they'd likely be trapped in their cars for hours before Llansantowain's one tiny street became unclogged. If only the rain could just keep falling, she thought wistfully, everything would be all right.

Bleary from jet lag, and wearing only a light bathrobe, Bill stood in front of his refrigerator, staring at the nearly empty shelves within. He'd slept 'til noon, and now his stomach ached with hunger. He'd had nothing to eat since the flight. He'd spent a lifetime eating meals out, so there wasn't usually much to chose from besides the six pack du jour or some of the Girl Scout cookies he bought by the case. Today, though, even that was unavailable.

He strolled over to the pantry where the story was much the same. An open box of graham crackers and a jar of peanut butter held out the most hope, and there was enough instant coffee to satisfy the 3rd Army, compliments of a client he'd helped somewhere along the way.

Carrying this meager provender, he headed for the living room and the recliner that sat in front of his big screen TV. He had only just turned it on, and with any luck, he'd have already missed most of the soap operas. It had been so long since he'd watched television in the daytime, he couldn't remember what else was on. Game shows, most likely. He might also try the cable sports channels. Even though it was the middle of the day in the middle of the week, there ought to be something on somewhere. Sumo wrestling, perhaps, or rugby. Maybe even a Welsh rugby match. That thought gave a slight rise to his spirits.

He settled in, opened the peanut butter, which by all accounts had a shelf life of just slightly less than forever, and the graham crackers. The latter, despite being distinctly soft and bland, weren't too bad given a heavy enough layer of Georgia's finest. Bill was on his third and watching the second half of a "Crocodile Hunter" rerun when the doorbell rang.

With peanut butter in hand, he stepped to the door and put one eye to the peep hole. David Jones stood outside rocking back and forth on his heels. Bill yanked the door open. "David! This is a surprise."

Bill ran his fingers through his hair as a makeshift comb. "I just got up."

"So I see," David said, appraising Bill's attire, his eye making the trip from neck to knee and back in silence. "May I come in?"

"Of course."

Bill barely had time to step aside as the older man cruised past him and went straight to the TV set. David grabbed the remote control and flipped through half a dozen stations before surrendering it in frustration. "Put it on cable news, will you please?"

Bill complied. "What's going on?"

David waited until a commercial ended, then

pointed at the set. "I was watching this a couple hours ago. It surprised me they had some BBC footage from Wales."

Bill tensed. News from Wales that would get David out of his posh neighborhood and knocking on Bill's door couldn't be good. "And?"

"It seems there was some kind of protest near Llansantowain. If it hadn't been a slow news day, I doubt the story would've gotten as far as London. Unfortunately, that wasn't the case. It seems to be generating a lot of human interest."

"What kind of protest was it?" Bill asked.

"I'm not entirely sure, but there appeared to be elements of several different interest groups present including an anti-porn outfit and representatives of some lunatic fringe religion."

Suddenly Bill had a very good idea of just what was happening, and where. Caitlin had already warned of extreme bad karma if anyone disturbed the spirits around Owain's rock. And Rhia must have riled the anti-smut crowd by her efforts to cause an erection in the great granite tallywhacker. It all cheered him immensely. "Sounds... interesting."

"I thought so, too, and even cracked a smile as I listened to the BBC journalist on the scene, until I saw my daughter on center stage being interviewed." David shook his head in dismay. "All I can say is, she looked and sounded a whole lot more ridiculous than any of those people running around with signs and rainbow-colored hair."

Caitlin's hand was definitely showing, and Bill bit his lip to keep from laughing. "No kidding?"

David scowled. "No kidding. You seem less

surprised than I expected."

"I did try to tell you there was some trouble in Wales."

David nodded. "So you did. Now it seems I should have listened to you."

"So, how can I help? I thought you didn't want to do anything behind Rhia's back."

"I need you. I don't know my way around Wales. Despite the fact I've wanted to go there for decades, I never have. Now I find I must get there in a hurry before my only child screws up everything and puts my business out of business. I'd like you to go with me. You know the players; you know where everything is, and you can fill me in on exactly what's been going on all the time I was locked up in that stupid hospital."

Bill reached for his coffee. Vindication felt very good--better than he'd imagined. He wanted to stretch this moment out and savor it.

David pulled two airline tickets from the breast pocket of his suit coat. "I've got two first class tickets to Manchester on the three o'clock flight. Are you coming with me?"

Bill glanced at his watch. There wasn't much time. "I'm in," he said.

"Good. Pack a bag as quick as you can. Don't worry about anything but essentials. We can buy anything else you need once we get there."

Bill put down his coffee, stepped into his bedroom, and came out with his suitcase in hand. "Let's go."

"Damn!" David exclaimed. "That was fast."

"I haven't unpacked from the last trip," Bill said.

David smiled for the first time as he looked at Bill's bathrobe. "You might want to pick out something a little less... uhm... eccentric to wear on the plane."

~*~

Eleanor Pynchon sat behind the wheel of her Mercedes with the motor purring and the heater running. How, she wondered, had North England ever managed to capture the climate of a polar ice cap and still produce greenery? She shivered despite the cozy warmth of the car. It would've been vastly better, of course, if she could have made the trip with her driver, but then prudence dictated she not take the man into her confidence. He did, after all, come from a questionable neighborhood and had never expressed an interest in either birding or maintaining the cultural purity of the kingdom. He was, nonetheless, an excellent driver. Her skills had softened from lack of use, but remained adequate, at least for this mission.

She gazed out the windshield at the fog-shrouded diggings. The dark opening of a tunnel in the making wavered through the mist. Her husband had complained more than once to her of the suspension of the second and third shifts; the Crown wanted the road and the tunnel, it just didn't want it badly enough to pay for round-the-clock labor. That suited Eleanor just fine. The only person she was interested in was an off-duty supervisor at the site, a man named Darby, who had agreed to meet her at the supply shed just outside the tunnel entrance.

Eleanor checked her watch for the thousandth time. Where could the dreadful man be? She strained to see through the growing fog and wondered if he might not have backed out after all. It was bad enough she had to deal with a man of his caliber; the least he could do was show up on schedule.

Headlights in the distance put her heart into a higher gear. If it was anyone but Darby there'd be hell to pay. The oncoming vehicle stopped. Its lights went out. Eleanor clutched the wheel tightly, her breath coming in short gasps as the crunch of footsteps on gravel grew louder. A tap at the window made her realize she'd closed her eyes. She turned to look over her shoulder.

A bewhiskered man in his fifties, with loose jowls and full lips leered at her through the glass. Eleanor stabbed the window button and lowered it a few inches. Cold air poured in. "Yes?"

"I'm Darby," the man said, the working class accent of central London strong in his speech.

"Have you got it?" she whispered.

He nodded.

"How much? I want enough to do the job properly, and I'll only get one chance."

"Three sticks should do it, if ye' place it right. Can't just throw it about and expect a decent blow." He squinted at her through the narrow opening at the top of the window. "D'ye have any idea how to use it?"

"I presumed all I had to do was place the charge and press a button."

He shook his head. "Only in the movies, luv. Ye'll have to make do with less elegant arrangements. 'Ere now, get outta the car, and I'll show ya."

Eleanor reluctantly left the warmth of the big sedan to stand beside him.

He held a wire from a spool in one hand and a stick of dynamite in the other. "This wire goes 'ere, see, like this." He attached it to the blasting cap which fit down over the end of the explosive tube. "The other end goes into this." He held up a box not much larger than a pint carton of milk, then connected the wire to a terminal on the side of the box. "Ye run the other wire to the other terminal," he said, without connecting it. "Put the charges wherever you need 'em, and reel out the wire to someplace safe."

"My husband said all his blasting crews triggered their explosions by radio signal. He didn't say anything about wires and--"

"Lady, this is the best I could do. If ye want somethin' sexier, ye'll have to look elsewhere. But if ye just want to blow somethin' up, this here'll work just dandy. Ye've got me word on it."

She eyed the box with suspicion. Wires meant something to clean up before she made her getaway. She'd been counting on setting off the explosion from the comfort of her car.

"Open the boot, and I'll pile it in," Darby said.

"I'm not sure--"

"Of what? That it'll work? Don't be tellin' me ye' want a demonstration now. I didn't bring any extra."

"No, no. It's not that. It's just--"

He gave her a savage look. "Ye've changed yer mind about talking to yer husband about me promotion."

She waved the remark off. "Don't be silly. We made a bargain. You think I'm the kind of person who'd back out of an agreement?"

"I've no idea what kinda person ye' are," Darby

said. "Ye' want to fiddle with dynamite, and you clearly don't know what you're about. Ye' can't hardly blame me for protectin' me interests."

She exhaled impatiently. The man was hopelessly pedantic.

"Ye've spoken with him, haven't ye?"

"Not yet," she said. "Nor will I until I know the goods you've provided actually work."

He grinned, exposing two rows of badly misaligned teeth. "They ought to; I got 'em right outta your husband's stores. You just wire 'em the way I showed ya, and they'll blow. Just make sure you aren't too close when they do."

Eleanor stood by the rear of the car as Darby loaded the explosives, a spool of wire, the blasting caps, and the detonator into the trunk.

"Make sure ye get rid of anythin' left over," he said. "And do it where no one'll ever find it. All this stuff can be traced."

She gave him her sternest look. "What makes you think I'd need to hide anything?"

"'Cause there are only so many legit reasons to use dynamite, and I can't think of a single one that'd send a lady like yourself creeping around in the middle of the night."

"Hmpf," she said and slammed the boot shut.

Darby walked beside her--uncomfortably close beside her--as she made her way to the front of the car. "Ye won't forget to talk to Mr. Pynchon, will ye?"

She climbed in, rolled the window down half way, and cranked the heater to high. "Of course not. I'll be happy to inform him what a bright, capable, and considerate man you are. If he doesn't elevate you to a position commensurate with your ability within a fortnight, I expect you to let me know."

"Oh, I will," Darby said. "Rest easy on that."

As she reached for the button to close the window, he put his hand on the door. "I sure hope you know what ye're doin'."

"I do," she said grimly. "I most certainly do."

Chapter Eight

Mali sat beside Dylan Davies in the back of Brenna's pub under the great green and white flag of Wales with its fiery red dragon. Mali felt anything but fiery. The rain had come non-stop for two days and no mere drizzle. Thunder and lightning accompanied torrent after torrent. Dirt roads had become quagmires; paved roads became black-bottomed streams. Day was just a wet dingy version of night.

Dylan knocked back the last of his beer and set his empty glass on the table with a resigned belch. "Oh dear. Sorry, Mali. I--"

"What?"

"I bel... I, uh... never mind."

Mali shook her head. "Get another if you need it."

Dylan rubbed his stomach. "Food, I think, is more in order. I wonder if Brennie's got anything on for this evenin'."

"Wouldn't surprise me," Mali said, eyeing the foreigners crowding every corner of the little pub. "She ought to make a small fortune feeding this mob."

"Want anything?"

"No," she said. "I'm not hungry." Nor had she been since William rode the Manchester non-stop back to the States. No matter how she replayed it in her mind, she couldn't imagine what she'd done to make him feel he needed to leave the country at a dead run. Things had been going quite well, she thought. All right, she'd been a little argumentative, but wasn't that a woman's prerogative? What sort of man was in such a hurry he didn't give a lady enough time to change her mind?

"You sure?"

Mali looked up at Dylan in surprise. "Huh?"

"You sure you're not hungry? You look like you could use something. If not food, then maybe something stronger."

"I-- No. Yes. Hell, I don't care."

Dylan leaned close and looked her right in the eye. "You're startin' to scare me, Mali Rhys. I've never seen you act this way--passing on an ale and no appetite for Bren's stew. Have you thought about seein' the doctor?"

"Doctoring is the last thing she needs," Caitlin said as she cruised between the tightly packed tables and squeezed into a spot on the bench between them. "I know what ails the girl." She flipped two bright pink braids over her shoulders. They settled starkly against the umber and purple plaid of her shawl.

Dylan looked at her from the corner of his eyes. "You didn't give her one of your mad potions, did you?"

"Of course not. Her heart's broken; can't you tell?" She patted Mali's shoulder and scowled at Dylan. "You go on and do something useful. I'll keep her company."

"I'll just fetch a bite, then. Want anything?"

"No, thanks," she said gently, her attention riveted on Mali. When Dylan put a few feet between them, Caitlin leaned close to Mali's ear. "What'd that bastard Yank do, luv? I've got a few friends in the States. I could arrange for a spot of payback, if ya know what I mean."

Mali wanted to cry, but fought down her growing frustration. "Thank you, Cait, you're a darlin', but he didn't do anything. I drove him off."

"I'm finding that hard to believe."

Mali gave her a quizzical look. "You've talked to Aunt Glynnis, haven't you?"

"Not yet, but I will."

"Don't bother," Mali said. "She won't say anything I wouldn't say myself."

"But--"

Mali waved her hand at the crowded pub. "I'd rather not talk about it in front of so many strangers." She looked at the odd assortment of Londoners who made up the film crew, many of them younger than herself, and most of them dressed in jeans, T-shirts, and leather jackets, and all of them vying for the attention of the Spanish film star. Mali wondered how the man could even breathe with Rhia Jones wrapped around him. Rhia may have had recognizable advertising expertise in America, but here in Llansantowain she was appreciated only for her sex appeal. No one but Mali, and a few other local women, recognized she was more viper than anything else.

Rhia's crew weren't the only ones vying for space in the pub. Caitlin's friends from all over the valley and some from as far as Swansea, a phalanx of bird watchers, and a squad of smut protesters filled all the left-over seats and standing room. None of them acknowledged the presence of the other groups.

Gillet, the odd little man leading the birders, fluttered from table to table like a nervous hen counting chicks. Caitlin, too, had circulated among her followers, though without the fidgety distress of Gillet. Eleanor Pynchon, majordomo for the purity patrol, was nowhere in sight, and for that Mali was truly grateful; the woman showed evidence of being even more volatile than Rhia.

They'd all camped in and around the Cock and Bull for two days waiting for the rains to abate. Brenna had called for extra deliveries of everything she sold, but Mali still marveled she had anything left to eat in the place.

Cars and vans occasionally arrived with relief troops for the various factions, but the totals remained largely the same--far too many.

Boredom had set in, and Mali feared tedium would lead to trouble. One could only throw so many darts or play so many hands of cards.

Already, bird calls were answered with cat calls, and obscenities with slogans. Every time the rain threatened to let up, a delegation from each camp grabbed their gear, be it placard or klieg light, and headed for the door. The resulting jams had thus far been comic, but it only required one hot head to set the mob a boil. Dylan managed to get a constable from

Bedgelert to spend a few hours keeping an eye on things, but he left when his shift ended, and there weren't enough officers on the force to leave one in Llansantowain at all times. Luckily, there'd been no serious trouble, yet.

Eventually Dylan worked his way back to the table with a beer and a platter loaded down with steaming sausages and a veritable mountain of mashie peas.

Caitlin glared at the combination as he tucked a napkin into the neck of his shirt. "Bangers'll kill ya," she said. "Very unhealthy."

"That's why I drink so much beer. I know I'll be smiling when they drop me in my hole and cover me with a dirt duvet."

"You've been hangin' around those movie types too long," Caitlin said. "You need to go back outside and get in touch with reality."

"Reality is a bit too wet just now. Besides, I need to disperse this rabble before I do anything else. And I can't do any work on an empty stomach." He took a large mouthful of peas, closed his eyes and sighed in pleasure.

Caitlin shook her head. "I said as much to Brenna, but she disagreed. She's perfectly happy to let things stay as they are--her business has never been better."

"She can thank the rain," Dylan said, shoving a bite of banger into his already full mouth. "Can't expect me to control that."

"Fraternizing with the enemy," Rhia said. "Can't say as I'm surprised."

Mali started at the sound of her voice.

Rhia had walked right up to their table without

anyone noticing. At least, no one at Mali's table. The laws of nature precluded the chance of Rhia moving anywhere without drawing someone's attention. Today's wardrobe favored the usual assortment of tight-fitting garments, this time bearing designs taken from serpents. Snakeskin boots matched the band on her hat, one which no fashionable Fifth Avenue cowgirl could do without.

Mali considered the snakeskin motif quite apropos. "I suspect we might have differing views on who or what constitutes an 'enemy' just now," she said.

Rhia ignored Mali, curled a lip at Caitlin as if she were carrying disease in an open container, then nodded at Gillet several tables away. "I see the whacko leadership is on duty, but who's in charge of the bible thumpers?"

"You've no reason to make disparaging remarks," Dylan said.

Rhia put on a theatrical smile and waved her arm in equally dramatic fashion. "You're right, of course. What was I thinking? I'm only trying to save this hick town from perpetual boredom, put it on the map, and create a few thousand jobs. Why should I expect any sort of appreciation, much less cooperation?"

"You needn't upset the balance of nature to do it," Caitlin said. "There are forces--"

"Oh please," Rhia sighed. "That Force nonsense went out a long time ago." She looked at Clive Gillet who contorted himself to pass through a maze of tables and chairs to reach them. Along the way, he was joined by Mrs. Pynchon's lieutenant, a tall woman in khaki slacks and a sweatshirt festooned with slogan-bearing buttons. "Oh, great, now we get the head stork and the head dork, too. We can have a party."

"Ms. Jones," Dylan began, "tensions are already running a bit high. As your client, I'd appreciate--"

She stabbed his chest with the long, crimson nail of her right index finger. Silenced, Dylan stared down at it in surprise. "I'd appreciate it," Rhia hissed, "if you cleared these idiots out of my way so we, the professionals *you* hired, could get on with our work."

Mali reached for Rhia's finger and pushed it away, none too gently. "No one's going to do anything in this rain. Why don't you just relax and give us time to work things out."

"Because I don't have that luxury. In the real world, people operate on schedules. We have these things called calendars--you might have heard of them--civilized people use them to organize their time. People whose time is in more demand than the average sheep farmer's."

Dylan regained his calm and casually sliced a chunk of sausage which he held between himself and Rhia like a talisman. "I can't help you much with the weather. It tends to rain here. A lot."

"I've noticed."

"What would you have us do?" Dylan asked as he munched the sausage.

"Don't even consider asking us to provide an anti-rain dance," Caitlin said to Dylan.

Dylan finished his sausages, wiped his mouth with his handkerchief, and rose from his seat. He bowed stiffly from the waist. "Ladies."

Rhia's disdain for Caitlin spread into a full blown glare. "I have a better idea. How 'bout you dance your little moonie friends right out of town? At least then, when the rain stops, they'll be out of my way."

Caitlin laughed. "Why in the world would we want to do that? Besides, I live here."

Rhia lowered her voice and stared intently at the hairdresser. "To avoid arrest? My attorneys have been busy. They're on their way with restraining orders, or whatever you people call them over here." She turned the full force of her heavily-made up eyes on the diminutive Gillet who finally finished his circuitous journey to the table by collapsing on the bench just vacated by the Town Councilor. "I'm willing to bet neither you, nor that bunch of saints over there bothered to get permits before you started your petty little demonstrations, did you? It might take a whole fleet of paddy wagons to haul the lot of you away."

"Permits aren't required here," Mali said. "You can't threaten us."

Rhia's brows drew down like a crossbow, her stare a steel-tipped arrow. "Try me."

"We know our rights," Gillet piped. "There's no law against peaceful demonstrations."

Rhia suddenly gave them a cobra leer, and her voice dropped to a barely audible level. "I'd hate for this to turn ugly. The town hired me to do a job, and I intend to finish it. Until the council says otherwise, you're the ones who need to back off, not me. If necessary, I can hire people to clear the film site, and quite frankly, the people I have in mind won't be terribly concerned about anyone's rights but mine."

"Why are you doing this?" Mali asked. "Why is it so important for you to upset everyone? This is a far cry from what the town hired you to do."

Rhia drew herself upright, her breasts straining at their tight silken restraints. "This is bigger than your little town now. The public must know. Besides, that's my relative lying out there under that rock. He's been ignored long enough. When I'm through, he'll be more famous than Saint Patrick."

"And so will you," Mali muttered, suddenly very happy to know the legend was hogwash. When no remains of anyone were found under the Rock, things would settle down, and Rhia would just go away.

Just then, a nondescript young woman with plain brown hair and clothing as demure as Rhia's was excessive tapped Rhia on the shoulder. "Your contact in London said he could have a private security force here by tomorrow morning if you still want it." By the clouding on Rhia's face, Mali figured the woman had said it more loudly than Rhia wanted.

Rhia forced an icy smile. "I want it, Stacey." She put her hands on her hips, her expression again smug. "Well, folks, what's it going to be? You or the boys from Bristol? Someone's going to drive the riffraff off my production site, and frankly, I couldn't care less who does it."

Mali looked from Caitlin to Gillet to Mrs. Pynchon's delegate. "We don't seem to have much choice."

~*~

A lengthy nap on the flight back to Manchester, coupled with decent food and a self-imposed ban on alcohol, left Bill feeling nearly refreshed, despite the lack of a shower in the past God-only-knew how many hours. He slipped into the washroom near the end of the last in-flight movie and did the best he could with a wash cloth and the tiny sink. It was enough. He used his electric razor, splashed on liberal helpings of after shave and deodorant, then changed into a clean shirt and slacks. By the time he stepped out of the miniature rest room and walked past a growing line of waiting passengers, he felt nearly human.

He slid into his seat, then turned to his former boss sitting in the seat beside him. David appeared lost in thought. "I'm glad you decided to check into this yourself, David."

"I had no choice, really, after what I saw on CNN. I love my daughter, but I'd hate for her to make a total ass of herself. God knows it won't be the first time," he added. "I think she gets some of her people skills from her mother--the woman can raise hackles on a dead dog."

Bill decided no comment was better than anything he wanted to say, so he just nodded and looked out the window. The airplane slowed and began an uneventful descent and landing at Manchester International Airport. They passed through Customs without incident and proceeded to the car rental counter. While the clerk fussed with details of the rental, Bill called Mali's number on his wireless, but there was no answer. He left a message.

On their way out to the car, David surrendered the keys. Bill couldn't help but smile when he discovered David had rented a vehicle with an automatic transmission. Unlike the Peugeot he had struggled to shift wrong-handed during his previous trip, the sleek Mercedes David obtained responded instantly, quietly, and with precision.

"You're sure you don't mind driving?" David

asked.

Bill just laughed. The leather-wrapped wheel in his hands felt as if it had been crafted especially for him. For once, he actually looked forward to reaching the narrow, twisting roads of the Welsh hinterlands.

"I don't drive all that much at home," David continued, "and I'd rather not have to get the hang of driving on the left."

"That's not the tough part," Bill said. "Wait 'til we get out into the boondocks."

"I've been looking forward to doing precisely that." David pulled a handkerchief from his pocket and wiped a circular peep hole in the fogged windshield. "I hope this rain lets up soon."

"Me, too." Once clear of the airport complex, Bill punched the accelerator and swiftly joined the traffic on the interstate-like motorway heading for Wales. "Just relax. I'll let you know when we're getting close. First stop: the Rhys estate."

"That's where your lady friend lives?"

Bill nodded, hoping they were still friends, and praying that they could be much more than that.

With the wipers slapping out a steady beat, and the hum of the Mercedes engine filling the background with white noise, David soon fell asleep. It left Bill time to think, time to decide what he might say, and how he might approach Mali this time. For once, he could represent just himself, not an employer. Rhia Jones, for all he cared, could take a flying leap at a rolling doughnut.

The rain slowed to a steady drizzle, but evidence of much harder downpours surrounded him. The streams and rivers flowed at capacity; fields which he'd last seen green and vibrant now appeared swampy; dirt roads which he bounced over before now squished and splashed beneath his tires. He didn't care. It was Mali land, and that was all that mattered.

Once they reached the wretchedly twisted, single lane road leading to Llansantowain, Bill roused David. "This is the village," he said, as they cruised toward the Cock and Bull. Bill pointed to it. "That's where I stayed."

"In a tavern?"

"It has some rooms upstairs and is the closest thing to a hotel around here."

"Then I hope they'll have room for us tonight."

Judging by the number of cars parked out front, Bill doubted that would be the case. They'd likely have to drive to Bedgelert or Betws-y-Coed, both renowned for their Bed and Breakfasts.

"I thought we'd visit Mali first," Bill said. "She'll be able to tell us exactly what's happening."

"Bill, I appreciate your eagerness, but I came to muzzle Rhia and salvage the firm's reputation, not put that on hold while you renew your love life."

Bill drove past the pub without even applying the brakes. "I understand, but the fact is, David, you know nothing beyond what you saw on TV. We both know there's always more to the story. Wouldn't you rather find out exactly what's going on before you do anything?"

David gazed out the window as the pub, and then the village, drifted away behind them, then sighed. "You're right, of course. Being a father isn't always easy, especially to a daughter like Rhia."

Bill didn't look at David, but nodded as he sped up.

"I assume Rhia will be staying there?"

"Probably," Bill said, "but I'd rather get the lay of the land from Mali before we arrange face time with Rhia."

David looked at him with uncertainty but said nothing.

The road was in considerably worse shape than when Bill had last driven it on his way to Manchester. Now, thick mud oozed down the length of the pavement in twin lines. He tried to stay out of them, but the effort pushed him too close to the stacked slate walls which bordered the tiny road. He stayed in the middle, intent on reaching Mali before David could change his mind and demand that they go back to the pub.

"Not much room through here, is there?" David said as Bill guided the car down the road with ever-increasing speed. "It's a little like threading a needle."

Bill concentrated on the road ahead.

"I've found it's easier if you thread the needle slowly," David said.

"Me, too," Bill said, drifting slightly as he powered through a curve.

"And you're far less likely to stab yourself."

"Uh huh."

"Or anyone else."

"Gotcha."

"You must be looking forward to seeing this woman."

Bill nodded. "More than you can imagine."

"Then will you please slow this damned car down

so we'll have at least an even chance of getting there alive?" David's voice was locked into a forced, but even pitch.

Bill quickly backed off the accelerator. "Sorry. I--"

"Apology accepted. Now keep going; I've no desire to take over."

The driveway leading to Mali's cottage appeared on the left. The ground was so thoroughly soaked that instead of crunching, the gravel made a squishing sound when they drove on it.

The rain had nearly stopped as they pulled up in front of the little house. Only then did Bill think about failing to bring an umbrella. David, meanwhile, had gotten out of the car and stood alongside it, stretching. Bill joined him.

"It's dark--doesn't look like anyone's home," David said.

Bill glanced up at the chimney, relieved to see a steady supply of smoke. And Mali's little car sat up to its hubcaps in a puddle at the end of the drive. "They must not have heard us pull in. If it weren't for the rain, Samson and Delilah would've greeted us."

David gave him a puzzled look.

"Mali's dogs," Bill said. "Real charmers. Think Mutt and Jeff, only female."

"Samson, too?"

Bill chuckled. "Go figure."

They were halfway to the front door when it opened and Mali burst out, followed by the dogs. She ran straight for Bill and wrapped her arms around him. Samson and Delilah danced around them alternately barking and pawing at Bill's legs. She clung to him like someone just back from the dead and Bill realized with no great surprise he really liked it. He stroked her hair with one hand and squeezed her to his chest with the other.

"I'm so sorry," she said at last. "I had no idea what you were trying to deal with. I didn't mean to send you away. I was afraid I'd never see you again, and then I got your message on the answering machine just as we came home, and now you're here, and the rain has stopped, and that horrible woman is going to take over everything, and--"

Bill gently pressed his finger to her lips. "It's going to be all right. Honest." He gazed down into her bright hazel eyes, his heart still thumping madly. "I promise."

Glynnis called from the front door. "Come in you two. The rest of us have more sense than to stand out in the rain."

Bill looked away from Mali to see Glynnis and David smiling from the doorway. She waved them indoors. "I think we'll all be more comfortable inside."

Bill let Mali lead him into the fire-warmed cottage. They crowded in the narrow entryway, slipping their muddy shoes off and padding with sock feet to warm themselves by a blazing fire.

"William, dear," Glynnis said, smiling at David. "I think it's time you made some introductions."

Reluctantly, it seemed, Bill released Mali and looked at his companion, his arm around her waist protectively. "David, this is Mali Rhys. And her aunt, Glynnis Rhys. Ladies, David Jones."

"Delighted to meet you," he said, taking Mali's hand in both of his for a moment. He moved to Glynnis who offered him her hand. He delicately lifted it to his lips, and she blushed. "Bill, I must apologize. Now I can appreciate your eagerness to get back. You should have told me how lovely the women are here."

Glynnis turned beet red, but the smile on her face heightened her charm. "With a name like Jones, and compliments like that, you must certainly be a Welshman. Next you'll be telling us you speak *Cymraeg*."

"*Y'dw, tipyn bach*," David said with a wink.

"Fancy that! A little bit!" Glynnis clapped her hands in delight. "Ah, Mr. Jones. Sit yourself down by the fire, and I'll make us all a nice cup of tea."

Mali's gaze followed Glynnis and then turned to David. "Mr. Jones. Any relation to Rhia Jones?"

David nodded, his expression somber. "I'm Rhia's father."

Mali's eyes went wide. "You--you're *that* David Jones? The one who started all this madness?"

"Easy now," Bill said. "He's also the one who's come to put things right."

"I'll believe that when I see it." She retreated toward the kitchen and nearly bumped into Glynnis pushing a small tea cart.

"Would you like some tea, Mr. Jones?" Glynnis asked as she waved them all into seats at the minuscule built-in table and poured the tea without waiting for an answer.

Sitting directly across from Mali, David said, "Bill tells me you're quite a history buff."

Bill was suddenly very aware of how professional David was. Some executives would have jumped right into the issue. David seemed content to set Mali at ease first.

She smiled at David for the first time. "My degree

is in history, but it was a poor choice, I'm afraid. It hasn't provided me with much of an income."

"But it's such a rich field. We think we know so much, and then we come across something which completely changes our views."

Mali looked at Bill. "I gather you told him about the letter."

Her insight startled him. "Yes, but he doesn't think it's genuine."

"Don't go putting words in my mouth, Bill. I merely said that one can't always assume every old document is legitimate, either by origin or intent. The rules could change quite rapidly back then, depending on who held the throne."

"And which throne was held," Mali added. "You're quite right. But we're talking about people living far from the center of court intrigue. They were simple folk with little skill in subtlety." She walked over to the glass case containing Meleri's damning testimony and carried it back to David. She set it in his lap and returned to her seat. "There is no reason to doubt the authenticity of this document. I'm truly sorry if it puts Owain in an unsavory light, especially if you're related to him. But on that score, you won't be alone; it casts the same light on its author, my own ancestor, and most of the people living hereabout."

"I'm sorry I had to spill the beans," Bill said, feeling entirely responsible for the whole mess. All things considered, Mali was taking it very well, he thought. "I know you would have preferred to keep it quiet."

"It's all right," she said. "I only wish I'd been more candid about it when you first arrived."

David squinted at the document in the case. "Well, it certainly looks genuine," he said at length.

Mali sat back against the loveseat and pressed close to Bill. "It is. For a long time I hoped it was a hoax, and during my studies for my degree, I asked the head of the Welsh Antiquities department to examine it. He concurred. He wanted me to donate it to the university, but I refused. In hindsight, that was probably a mistake, too."

Bill put his arm around her. "Maybe not."

"My Welsh isn't bad," David said, "but this lettering is hard to read. Do you have a translation?"

Mali went to her desk, opened a drawer, and extracted several typewritten sheets. "It's here in both Welsh and English," she said, "but you're welcome to examine the originals."

David compared the first few sentences of the typed version with the handwritten document in the case. "If the rest is as good as these opening lines, I have no reason to doubt your work at all. May I keep this English copy?"

"Keep them both," Mali said. "I have more."

"I hope you'll give me a chance to talk history with you at a later date," David said, "but right now I'm more concerned about what my daughter's been doing."

"I don't know what she's done to anyone else, but she used her banking connections to threaten me-- either I let her do whatever she wants with Owain's Rock in exchange for bringing the mortgage up to date, or she has the bank call in the loan."

David's face clouded with anger as she spoke. "I daresay I'm not surprised, though I wish to God I was.

Just like her mother," he added. "The woman never used a feather when a brickbat was handy."

"I'm perfectly willing to cooperate with the filming," Mali said. "And I suppose I must now go along with an archeological inspection of the whole area, if only for the sake of the town. But I think the Ornithological Society makes a good point when they say the timing needs to be such that their rare little birds aren't disturbed."

"Rare birds?" David seemed baffled. "I didn't see anything about birds in the news."

Bill explained about Clive Gillet's rat-faced wren. "And there's more."

"Come to think of it," David said, "there were a lot of hippies running around in the background, too."

"Caitlin, one of our locals," Mali said. "Her group follow a neo-pagan religion which holds the Rock sacred. She leads a bunch of worshippers who don't want the Rock moved. They think it'll upset the spirits."

David squinted at her. "And where does pornography fit in with any of this?"

"More tea, Mr. Jones?" Glynnis asked.

"No thanks. Now, about this rock--"

"It's the lemon, isn't it?" Glynnis said. "I used too much."

"What? No, thank you, Miss Rhys, it's fine. What about the rock?"

Glynnis dropped a sugar cube in his cup. "Try it with that."

"Aunt Glynnis!"

"What, dear? I'm merely trying to be civil."

"You're doing fine, Glynnis," Bill said. "It's the rock

Owain's under."

"*May* be under," amended Mali.

David waved his hands in the air. "Why is everyone so upset about it?"

"We aren't upset," Mali said. "We've grown used to it."

Glynnis frowned. "Speak for yourself."

David's frustration surfaced. "What's the problem with the confounded rock?"

"It's shaped like a penis," Bill said. No sense in pulling his punches now.

David shook his head in consternation. "Aren't they all? It seems pervasive in the form."

Glynnis added two more lumps of sugar to her cup and stirred vigorously. Mali cleared her throat and neatly folded her hands in her lap before looking pointedly at Bill.

"It's not just phallic, David. It's... anatomically correct."

"It's so--" whispered Glynnis, searching for the right word, "--so penile!"

David looked at them in astonishment, but his gaze centered on Glynnis. "Are you with the anti-pornography group?"

"Of course she's not," Bill said.

Mali thumped him on the shoulder. "What's *that* supposed to mean?"

"Not that she likes-- You know what I meant! She's not part of any protest group."

"Some people are bothered by the shape of the Rock," Mali said. "I'm sure you saw it on the telly."

"Not really," David said. "I wasn't paying all that much attention until I saw my daughter force herself on the reporter. At that point, whatever was going on in the background ceased to be of interest to me. And that brings me to the whole reason for my visit. I've got to--"

A great roar shook the cottage, rattled the windows, and knocked a vase of flowers to the floor.

"My goodness," Glynnis said. "That lightning must've struck very close. And I was so hoping the rain was over for a bit."

Bill and David stared at each other. Bill spoke first. "Usually there's lightning, *then* thunder. Did any of you see a flash of light?"

The women shook their heads.

"Me neither," David said, rising to his feet. "That wasn't thunder."

Bill put it together. "An explosion."

Mali gripped Bill's arm. "It sounded like it came from the Rock."

He stood and fished the keys to the rental car from his pocket. "I think we'd better go have a look."

Glynnis dashed out of the room and returned with a pair of umbrellas and two pairs of wellies. "I wish I had something you gentlemen could wear." She quickly slipped her feet into one pair and held the umbrella out to David. "Are we going now, or not?"

~*~

The renewed drizzle pummeled them as they dashed from the cottage toward the Mercedes. David held the rear door open for Glynnis who, with one smooth motion, neatly folded her umbrella and slid completely across the seat. She patted the leather upholstery at her side and David, smiling, climbed in beside her.

Bill, surprised by Glynnis's bold move, held the passenger door open for Mali. With practiced ease, she also folded her umbrella as fast as she settled into the seat. By the time he hurried around to the driver's side of the car, he was nearly soaked. When he slid in behind the wheel, she smiled and squeezed his hand. He turned in a tight circle and headed back up the drive, slaloming out onto the narrow hardtop. As mud flew from the tires, the car fishtailed. Mali gasped and David coughed nervously. Bill quickly corrected for the slide and gunned the accelerator.

David leaned forward and spoke over Bill's shoulder. "Whoa, Andretti!" he admonished. "I'd like to get there in one piece. No need to break the speed limit."

"Nonsense," Glynnis said pulling David closer, "step on it, William."

Bill goosed the Mercedes toward the village and the only place he knew of where a car could approach the Rock--a break in the ever-present slate wall, roughly half way between Mali's cottage and town. Bill slowed and saw another Mercedes, larger and older than the rental he drove, parked under some trees.

Mali waved him on. "Keep going. There'll be a stream and then a sharp bend," she said. "You should be able to park on the right under an old oak."

He'd not noticed it before, but her advice proved accurate, and Bill slowed the car to a halt next to an enormous tree that marked the end of the wall. The ground around the tree had been churned into a quagmire by a crane whose bulk now obliterated the path leading toward the Rock. Fortunately, the rain let up considerably. As they exited the car, a truck approached from the opposite direction. It bumped off the road to park behind the crane.

Mali squinted at the new arrival. "I know that lorry! Michael Wells?"

Bill was more surprised by the electrician's companion. *"Stacey?"*

Together they all asked, "What are you doing here?"

Stacey tried to pick her way across the mud. She only succeeded in slipping and would have fallen if not for Michael's firm hand on her elbow. She shot him a wide smile of thanks then turned back to Bill. "Rhia sent me." She looked up at Michael. "Us, I mean."

"Michael," Mali said, pointing accusingly at him, "don't tell me you're working for that... that..." She paused, her cheeks flushing pink with anger. "That bi--"

Bill put his hand on her arm and whispered, "Easy, now. Daddy's here."

She took a breath and nodded. "--that busybody from the States, are you?"

"No," Stacey said before Michael could respond. "I work for Rhia and asked him to give me a ride."

"Where's everybody else?" David asked. "We figured everyone heard the explosion and would come running."

Stacey blushed. "We were already in the truck--so, uhm, we got a little head start."

Mali leaned close to Bill and whispered, "Should we warn her off Michael?"

He shook his head. "Trust me; any daughter of my Aunt Nell can take care of herself."

"You're related?" Mali asked.

"Yeah. I'll explain later."

They watched with amazement as Michael, like a perfect gentleman, offered Stacey his arm. He helped her negotiate a series of puddles between the trees that screened Owain's Rock from the road.

"I'd never have believed it if I hadn't seen it with my own eyes," Mali said.

"Are you two coming?" Glynnis called. She hung onto David's hand, and he was all but dragging her toward their destination.

"Absolutely," Bill said, taking Mali's hand. He didn't dare look at her, but her fingers intertwined with his as if they had always been there. He wanted to pull her to him, but David and Glynnis had already passed behind the trees. He'd make up for it later. They hurried after the older couple and went through the screen of trees at about the same time as Stacey and Michael. They nearly bumped into Glynnis standing alone at the edge of the wood.

Owain's Rock had been reduced to rubble. A score of large boulders and half a dump truck's worth of rocks, gravel, and dust blended in with the mud. David knelt down at what must have been ground zero.

"Holy cow," was all Bill managed to say.

"Who could've done such a thing?" Mali asked.

"Off hand," Stacey said, pulling Michael toward the far side of the largest surviving boulder, "I'd say he had something to do with it." She pointed several yards away to the prone form of a very short, very stout person in workman's coveralls, mud-covered Wellingtons, and a heavy raincoat.

Mali bit her lip and gripped Bill's hand more tightly. "Is he dead?"

"I dunno," Bill said, hurrying toward the body, "but we'd better find out fast. We may need to call an ambulance."

"Don't touch anything," David said to the rest of them. "This is a crime scene; the police will want to investigate."

"What police?" Glynnis asked, alarmed.

Bill reached the body first, knelt beside it, and put his finger against the figure's throat. A strong pulse rewarded him, and he sat back on his heels. Stacey joined him and put her ear to the figure's back.

"Can ya hear anythin'?" Michael asked.

"Only his stomach growling," she said.

Bill looked more closely to make sure nothing interfered with the man's breathing. "His nose isn't in the mud, so I don't think he'll drown, but I'd hate to move him. He might--"

"I'm not a he," said the body. One baleful eye opened and glared at him.

"Mrs. Pynchon?" Mali asked. "What are you doing here?"

"Look at this!" Michael held up an explosives detonator. A pair of wires trailed away from it toward the remains of the Rock. "I don't think she was out lookin' for blue-footed boobies."

Stacey chuckled, and Michael stood a little taller, a look of satisfaction on his face.

"Help me up," said Mrs. Pynchon.

"I'm not sure that's wise," Bill replied. "You might be injured. The blast must've been--"

"Nonsense. I tripped over a ruddy tree root," she said between grunts as she rolled to her side and struggled to get up without actually putting her hands in the muck. "I'd know if I broke anything."

Bill and Mali scrambled to help her to her feet. By that time, many more people began filing into the area.

"Stay back, everyone, please!" Bill shouted, but no one paid him any attention. Every person staying at the pub showed up, and a few more who'd parked their cars and trailers in every available space in and around the village. Birders, neo-pagans, smut protesters, villagers, and cinema folk intermingled among the wreckage of the Rock, and all seemed to be shaking their heads at the extent of the destruction. Caitlin sobbed with what looked like genuine grief. Bill surveyed the onlookers. No one knew what to say or do.

He spied Rhia, accompanied by Dylan, Dai Thomas, and the Spanish actor at the edge of the clearing. Rhia, supported by Fernandez, was taking deep breaths and appeared to be on the verge of a breakdown. The actor seemed distinctly out of place comforting her. Dylan edged slowly away until he spotted Bill and Mali at the far side of the blast zone and hurried toward them.

"You! Where are you going?" Rhia shouted at Dylan.

"I'm trying to find out what happened here," he called over his shoulder.

She trembled and pointed at the people milling about. "Get all these people out of here."

"Right," he said, waving her off. "In due time."

"In due time, hell!" she screamed. "Do it now!"

"Calm down, Rhia," David said, his voice quietly firm and insistent.

"Daddy?" Rhia asked, her voice instantly softening. "What are you doing here?"

"Seems to be a popular question," Michael said to no one in particular. Stacey pinched him, and he winced.

David embraced his daughter and gave her a light kiss on the cheek. "I originally wanted to come here to learn something about Owain y'Craig. That was before I saw your performance on the news."

"My performance?"

"Yes. The one where you put your posterior on display for the world."

She looked confused. Bill suspected she was so used to showing off her shapely legs and hips she wouldn't be able to comprehend her father's reaction.

David patted her on the hand in a way that left Bill's mouth agape. He'd never seen Rhia back down from anyone. Ever.

"Anyway, now I'm here," David said, "and you don't have to worry about this project anymore."

"But Daddy, I--" Command tones were already creeping back into her voice.

"No need to thank me," David said, his gaze back on the scattered remains of the Rock. "I've always wanted to come here and study Saint Owain, though I never dreamed until tonight I might actually find him."

What the hell? Bill thought. Mali inhaled sharply and grabbed his arm.

"What are you talking about, Daddy?" Rhia asked.

"Look there, but don't touch anything. I've found something interesting in the dirt where the Rock used to be."

Bill craned his neck for a better look. "What is it?"

"It hasn't held its original shape too well," David said, "but I believe it's part of a human skull."

Mali fainted into Bill's arms.

~*~

Bill crowded at a table in the now quiet Cock and Bull tavern with Mali, Dylan, and David sipping an ale and listening as the others chatted about the excitement of the past few days. It felt good to just relax with a pint as things settled back into a comfortable routine. No big city potions, just the same brew the locals drank. Something roasted in Brenna's kitchen and filled Bill's nostrils with a promise of another satisfying meal soon to come. He hadn't been this relaxed since his childhood in Wetumpka.

It took nearly a week to clean up the mess and send most of the "foreigners" home. Archaeologists showed up the first morning with field kits to stake out the area where David found the skull. Four large tents went up in less than an hour followed by a huge canopy that covered the site, keeping the researchers as dry as the air would permit. One of Mali's friends at the university helped expedite things, and the students he brought worked non-stop to secure every bit of the remains. They did allow a few small samples to be whisked away for dating.

A handful of the neo-pagans lingered at Caitlin's, and every night they paced a candlelit circle just outside the canopy covering the rubble once known as Owain's Rock. What they chanted in Welsh, Bill could only guess, but Mali told him they worked to set the local spirits at ease. After three days Caitlin announced the area cleansed, and her followers packed up their tents and campers and drove away.

Mrs. Pynchon was arrested by the constable from Bedgelert. Surrounded by a cheering and applauding throng of well-wishers and an equally vociferous and angry mob of bird enthusiasts, she bravely weathered the indignity of handcuffs. According to news reports, her accomplice at the mine was also arrested.

Clive Gillet wandered like Diogenes through the field in search of some indication his precious wrens hadn't suffered the same fate as the Rock.

The film crew had packed up as soon as the police inspector was convinced they knew nothing about the illegal use of blasting materials. The rain finally stopped on the fourth day, and the crane disappeared from the pasture which was likely to bear a criss-cross of deep ruts marking its passage for a long time. Rhia disappeared with Antonio at about the same time, and even David had no idea where she was.

Now, nearly two weeks later, the Cock and Bull seemed empty without the hordes of people from the film crew and the various camps of protesters. Things were once again quiet, and Darts Night was two days away.

"Here's your supper," Brenna said as she delivered four steaming plates of roast lamb with potatoes, peas, and a jar of homemade mint jelly.

"If my doctor could see what I'm eating, he'd have my hide," David said as he shoveled Brenna's handiwork into his mouth without waiting for the others to begin.

"I won't tell him if you won't," Bill said. He marveled at how succulent the lamb was. He'd never acquired a taste for it in Atlanta and couldn't recall if he'd ever even had it in Wetumpka. Here in a small Welsh pub however, it seemed the most wonderful meat in the world.

David munched lustily for a time before pausing for air. He wiped his mouth on a huge linen napkin and squinted at Bill. "Have you given any more thought to my offer?"

Bill smiled at Mali then turned back to David. "You know I'm flattered, but I'm not eager to go back to Atlanta, at least not right away. Besides, someday Rhia will take over the business for good, and she might fire me all over again." She'd take great delight in doing just that, too. He preferred not to give her the opportunity.

"That's a fair assessment," David said slowly, "and believe it or not, it's one I anticipated. What would you say to--"

Just then the pub door opened, and an extraordinarily dejected Clive Gillet walked in. His pathetic manner stopped all conversation. Bill and the others watched Gillet as he shrugged a knapsack from his thin shoulders onto the floor near the bar, deposited a toolbox-sized camera bag on the countertop and decamped on a stool. He slumped as he leaned against the polished wood. Dai and Michael were the only others seated at the bar, and they promptly relocated to a table near the darts boards.

Brenna appraised him sympathetically. "Somethin' to drown yer sorrows, Mr. Gillet?"

The birder gazed up at her with tormented eyes; the circles under them were as dark as bruises. "A Guinness, please," he said. "A big one."

Brenna laughed. "I was afraid you'd ask for

sherry. I still haven't restocked from the last fellow to ask for that in here. He polished it off."

Every day once the sun went down Gillet had returned in despair to the pub and drowned his misery in a double sherry. When the sherry ran out, he switched to stout.

"The bugger," Gillet opined, the first conversational words he'd spoken in a week.

"I dunno," she said convivially as she passed him a tall glass of dark brew, "he seemed like a nice enough sort. Big into birding from what I hear. Discovered a rare one hereabouts, too."

Gillet shook his head wearily. "Not that anyone'd believe me now. When Mrs. Pynchon blew up the rock, I'm afraid she blew up my specimens, too." A tear appeared in the corner of his eye. "Whatever punishment she gets for doing that, it won't be enough."

"You took some photographs, didn't you?" Mali asked from her table a few feet away.

"Oh yes. I got some excellent shots. In fact--" he paused to retrieve his knapsack and removed several large color prints which he spread out on the bar. "--I made another discovery. It wasn't a rat-faced wren after all. Look here." He tapped his index finger on one of the pictures.

Brenna leaned well over the bar for a better look. "What am I looking for?"

"A pale rosy-buff mark on the bird's throat."

Brenna turned the photo around and pulled it closer. "Can't see too much here."

Gillet pushed another toward her. "It's clearer in this one."

"Ah, right. Not much to it, is there? Looks like a finger. Is that important?"

"I should say so." He took a deep draught of his stout and squinted as he swallowed. "That marking doesn't exist on the rat-faced wren. It doesn't exist on any other known species, either."

"And that's bad?" she asked.

"No, no, not at all. It's excellent. It means I may have discovered a previously unknown species--a brand new bird."

"Good for you!" Mali said. "You should be very proud."

His despondent frown returned. "I would be proud if Mrs. Pynchon hadn't blown the only known nesting site to smithereens." He crossed his forearms on the bar, leaned his head on them, and wept.

"Oh, dear," Mali said. She looked at Bill. "There must be something we can do."

"It's a little late for that," he said. "Mrs. Phynchon was in the hospital under observation for a few days, and yesterday she appeared in court."

Mali sighed. "The woman needs treatment, not imprisonment."

Dylan interrupted. "You're too kind, Mali. There are at least two governmental groups who disagree," he said. "They intend to go after her. No matter what else it may have been, Owain's Rock was a prehistoric artifact. She had no right to tamper with it, let alone destroy it."

"I agree," David said. "But Mali has a point, too. Did you happen to catch the headline about Mrs. Pynchon in the Manchester paper?" He unfolded a section of newsprint, turned to an inside page and handed it to Dylan.

Dylan set it briefly aside while he donned his glasses. He held the paper at arm's length, then read the large type out loud. "Smut Fighter Faces Condomnation for Damage to Prehistoric Prong."

Dai called from across the room, "Is 'condomnation' a word?"

Dylan groaned. "It's a joke, you twit!"

"Now," David said to Bill, "about that job. I wonder--"

The pub door crashed open as if blown in by a hurricane. Bill and the others twisted in alarm. The hurricane was Rhia.

Dressed in a typically tight-fitting ensemble, this time featuring an African leopard motif, she entered like a conqueror rather than the failed producer of a non-show. A pair of suited briefcase-bearers flanked her. Stacey, with a suitcase and a pair of cell phones, brought up the rear. She smiled when she saw Michael, dumped her burdens on the nearest table, and headed in his direction.

"Ha!" Rhia said, staring at David like a predator assessing the food value of a lame gazelle. "I thought I'd find you here."

"Nice to see you, too, dear. I thought you'd gone home," he said mildly. "You know I'm not very happy with how you handled things around here."

She drew herself up as tall as possible and waved her hand in a familiar gesture of dismissal. "Whatever. I've spoken with Mother, and we've decided we don't give two hoots in hell about that stupid saint and his blown up rock. I came here to deliver some real news." She nodded at the two attorneys standing silently beside her. "You can confirm anything you want with these two. They know all the legal mumbo-jumbo."

David squinted at her. "What in the world are you talking about, Rhia?"

"Mother has given me a proxy for the shares she still has in the firm. While they're not as many as I'd hoped, when combined with the shares you gave me for my twenty-first birthday, I now have a controlling interest in Jones and Associates. I've decided to take charge--permanently."

"Congratulations," he said. Mali flashed him a worried frown, and he patted her hand.

His calm response seemed to douse a part of Rhia's fire. "You don't seem very upset about it, Daddy."

"I'm not. Your mother, however, must be very proud. This is so like her."

She glared at him. "I obviously didn't make myself clear." She stabbed her thumb at her chest. "I run the company now, not you."

"Yes, I see."

Bill and Mali looked at each other. David was up to something, of that Bill was certain, but to overcome shocking news like Rhia's controlling interest in the company should have enraged the man. Instead, he calmly took another sip of his beer then whispered something to Mali which wiped the frown of doubt from her face and replaced it with a rosy blush and a shy smile. She glanced at Bill and then away, the smile broadening.

Rhia was less calm, her abrasive manner honed to irritating perfection. "*Do* you see?" she asked, her voice dripping the same kind of disdain Bill remembered coming from Rhia's mother.

David leaned back in his chair, wiped his mouth with his napkin, then nodded--still calm, though no trace of amusement played on his face. "I figured you'd contact Sandra for her support."

"Did you also figure I'd fire you?"

He frowned, and bit at his lip as if contemplating saying something, then changed his mind. He said nothing.

"Well, I just did," she crowed, then turned to face Bill. "And just in case he hired you back, you're fired, too!" She whirled about in search of her assistant, then called to her across the room. "Stacey, make sure payroll knows about these firings. They're official as of today. In fact, Bill's is retroactive to whenever Daddy hired him back."

Stacey shook her head and took Michael's hand in hers. "I'm going to be busy for a while, Rhia. Why don't you call them yourself?"

Rhia's mouth dropped open, and her eyes grew wide. Then her brows took a sharp downward dip, and her cheeks flushed a deep crimson visible through her heavy make-up. "What did you say?" she croaked in disbelief.

"I said I'm busy. Call payroll yourself. It's not like you've got anything else to do."

"You ungrateful little bitch! You're too busy to do your job? Fine. You're fired, too."

"Speakin' of getting the sack, Miss Jones," Dylan said, "there's no need for you to hang around Llansantowain any longer. With the Rock in pieces, the council won't be needin' your services after all."

She glared at him. "Is that so? Well, I had no intention of doing anything else for this cesspool of a town anyway. You'll get a statement for services rendered as soon as I get back to the office."

"That should prove interesting," Bill said casually, "considering no one from Jones and Associates provided any services. I certainly didn't, and I was here the longest."

"Stacey," David called over his shoulder, "if you aren't doing anything later today, would you please come and see me? I'm going to need a good assistant."

"You can't give her a job. I just fired both of you," Rhia said.

David gazed solemnly at his daughter. "I've decided to work on the tourism campaign for Llansantowain myself. Dylan, the town council, and I, worked out the details last night."

Rhia stared from one to the other, and then tossed her head back in a throaty laugh. "You can't do that. You can't begin to make a go of it out here in the middle of nowhere."

He nodded. "Probably true. That's why I still expect most of the billings to come from my Atlanta office."

"What Atlanta office? You don't have one, remember? The business is mine."

"Sorry to disappoint you, honey, but I didn't have a chance to tell you," he said, "I opened a new business earlier this week. Grady Banyon's running it for me. Oh, and by the way, he's bringing just about everyone else on the staff with him. I daresay most of the clients, too."

Rhia's mouth dropped open again, and Bill had to

fight the urge to close it for her. For once she seemed at a total loss for words. The two lawyers exchanged worried looks and shuffled back and forth like a pair of nervous hens.

Glynnis opened the pub door and waved. "Hello all! Is David here?"

Brenna motioned her inside and pointed to the corner tables. "Over there, luv."

Glynnis swept into the room, made a wide detour around Rhia and her mute attorneys, then stopped beside David. He reached up and touched her tenderly; she flushed pink. Their fingers met briefly as she sat close beside him and handed him an envelope. "I hope you don't mind; I signed for it. It's a telegram from the University."

"Not at all, my dear." The adoring look he gave her could have melted concrete, and Bill exchanged a knowing glance with Mali. David slid his thumb under the envelope's flap and extracted a single sheet of pink paper. At first, his lips moved with the words, but they soon slipped downward into a frown.

"What's the matter?" Mali asked. "What does it say?"

"It's from your friend, Dr. Devon, at the university. He says the carbon dating puts the skeletal remains roughly to the time of Owain--give or take 40 years."

"My God," Mali said, an astonished smile forming on her lips. "It *was* him. After all these years I finally discover the letter was telling the truth. Owain really was under the rock."

David shook his head. "We can't be sure it's *the* Owain of the legend, though. The gold cross they found and the ornate ring suggest that whoever wore them was most likely a prominent person. But that's all. There weren't any inscriptions or other identifying marks."

"Who else could it have been?" Bill asked.

Mali shook her head. "Could have been any traveling lord or priest. I've no idea. But all the records suggest that any of the relatives wealthy enough to have rings and gold of any kind are accounted for. It's definitely someone from outside the valley." Wide-eyed, she took the report from David and scanned its contents. "All my life I've believed the letter, and that the story Meleri told in it was genuine. I knew Owain wasn't the saint they made of him, but I never really believed they toppled the rock over on him, either. All just to hide the body."

"How likely is it that it's really the same man? That it's Owain y'Craig?" Bill asked.

David shrugged. "After so much time has passed, I doubt we'll ever know for sure."

"The first DNA results are also back--looks like I can't prove my relationship to him after all. They couldn't get any usable DNA from the bone fragments. If the land had been boggier, maybe."

"So much for you being related to the saint, then," Glynnis said. "What else does the telegram say?"

David read on, and his jaw tightened. "While they were unable to extract any useable DNA from the remains, they made comparisons of the samples Rhia and I gave them."

"I'm sorry," Mali said. "I know you were hoping to learn something."

"Oh, but I did," David said softly, sad eyes studying his daughter. "According to the university experts, the DNA samples submitted for comparison testing with the skeletal remains weren't related."

Rhia frowned. "What are you saying?"

"Regardless of my kinship with Owain, there's no doubt about the lack of kinship between us."

Rhia's eyes widened, and she suddenly seemed very small. "Daddy?"

He shook his head. "It seems not, Rhia. The DNA proves I'm not your father."

She staggered into a chair and sent it sliding into the lawyers. "Then... Who is?" she stammered.

David sagged in his own chair. "You'll have to ask your mother. The list of candidates ought to be pretty lengthy." He looked at her with sympathy. "Rhia, there's a lot more to parenthood than biology and frankly, after your mother left and I discovered her usual method of making clients feel important, I became more than a little suspicious of your true parentage. But you *are* my daughter. I helped raise you, and in spite of your mother's influence, I love you. I do regret, though, not taking a firmer and broader hand in your upbringing. Maybe then you'd be a little less like her."

Rhia sputtered as if to say something, but instead she looked at the sorrowful expression on David's face and slumped into the chair beside him. Bill finally knew what it took to shut the woman up.

With her usual perfect timing, Caitlin wandered in and joined Gillet at the bar. Wearing a smock of brilliant orange and with her hair resplendent in bright purple, she resembled something tie-dyed. Gillet barely looked at her before lowering his head once again to his crossed arms.

"What's wi' him?" Caitlin asked Brenna.

"He's upset over his birds," Brenna said. "Some ratty little wren or something. Its nest was on Owain's Rock when it-- You know."

"It's not a ratty wren," Gillet said between sniffs. "I merely thought it was a rat-faced wren. It wasn't. It was something even more rare." He slid an already well-worn photograph across the bar to Caitlin. "There it is," he said, his reddened eyes tearing up again. "And now it's gone."

The hairdresser lifted the picture carefully and examined it in the light. "What's so special about this bird?"

"It's rare, probably a new species," he said. "That marking on its neck is highly unusual. It's not--"

"It's not rare around here, luv. I've seen plenty of them," Caitlin said matter-of-factly.

Gillet stared at her, his jaw slightly askew. "You *what?*"

"There's a bunch of 'em out behind my shop," she said. "They hang around the tub where I clean out the casks I make beer in."

Gillet's face lit up, and he rose in excited expectation--his grief vanished. "Please don't tell me you're joking!" Gillet put his hand on her forearm, his eyes pleading.

Caitlin's finger traced an X over her heart. "It's true, Clive. I've seen 'em in the cemetery, too. They seem to enjoy pooping on Owain's memorial." She laughed. "They've almost buried it."

Hastily grabbing his camera bag and knapsack, Gillet raced for the door, and disappeared. About five seconds went by before he rushed back in. "Which way is it?" he cried.

Caitlin ignored him and instead picked up the remains of his beer. "Are you going to finish this?"

"Are you serious? Of course not! Which way?" His voice bordered on hysteria.

Caitlin rose to her feet. "I'll show you. Don't get your knickers in a knot," she said carrying the beer with her. She winked at Brenna. "I'll bring the glass back later."

Gillet grabbed Caitlin and hurried her through the door. The maneuver would have been easier if not for another patron on his way in. They squirmed past him and disappeared as a man in painfully proper attire entered the building. Bill winced at the idea of wearing such formal clothing anywhere, much less in a rural pub on a weekday evening.

"It's getting busier than darts night," Brenna muttered from behind the bar. "But at least there aren't any more film crews."

The over-dressed gentleman removed his hat and surveyed the room with quiet dignity until he spied Mali, then wiggled his fingers at her.

"Oh my God, it's Smythe-Webley," Mali whispered into Bill's ear.

He blinked. "Who?"

The man hastened over to their table before she had time to explain.

"Ah, Miss Rhys," the newcomer said, bowing slightly. "I had hoped to catch you at home, but when I arrived a pair of dogs assailed my vehicle, and I was afraid to get out. I came here to call you on the telephone."

"I'm so sorry," she said. "But you had nothing to

worry about. Samson and Delilah wouldn't hurt anybody. If only I had known you were coming, I--"

"I called. Didn't your aunt tell you?"

Glynnis looked up from her conversation with David and blushed. "Oh, Mali, I'm sorry. I completely forgot. Mr. Smythe-Webley called yesterday, and--"

"Not to worry, Miss Rhys, not to worry," he said congenially. "What's done's done. I've caught up with you now, and that's all that matters." He cleared his throat. "In light of the news coverage your little village has received in recent days, I thought it prudent to contact some of my better customers and inquire as to their interest in acquiring your letter."

Mali's eyes went wide. "You told them about the letter? How could you after I asked that it be kept in complete confidence!"

"I didn't mention anyone's identity," he said, completely unflustered. "I hinted at what the letter contained, and that it might soon appear on the open market. If it did, I wanted to know if they'd be interested." He paused for dramatic effect. "There are at least four serious collectors ready to make substantial bids, sight unseen." He gave an almost imperceptible bow. "And if you'd permit me to act as your agent and let them see the actual document, I've no doubt the bids will soar."

Mali pressed her lips together and looked at Glynnis. Bill knew she sought her aunt's acceptance. Keeping the letter away from public scrutiny had been Mali's goal for years. Now, it seemed, Glynnis didn't care about it anymore, scandal or no.

"Now that everything's out in the open it doesn't much matter anymore, does it? If I were you, dear,"

Glynnis said, "I'd sell the silly thing and spend the money on something important."

The words hit Bill like a toppling monolithic stone--forcing the breath out of him. *Something important.* With rare clarity he realized that was the key he'd been looking for all his life. He knew without hesitation what this meant for him. And for Mali. It wasn't the money for its own sake, it was what the money could do.

"Something important?" Mali asked slowly.

"Like refurbishing the manor house," Bill answered for Glynnis with a wide grin, "and opening that tourist resort your father planned."

Mali looked from Bill to Glynnis. "Are you sure you don't care about the letter anymore, Aunt Glynnis? What about the things people will say? What about moving in humiliation to Cardiff?"

As David squeezed her hand Glynnis shot Mali a satisfied grin. "Right now, dear, I'm far more interested in the future than the past."

"That's my girl," David said, kissing her on the cheek.

To Bill's mild surprise, the elder Rhys didn't blush this time, and lightly brushed David's cheek with the back of her hand. He turned with a grin to Mali.

"It's up to you, Mali. The family secret or the family home?" Bill asked.

She hesitated only a moment. "All right, you have a deal," Mali told the Londoner. "What do I need to do?"

"Just sign this consignment form and auction agreement," Smythe-Webley said, pulling a prepared set of documents from his breast pocket. "And let me take the artifact back to the city."

Mali took one last look at Glynnis then signed the papers. "I can't believe there will finally be enough money to make some real progress on the house."

Bill took Mali's hand and closed his fingers around hers protectively. He never wanted to let go. "I don't suppose you could use a construction foreman, could you?"

Her warm smile rewarded him. "Why, Mr. Thomas, do you know anyone looking for such a job?"

"As a matter of fact, I do," he said. "And he just happens to be available right now."

David looked up from his close conversation with Glynnis. "If he's the guy I'm thinking about," David said, "he's got another offer in the wings."

Bill stared at him, sure he'd already told David no. "I do?"

David nodded.

"I thought we had resolved that."

"Not exactly. You turned down my first offer--for a job. I think you'll find my second offer is a little better."

Bill looked at him sideways. David could be hard-nosed and devious, but Bill couldn't imagine what he was driving at. "I'm going to need time to work on Mali's house. I'm really not looking for a job--"

"Not a job, Bill. I want you as my partner," David said. "Like you, I have no intention of working full time. We'll let Grady and the others in Atlanta take care of that. Meanwhile, you and I can tackle the project here and take our time doing it. What d'ya say?"

Tension Bill didn't even know he carried drained

from him like someone had pulled a plug. He felt fresh and rejuvenated. A partnership meant freedom to be where he wanted to be. With Mali. "I--" He looked at her. "If-- That is--"

Mali gently pressed a finger to his lips, then kissed him.

It was the only answer he wanted. He turned to David with a satisfied smile. "I accept; thank you. Mali wouldn't want to marry someone who's unemployed, no matter how much he loves her." Then Bill enfolded Mali in his arms and returned her kiss.

~End~

About the Authors

Josh Langston and Barbara "B.J." Galler-Smith have been collaborating on top quality fiction for well over a decade. How do writers who live so far apart-- Josh in Marietta, Georgia, and BJ in Edmonton, Alberta--manage to work *together?* It's called the internet. They began their collaboration as an outgrowth of their participation in an on-line writer's group, the CompuServe IMPs.

Their first published collaboration was a short, contemporary fantasy. For several years they worked on a series of historical fantasy novels set in the 1st Century BC. The first two books, ***Druids*** and ***Captives*** are available now in both paperback and E-book formats from Edge Science Fiction and Fantasy Publishing. The final book in the trilogy, ***Warriors***, is scheduled for publication in May, 2012. The series has garnered much praise and a wealth of glowing reviews. **Captives** appeared on multiple bestseller lists in the spring of 2011.